Within the Shadows

by

J.D MCG

Dedication

For all my family, friends and fans. Thank you for
making this journey so special and I hope you all
enjoy what's to come in the future.

Prologue

December 2019

Jack Roberts loves to run. Whether it was a bright sunny day or wet, rainy and miserable. Whatever the weather, he loved to be outside. Whenever he would get the chance, he'd sign up for any marathon and charity run he could. One thing people would say about Jack was he had a huge passion for running.

He kissed his wife on the lips like he always did before his late evening run. It was cold when Jack set off from his house but he soon warmed up after a few metres; sweat dribbling down from his forehead. Jack couldn't resist wiping the sweat with his wrist as he carried on running.

Before he knew it, a mile had passed and he still had more than enough energy to go further. Nothing could stop Jack, not while he was running anyway. He approached the woodlands as 'Eye of the tiger' burst through his earphones. Standing still for a moment, he placed his hands on his knees and took deep breaths. He needed a rest. After a few more long, deep breaths, he straightened his back and stood tall, lifting his head to look up at the night sky which peered through the trees. *What a beautiful night*, he thought. The moon shone brightly through the trees, lighting up the woods below.

Jack began to move again slowly but picking up the pace a few steps at a time. Ahead of him, he could see the end of the woods through to the open parkland. He kept his breathing regular, and his feet in rhythm with one another. Something stopped Jack in his tracks. A feeling as if someone was watching him, a feeling like no other he'd experienced in his lifetime. He stood still on the path surrounded by the tall trees and leafy bushes. The perfect spot for someone to be hiding. He removed his earphones from both his ears and called out.

'Hello? Is anybody there?'

But nothing, just the silence of the woods. The wind gently rustled the leaves and moved them around him. As Jack put his earphones back in, his eyes caught a glimpse of a bush rustling to the left of him. He removed his earphones once again and dangled them outside of his top.

'Who's there?' he yelled. 'This isn't funny. Show yourself.'

Jack's pulse was racing. His fitness watch was monitoring his heart rate, which shot up like a rocket as he kept his focus on the rustling bush. His eyes remained on the undergrowth, ready for somebody to jump out and mug him, but nothing happened.

A minute passed, and nothing else happened. *What am I doing?* he asked himself. *I must be going mad.* He placed his earphones back into his ears and started jogging again. The end of the woods was just within sight. Just a few more steps and he'd be out of there, but something else caught his eye. He could see someone hiding behind a tree as he stopped for the second time.

'What do you want?' he shouted at the top of his lungs, making sure the person could hear him.

The mysterious figure removed themselves from behind the tree and into the open. Jack couldn't quite see their face. They'd hid in the darkness of the unlit woodland where the bright moonlight was unable to lighten them up.

'Who are you?' Jack asked, but the figure said nothing. 'Why have you been following me?'

But again, the figure was unresponsive. They just stood in one spot staring directly towards Jack. He felt scared and he didn't scare easily.

Jack began to walk away slowly and kept his eyes fixed on the figure. One step, two steps and then picking up the pace slightly, he was almost at the end of the woods. The figure had gone from his sight.

He stopped while looking anxiously around to find the person. Jack was two steps away from the end of the woods. It was silent. All Jack could hear was his heartbeat thumping in his chest. He turned his head from side to side when he caught sight of the person standing right in front of him. Their face lit up brightly in the moonlight. He could see every feature on their face. *What do they want?* he thought as the person approached him.

Chapter 1

January 2020

Jacob waited for Barnes to arrive at the wake of his father and step-mother. He held a drink in his hand while tears filled his eyes. Memories of his mother and father flooded into his head as he sipped from his glass. The memory of him getting into the police force and seeing the proud look upon his fathers face. Remembering what his father had said to him at that precise moment was all he could think about.

'Your mother would be so proud of you, son. Just as proud as I am.'

Jacob snapped back to reality as his brother, Adam, sat next to him with a pint in his hand. Kate sat on the other side of Jacob, staring downwards at her phone like usual.

'Are you okay?' Adam asked him.

'No, but are any of us?'

'True,' Adam replied. 'I can't really remember half of these people,' Adam said while looking around at all the guests.

'Me neither,' replied Jacob. 'Dad never really had any family, well none that we know of anyway. I'm sure all of these people are from Maria's side of the family.'

'Where's your boss anyway? I thought he said he was coming.'

'I'm sure he'll be here in a minute,' Jacob said with certainty.

Ally Miller suddenly made an appearance, as she walked through the door to the pub. Everyone inside turned and stared at her, before returning to their conversations. She made her way towards Jacob's table and took a seat.

'I'm sorry for your loss,' she said as she approached Jacob and his family.

'Thank you, Ally. That means a lot,' Adam replied.

'Would you three like a drink?'

'No, thank you,' replied Kate, sat with her head down.

'I'm good, thanks,' said Adam.

'How about you?' she looked at Jacob.

Jacob was elsewhere. His mind was all over the place, reminiscing memories of him and his father. He flashed back to reality to see Ally staring at him.

'Sorry, Ally, did you say something?' he said.

'Would you like a drink?' she repeated.

'I wouldn't mind another pint,' he said after looking down at his empty glass.

Ally made her way over to the bar and ordered herself and Jacob their drinks when she noticed Jacob stood to the side of her. His phone was in his hand texting somebody, but she couldn't quite see who. She didn't want to appear nosy by looking over his shoulder or by asking who he was texting but she was curious.

'Have you heard from Barnes?' Jacob asked her.

'Not since the funeral. He said he was going to meet us here.'

'I know but he should be here by now. I've texted him a few times but no reply,' explained Jacob.

'I'll give him a call,' Ally told him. She pulled out her phone, found Barnes' number and placed it against her ear. No more than two seconds later, Ally moved the phone from her ear. 'Straight to voicemail,' she told him.

'I think something may be wrong, Ally.'

'I'm sure it's nothing,' she said while studying the worried expression on his face. 'But we'll go and check out the cemetery since it was the last place any of us saw him.'

'I'll ask Ethan to see if he can trace Barnes' phone,' Jacob said before making his way over to Ethan.

Ethan, Brian and Sarah were all squashed around one small table with Chloe Fisher, the forensic investigator, who perched with them. They all took their attention off one another and turned towards Jacob.

'I think Barnes may be missing,' he informed them of his suspicion. 'Ethan, would you be able to trace his phone, please? Me and Ally are going to check the cemetery as it's the last place any of us had seen him.'

'Yes, Jacob, no problem,' replied Ethan.

'What do you want us to do?' Sarah asked.

'Would you be able to check to see if Barnes went home?'

'Of course,' replied Sarah, 'But I don't know where he lives.'

'I do,' Brian piped up.

The three of them finished up their drinks quickly before grabbing their coats and heading out the door. Jacob made his way back over to Ally who was now back at the table with his family. He grabbed his pint from the table and downed it as quick as he could.

'Let's go,' he uttered.

Ally finished up her drink and picked her coat up from the back of her chair. She gave Adam and Kate a slight wave before following Jacob out of the door. Jacob ran over towards his car as Ally caught up and snatched the keys out of his hands.

'I think I'd better drive, don't you?' she informed him with a rhetorical question.

Jacob glared at her before moving over to the passenger side. They both entered the car and drove to the cemetery. He had no idea what he would find, but he was hoping it would be something that could help them in the disappearance of their DCI.

It turned 3.44 pm by the time Jacob and Ally arrived in the cemetery car park. They both exited the car and made their way over to where Barnes had parked his car when Jacob received a call from Ethan.

'Jacob, I tried tracing Barnes' phone but no such luck. I think the phone is off. The last location was the cemetery,' he informed Jacob.

'We're here now, Ethan. Barnes' car is gone. Do you know if there is any way of tracking it?'

'Barnes' car was never fitted with a tracker, so I'm afraid not. We could track his car through CCTV images but that could take days, even weeks, by which time he could be gone. Have you heard anything from Sarah or Brian yet?' Ethan asked.

'Not yet, but we'll keep you updated,' Jacob replied before putting the phone down. 'Ethan said the last place Barnes' phone could be traced was here,' he relayed to Ally.

'Right. Let's search the area. There has to be something that can help us explain what happened.'

The pair of them looked around the car park. Five minutes had passed before Jacob noticed something on the floor below him. He crouched down, his eyes trying to analyse what it was. But he knew deep down. Bright red spots of liquid. He was just hoping Barnes was still alive.

'Ally, over here,' he yelled.

She came running over to where she saw Jacob crouched over red spots on the floor. She looked at Jacob who was staring directly at her with a sad look upon his face.

'Do you think it's his?' she asked, knowing she knew what his reply would be.

'Without a doubt,' he replied. 'We need to find him, Ally, and fast.'

Sarah and Brian pulled up outside Barnes' home address. His family had moved out a year ago when he and his wife went through their messy divorce. Brian had known Barnes for many years and visited his house on many occasions.

They both walked up the pathway towards the house. Barnes' car wasn't on the drive so they knew the chances were he wasn't there. But that didn't stop them. Sarah tried the door handle to see if it was open, but it wasn't. *No surprise there. Who leaves their door open?* she thought.

Brian knew exactly where to find a spare key. He walked through the back gate and into Barnes' garden and lifted up a plant pot, which had seen better days. It was crumbling with cracks throughout. Sarah made her way into the garden to see Brian holding a key in front of him with a smile on his face.

'Where did you find that?' she asked him.

'You forget how many years I've known the man,' he smiled.

'True,' she also smiled along with him.

Brian placed the key in the back door, and they entered the house of their boss. The house was dark. Curtains and blinds were closed, empty beer bottles, dirty bowls and plates surrounded every surface. *Barnes lives like a slob*, Sarah told herself.

'Barnes is a very respectable man,' she began, 'but looking around, this is not the life of the man I know.'

'You think you know,' Brian commented.

'Well yes. I don't get it,' she continued. 'Barnes is well presented. Clean-shaven and well dressed. I'm looking around his home, and I'm disgusted by the mess he's left.'

'Don't judge the man,' Brian yelled at her. 'You don't know what he's been through.'

'Oh and you do?' she replied with a question, not taking any shit off her partner.

'As a matter of fact, yes I do,' he answered. 'He went through a very hard time when his wife left him and asked for a divorce. That's what broke him. I don't think he ever really recovered. Then recently, losing his old partner, his friend, to the one person they both helped after the death of her sister, really crushed him,' he explained to her.

Sarah began to feel bad. She wished she had just shut her mouth. *Why do I always get myself into these situations?* she asked herself.

'I'm sorry,' she apologised to Brian. 'I just open my mouth sometimes and say really stupid shit.'

'It's okay. Let's just search for anything that can help us find him.'

The pair of them searched Barnes' home but couldn't find a single thing that could help them. Barnes was missing, gone and they had no leads, nothing to go on. The search for Barnes was beginning to look like a dead end.

It was 5.43 pm by the time the forensic investigators arrived on scene at the cemetery. Jacob and Ally needed them to take a sample of the blood for testing, to see if it truly was Barnes' blood. Chloe Fisher was also there taking photos. While Jacob and Ally left the forensic officers to do their job, the pair of them took a walk over to the nearest bench, overlooking the whole cemetery, and sat down.

'I really hope the others find something that can help us,' Jacob said.

'Me too,' replied Ally.

They sat there for only a few minutes before Jacob became restless and raised himself from his seat. He couldn't sit still, he felt he needed to do something. Time was slipping away and they were no closer to finding Barnes.

'I can't just sit here,' he shouted. 'I need to find him. That man has done so much for me this past couple of months. We need to find him.'

'I know, Jacob,' she said, 'but we have no other leads. We have to see whether this is his blood first. We've got Barnes on a missing alert so every officer in Birmingham is on the lookout for him and his car. Don't worry, we'll find him,' Ally consoled him.

'You're right, Ally,' he said as he began to sit back down.

Something caught Jacob's eye before his bum hit the bench. His eyes were diverted to the bin at the side of the bench. Something in the bin might be of some use in helping them find him. Barnes' phone was peeking out from under a dirty piece of tissue.

'Ally. I think I've found something,' he informed her while reaching into his coats inside pocket and retrieving a latex glove.

'What is it?' she asked.

'I think it's Barnes' phone,' he answered, before shouting out to Chloe to take a photo for evidence.

He placed the glove on his hand while Chloe took the pictures they needed. Then Jacob pulled the phone out of the bin. The screen had been smashed and scratched like it had been stamped on by somebody's foot.

'I need an evidence bag over here,' he shouted to the forensic officers. 'I hope this can help us find him,' he said to Ally.

Chapter 2

Jack Roberts hadn't run in over four weeks, ever since his experience in the woods. He was so frightened, he'd forgotten how he'd got home. That night had terrified him for weeks, making him give up his passion for running.

His wife had asked him many times what was wrong, but he always insisted he was fine. She noticed his behaviour had become erratic over the past few weeks; looking out of windows and making sure doors were locked.

'Are you not going out for your run tonight?' she asked him.

'No,' he replied. 'I think I'll just stay home again tonight.'

'Why? You used to love running,' she reminded him. 'What's going on with you?'

'I just don't fancy going running, okay,' he yelled while peeping through the blinds.

'You've been acting so strange ever since your last run. What happened?' she asked, edging closer to him. 'You know you can talk to me, Jack.' She placed her hand on his back.

He jumped as her hand gently touched his shirt. 'I'm fine. Just stop asking me!' he yelled again before storming out of the house.

His wife, Charlotte, stood in shock as she watched him leave the house. *What is going on with him?* she thought. *What is going through his head?* She had no idea and he was beginning to scare her. She peered out of the window to see her husband walking down the street. *Where would he be going at this time of night?*

Jack needed to go on a walk to clear his head. He hated himself for shouting at his wife like that, but he was scared of what he saw that night. He watched his back as he walked down the street, and turned his head in every direction.

Nothing had ever frightened him so much before that night. The person he saw stood in front of him still scared him, even though his memory was blurry when he tried to remember their face. The whispers that surrounded him still haunted him, during the day and in his dreams.

Jack came towards the end of his street and turned left on to Russell Road. He just kept walking, not realising how far he was going. All that was going through his mind was that night.

'Jack,' a voice whispered down a cold, dark alleyway. 'Jack, come here.'

Jack glared down the alleyway, uncertain of who was calling him into the dark. Tears of fear filled his eyes. He was terrified. *Is this that guy again?* he wondered, but not remembering what their face looked like. He wiped the tears from his eyes, put the fear to the back of his mind and followed the sound of whispers into the dark alleyway. The moonlight revealed a shadowy figure in front of him. His hand began to tremble, but he tried to forget about it, wanting to move forward.

The whispers kept calling to him as he continued to walk forward. The voice sounded familiar. It was the same voice from that night. The same voice he'd been hearing in his dreams.

'You're almost there, Jack,' the whispers continued. 'A few more steps.'

As he got closer, he was able to see the person's face. *Maybe the reason I can't remember their face is because it's disfigured*, he thought. As he glared at their face, his vision became blurry, and he began to slowly lose feeling in his legs.

'What do you want?' he asked before dropping to the floor.

But he didn't get an answer. He passed out before the person could speak. Laying on the floor in front of his stalker, who he'd been scared of for weeks, Jack was now in a vulnerable position.

An hour had passed and Jack came back around. The floor was cold and wet. His body ached as he pulled himself onto his feet. *What happened?* he asked himself. He was all alone in the alleyway. Only the sound of passing cars could be heard. No whispers, and nobody stalking him. The fear crept back into his mind. Jack stared down towards his hands, which were shaking viciously from fear. He started to sprint home, though he couldn't run for long as his legs ached.

As he reached the end of Russell Road he turned back into The Russells and continued down the street until he reached his house. He stood at his front door for a moment, turned his head to stare back down the street before entering his home.

Before he could shut the door behind him, Charlotte came rushing towards him with a face full of anger.

'Where have you been?' she shouted at him. 'I've been sat up, worried sick about you.'

'I just went out to clear my head,' he responded with sadness in his voice.

'Why did you just walk out like that? What's going on in your head?'

'I don't know,' he cried, placing his face in his hands and sitting on the floor.

'I just want you to talk to me,' she pleaded, changing her tone with her husband. She sat on the floor beside her husband and held him tight within a hug, caressing and comforting him.

Back at the CID, Jacob and Ally were still on the hunt for Barnes. It was late, but Jacob remained focused on the task at hand. They were awaiting the results from the blood found in the cemetery, even though they already knew who it belonged to.

Officers were still patrolling the streets, looking out for Barnes' car. Jacob wondered if he'd ever see Barnes again. He saw him as a father, especially since his own father had been murdered by his fiancee. The fiancee who had become their number one suspect for Barnes' disappearance, let alone for the brutal murders that took place before that. Lily deceived Jacob and his entire family. She crushed his heart the day she decided to kill his father and step-mother and he learnt the truth about who she really was.

Ally patted him on the shoulder. 'I think I'm going to go home,' she informed him. 'Good night, Jacob.'

'Good night, Ally,' he replied.

She swiftly stepped out for the night, leaving Jacob all alone in the office. The lights were off and he was working in the dark. The only light he had was from the computer monitors. But Jacob didn't mind. He quite liked the dark lately. His life had become very much the same since the beginning of the last case. Darkness seemed to follow him wherever he went.

He moved his eyes away from the monitor and onto the clock. *Oh my, look at the time.* Jacob shot up off his chair and logged off the computer, before exiting the station for the night.

He entered his car and drove home. He couldn't bear to think he used to share his home with that monster. His entire life with her had become a lie just so she could get close to his father and seek her revenge. Now his home and life felt empty, even though it was far from it. He had his family, his friends. But the feeling was always there, no matter how he felt.

Thirty minutes had passed before Jacob pulled up outside his apartment. He sat there for a minute before leaving his car. Thoughts kept playing on his mind. *Where would she take Barnes? She must have found a place well before any of this.*

He pulled himself out of the car and strutted into the building. No ghosts following him, no stuttering lights, just Jacob. He placed his key inside the lock and entered his apartment.

Everyone was in bed. The apartment was silent and dark. He felt the wall for the light switch. The light beamed brightly as the bulb flashed on, blinding him. He glanced around at the surprisingly clean apartment. *Wow, Belle must have been busy*, he thought.

Jacob headed for his bedroom, stripped off his clothes and entered the bathroom. He stared at himself in the mirror, noticing how tired he looked, before hoping in the shower. He washed the day off, before breaking down into tears. His mind couldn't stop thinking that the nightmare he was living. Lily was set out to destroy him and his entire life. He hoped Barnes was alright wherever he was.

Jacob got ready for bed. He stood there once again, staring at the bed he once shared with Lily. A tear released itself before he wiped it from his cheek. Deciding to sleep on the sofa for another night, he pulled some blankets out of the wardrobe, before leaving the bedroom. He lay down on the sofa and placed the blanket over his tired body. His head hit the pillow and he was gone. He had fallen asleep within seconds.

Chapter 3

It was freezing in the abandoned warehouse. The temperature had plummeted since the sunset. Barnes hung from his wrists, with as little as just his shirt and trousers on. The handcuffs that bound his wrists had created cuts. His arms ached from being raised above his head, but there was nothing he could do about it. Small amounts of blood trickled from his wrists from where the handcuffs cut him.

His shirt had been ripped open so cuts could be made on his chest. Barnes' breath created smoke as it left his mouth from the drop in temperature. He was so cold, but his captor didn't care, in fact, she relished in the idea of Barnes being frozen.

Barnes was out cold. He had been most of the day. Lily sat watching him, knowing she was in the final stage of her plan for revenge. She pondered on what she was going to do to him. Barnes was the last person to be a part of her plan and she wanted to make him suffer.

Lily lost patience in waiting for Barnes to come around. She picked up a bucket of ice-cold water and threw it over him.

'Wakey, wakey.'

Barnes sprung back to life and gasped for breath as the freezing water took his breath away.

'What? Where am I?' he asked, trying to catch his breath back.

'You're at my new crib. What do you think?' she joked.

'Why am I here?'

'I think you know the answer to that.'

'I had nothing to do with your sister's death,' he tried to explain, but she wasn't having any of it.

'Oh please. I remember you were both there that night. I watched your partner push my sister off the rails of that car park.'

'What? He never pushed your sister, she jumped,' he informed her.

'She wouldn't do that,' Lily dismissed what he'd told her. 'She wouldn't leave me behind.'

'Well, she did. No matter how much you try to deny it, she had no choice. It was either that or be put away for the crimes she'd committed. We'd have preferred her to have come with us, but it was her decision in the end, and that was the decision she chose, whether you like it or not.'

Lily didn't like the comments coming out of his mouth. She retaliated, smacking him in the cheek with the back of her hand, resulting in her engagement ring making a cut across his face. Barnes became mad.

'Do not talk about my sister like that!' she yelled. 'She loved me and she'd have never committed suicide. You're just covering your own arse.'

'Why would I lie? I've got nothing to gain. You're going to kill me either way. I know I'm not getting out of this alive.'

'Well it's nice to see you're right about something,' she smiled. 'I've got another question to ask you, Joe.'

'Fire away,' he replied.

'What did you do with the diamonds you found at the last crime scene?' she asked him.

'I don't know what you're talking about,' he lied.

'I know you took them into evidence. Where are they?'

'Look, I don't know what diamonds you are talking about.'

'Don't play stupid with me, Joe,' she raised her voice. 'I need those diamonds, so I'll ask you again before I get really creative. Where are they?'

'As I've already told you, I don't know!' he yelled back at her.

Lily pulled a surgical knife off a metal tray filled with other objects and pointed it directly at Barnes' chest, before making an incision. Barnes held back a scream of pain. He didn't want to seem weak, but Lily knew how to torture someone. She had been thinking about it for weeks. It was all she thought about.

'Now, I'm going to ask you again. Where are the diamonds?' she shouted.

No one was around to hear her shouting at Barnes. The warehouse had been abandoned and empty for years, deserted in an empty industrial section of the city. Holes in the roof let drips of rainwater splash on the ground below. Nobody would ever know Barnes was being held there.

'I don't know how many times I need to tell you this. I don't know what you are talking about.'

'Wrong answer,' she replied as she opened up a new cut in his chest.

Barnes kept his screams silent again and moved his head away from her line of sight. He didn't know how long he'd be able to hold out before giving her the answer she needed.

'You're stronger than I imagined, Joe. I honestly thought you'd have broken by now,' she laughed slightly.

'You're crazy, you know that? You threw away everything, just for revenge. Jacob, his family, they treated you like you were their own.'

'It needed to be done.'

'No, it didn't,' he retaliated. 'You could have just lived your life, knowing what your sister did was just plain evil. But you didn't and acted just as awful as she did. Jacob loved you. He still does love you, but you've broken his heart and completely destroyed the life you both built together.'

'I wish things could've been different, but they couldn't. I needed to do what I did. I owed that much to my sister. I needed to bring my mother back.'

'Back? Back from where?'

'My mother worked for a company. You must already know she worked with Ava's parents. Daisy found my mothers research, which is how she knew what she was doing would bring our mother back,' she explained.

Barnes laughed. 'What a fairy tale. Let me guess, this story doesn't have a happily ever after?'

'Not yet anyway,' she turned away from him.

'So where is your mother?' he asked.

'I have no idea. I don't even think Daisy knew. All I know is the diamonds are the key. That's what was in my mother's research.'

'But why the ritual killings? What do they have to do with the diamonds?'

'I never had the diamonds to begin with. The ritual was to bring the diamonds to me. It was the only way I would be able to get them,' she explained. 'So I need you to tell me where they are now.'

'I don't know,' he continued to lie.

She turned back around with a larger knife in her hand. 'You're doing this to yourself,' she said pointing the tip of the blade into his stomach.

It penetrated its way past his skin making a small incision. Barnes couldn't resist but to yell out in pain. His screams echoed throughout the warehouse, but only he and Lily could hear them.

Chapter 4

Another sunrise woke Jack from his slumber. 8.17 am displayed on the clock next to his bed as he decided to drag himself out of bed and make himself and Charlotte a cup of coffee.

He slowly made his way downstairs and into the kitchen, boiled the kettle and waited. His eyes couldn't help but stare out of the kitchen window. Minutes had passed and the kettle had boiled, but Jack continued staring out the window. Charlotte entered the kitchen and saw her husband standing completely still.

'So much for the coffee,' she joked.

Jack snapped out of his trance. 'Sorry honey,' he replied.

'What were you thinking about?'

'I don't know,' he stared at her with a confused look upon his face.

'What do you mean, you don't know?'

'I can't remember,' he admitted, trying his best to remember.

'It was only a few minutes ago, Jack. How do you not remember?'

'I just don't!' he raised his voice at her again.

'I think there's something wrong with you, Jack,' she expressed her concern.

'What are you talking about? I'm fine.'

'Then why have you stopped running? You used to go out every night for a run, but now you don't. Why?'

'I just don't want to do it anymore, okay?' he continued shouting at her.

'You're scaring me, Jack. You've never behaved like this our entire marriage. What happened that night?' she asked him, knowing something about it was bothering him.

Suddenly his head began to pound with an ungodly headache. He held his head in his hands and cried out in pain.

'Jack, what's wrong?' Charlotte asked with concern.

'My head is killing me,' he yelled.

'We need to get you to a doctor.'

'It's just a headache. I need some paracetamol and I'll be fine.'

Charlotte grabbed a glass from the cupboard and filled it with tap water, before grabbing the paracetamol.

'Here you go,' she said as she handed it to him.

Jacob shot up, sweating from his nightmare. Nightmares have become a common thing for him lately. His current nightmare was about his mother's murder. He and Adam were just kids when their mother was killed, and they could hear the whole thing from the closet they were hiding in. John Wright always believed she was murdered by Daisy

Blackwood's crazy killing cult, but there had never been any evidence to prove it.

Jacob could see Belle in the kitchen making her breakfast. He nipped off to his bedroom and headed straight for his en-suite bathroom. Jacob's body was covered in sweat. The nightmares he'd had, terrified him. It felt as if his own brain was trying to torture him as much as possible. His life wasn't getting any easier.

After Jacob got dressed, he headed for the kitchen. Belle was already halfway through her cereal when he joined her and noticed she was dressed in a uniform for the local cafe.

'How come you're dressed like that?' he asked her.

'Got me a job, didn't I?' she replied with a huge grin.

'Well done, Belle,' he congratulated her. 'I'm guessing it's for the cafe down the road?'

'Yep.'

'I'll have to pop by sometime.'

'Have you found your boss yet?' she asked, before pushing another spoonful of cereal into her mouth.

'Not yet. We've got no leads. I just hope he's still alive,' he answered her question while placing his head in his hands, trying not to get too emotional.

Belle patted him on the back. 'You'll find him. You're a fantastic detective and an awesome human being,' she comforted him. 'You took me in after Alex's murder. You didn't know me and could have thrown me into the system, but you didn't and I'm so grateful for that.' She hugged him.

He replied to her hug with open arms.

Jacob's phone began to beep. He glanced down to see an email from his father's solicitor. It was a date and time for the reading of his father's Last Will and Testament.

'I'll see you later,' Belle said while cleaning away her bowl.

'Yeah, I'll see you later,' he replied, not removing his eyes from his phone.

Belle left the apartment and headed to her new job. Kate still hadn't woken up. She took her parents death just as hard as Jacob and had stopped eating. She spent most days locked away in her room with the only contact she had being Belle, only because they shared a room together.

Jacob rose up from his seat and strutted to Kate's room, knocked on the door and waited for her reply.

'Come in,' he heard a muffled voice say from the other side of the door.

Jacob opened it. 'I've just had an email from dad's solicitor. His Will reading is tomorrow at noon. Make sure you're ready. They want all three of us to attend,' he informed her.

'Okay,' she replied.

'I'm off to work now. Are you going to be alright?'

'I'll be fine.'

'Are you sure?' She nodded. 'Okay. I'll see you later.'

Jacob left the room shutting the door behind him. He didn't know what to say to her, just like she didn't know what to say back to him. They were both mourning the loss of their family.

Jacob picked up his wallet and keys off the side before grabbing his coat. It was time for him to go to work.

Jacob pulled into the station at 9.34 am. He was greeted by Sarah who pulled in just after him. She exited her car and made her way towards him.

'Hey, Jacob. How are you?' she asked, already knowing the answer.

'I'm fine,' he lied. 'I had an email from my father's solicitor this morning. We've got to attend his Will reading tomorrow.'

'That's a bit late notice isn't it?'

'I know, but I don't mind. I just want to get it over and done with.'

'Yeah, I see your point.'

The pair of them entered the CID. Ethan and Brian were already sat at their desks. Sarah plonked herself down and logged onto her computer. Jacob scouted the office for Ally, but she was nowhere to be seen.

'Hey, Ethan,' Jacob tried to grab his attention.

'Yeah,' Ethan replied.

'Have you seen Ally?'

'I think she's in the briefing room,' Ethan informed him.

'Thanks.'

Jacob placed his coat over his chair, before heading towards the room. Ally was placing photos onto the investigation board of where Barnes disappeared as he entered.

'Morning,' Jacob greeted her.

Ally turned around and smiled at him. 'Good Morning, Jacob.'

'Have we got any new leads on Barnes yet?'

'Not yet. I just decided to set up the investigation board. We will find him.'

'I just hope he's still alive. I'm starting to think the longer we take, the less likely he is to be alive.'

'Me too, but we've got to have faith.' There was a pause before Ally spoke again. 'We had the test results of the spots of blood back. It is a match for Barnes. We think his abductor-'

Jacob cut Ally off. 'You mean Lily?'

'Yes. We think Lily must have knocked Barnes out and abducted him in his own car after smashing his phone and chucking it in the bin we found it in. The lab is also trying to find any prints on the phone as well as recover as much data as they can,' she explained.

'Hopefully, they'll be something we can go off.'

'Look, Jacob, I know life is very difficult for you at the moment, but you don't have to be here.'

'I need to be here, Ally. I need to help find Barnes. I can't leave him to die at the hands of my fiancee. I need to find him and that bitch.'

'I understand. Just remember, if you need anything, come and talk to me.' She smiled at him.

'Thank you, Ally,' he said before leaving the briefing room and returning to his desk.

Jacob noticed an A4 size envelope laying on his desk. It was addressed to him. He slowly opened it and removed the contents from inside. Photos appeared from the inside.

He couldn't believe his eyes. *What am I seeing?* Photos of him and Barnes at the crime scene of Sophie Mackenzie. *Is this some sick joke?* he asked himself as he flicked through the photos.

Jacob marched towards the briefing room where Ally continued to place photos on the investigation board. He stood there, silently, with the photos in his hands. Ally felt his presence in the room and turned to look at him.

'Is everything okay Jacob?' she asked. 'What have you got there?'

'Photos,' he replied in shock.

'Photos of what?'

'Me and Barnes at the crime scene of Sophie Mackenzie.'

'What?'

'Someone sent this to me.'

'Do you have any idea who?'

'Not sure who, but I think it's Lily and she's taunting me,' he began to explain. 'She must have been watching us the entire time, seeing how it played out. Or maybe she even got Mia and Ava to admire their work.'

'Has anybody else touched these photos?' she asked.

'I don't know.'

'Okay, we need to get it to the lab right away,' she explained. 'We need to see if there are any other prints on them.'

Jacob agreed and the pair of them headed down towards the lab.

It was noon when Jack decided to call his wife at home. He needed to apologise for his behaviour towards her that morning. His migraine had gone and he felt much better. But he still had a constant fear that his stalker was following him.

The phone kept ringing and ringing. There was no answer. *Maybe she's out*, he thought. He did think about calling her mobile, but he didn't want to bother her. He could always wait until he got home. Jack carried on with his work.

Minutes passed before another headache attacked. This time the pain was worse than the last. He opened his desk drawer and removed a packet of paracetamol and scouted his office for anything that could help him swallow them. The only thing he found was a cup of coffee which had been sat on his desk all morning. It was stone cold and made him gag while trying to swallow it.

He glanced out of his window to see a man staring at him. It was the man from the other night. The man with the disfigured face was just staring right through him like he was looking into his soul.

Jack kept rubbing his head. The pain was unbearable, but that didn't remove his focus from the man staring at him. Jack opened the window to feel the crisp breeze upon his face.

'What do you want?' he bellowed out the window.

The man just stood there, staring directly at him. His focus never wandered. Jack began to get goosebumps as the man smiled at him. It wasn't just any smile, it was the type of smile a sociopath would give. He enjoyed scaring Jack, and it showed.

Jack closed the window and shut his blinds. The man freaked him out. *Why is he following me? What does he want?* It chilled him to the bone. *Do I call the police?* He peered out of the blinds before making a decision, but the man was gone and so was his headache.

Barnes was starving. He'd been hanging for over twenty-four hours without any food or drink. Blood dribbled downward from his chest and wrists. Lily sat watching him, playing with the knife in her hands.

'Any chance of some food? Maybe something to drink?' he asked.

'Yes, when you give me some answers,' she replied.

Barnes chuckled. 'I'm going to give you a poor review. The service here is shocking,' he joked.

Lily smirked before rising to her feet. 'Do you think this is funny?'

'Well, I've got to lighten up a bad situation.'

'Just tell me where the damn diamonds are? I'm losing my patience with you Barnes!' she shouted.

'As I've said, I don't know anything about any diamonds.'

Lily sighed and walked off into a small, rundown office inside the warehouse. Barnes could hear whispers as if there was more than just himself and Lily in the building. He tried to listen carefully, but it was no good. They were too far away for his prying ears to hear.

Barnes looked around for anything that could help him cut himself down. The only items he could see that were of any use were those on Lily's metal tray. *If only I could reach.*

He swung his entire body in a rocking motion so the rope that was holding him up, would swing his feet closer to the tray. He had to be very careful, as one wrong move would alert Lily. The last thing he wanted was to knock the tray and its entire contents on the floor. *Here goes nothing*, he said to himself.

Just as he began to swing his body, Lily and another man exited the office and made their way towards Barnes. Lily's eyes immediately caught sight of Barnes' body swinging towards the tray.

'What do you think you're doing?' she shouted.

The estranged man stood beside her. It was the same man who helped her kidnap him from the cemetery. He stood tall frowning at Barnes with a vicious and terrifying expression.

Before Barnes could even open his mouth to lie about what he was doing, the mysterious man smashed his brick of a fist, straight into Barnes' ribs. A cracking sound echoed across the warehouse as the man's fist made contact with him.

Barnes let out a roar, swinging his head back. The pain was excruciating. The man's expression didn't change. There was no look of joy, or any other kind of emotion, other than anger. Barnes had no idea who this man was, or why he was assisting Lily. All he wanted was to just get the hell out of there as quickly as he could.

'Are you going to talk now?' Lily asked him.

Barnes swallowed his pain. 'I don't know what else you want me to say,' he replied.

'Very well. Just remember, I take no pleasure in this,' she smiled, knowing full well he knew she enjoyed every minute of her revenge.

Barnes let out a slight chuckle before the man ploughed his fist into the other-side of Barnes' ribs. Lily wanted the man dead, but she needed to know where he put the diamonds beforehand. Barnes knew the only way he'd get out of that warehouse alive, was by keeping that information from her.

Barnes coughed up blood and spat it on the floor before the man smashed his other fist into his chest, making Barnes throw up more blood. The remainder dribbled from his bottom lip, landing one drip at a time on the pool of blood below his feet.

'You don't have to do this, you know,' Barnes told the quiet but aggressive man.

'You'd better start talking then,' he replied with a forceful demand.

'Oh shit, he does speak,' Barnes joked at the man. 'So what do you want to talk about?' he continued joking around.

'Don't get funny, old man.' He had a strong London accent and was very well dressed and clean-shaven. Not the usual rough brute. 'Now are you going to give me that information, or are we going to have to get even more physical?'

'Ooh, that sounds like an offer. Shouldn't you buy me dinner first?' Barnes kept joking around, trying to hide his fear and pain.

The man said nothing. He just stood in front of Barnes with his sleeves rolled up to his elbows, ready to take another swing at him. Barnes closed his eyes tight, ready for another blow to the gut. But nothing happened. He opened his eyes to see the man walking away from him. Confused as to why he'd given up on the torture, Barnes yelled back at him.

'Hey, where are you going? You can't be tired already. I thought we were going all night.' He began to laugh at himself, then coughed as the pain hurt more with laughter.

'Oh, I'm not done with you yet,' the man replied seriously.

He turned back to look at Barnes. His hands clutched a battery with what looked like metal spark plugs.

'Oh man, come on. You don't want to do this,' Barnes pleaded with him. 'Do you even know who that monster is or what she's done? Do you even know the real Lily?'

'You don't even know who I am or what I'm capable of. Lily is nothing compared to us,' he answered while placing the clips on Barnes' toes.

'Us? There's more than one of you?' he asked.

'Yes. Four of us. My name's Cain, and my siblings are out there somewhere, wreaking havoc.'

'Who are your siblings?' he continued with his questions.

Cain laughed. 'Enough with your questions. This isn't how this works. Now, are you going to tell me where the diamonds are or are you going to test your pain threshold some more?'

Barnes knew this was it for him. He was either going to tell him or die a painful death.

Chapter 5

7.34 pm. The time Jack pulled his car on to his drive. He turned off his engine and walked towards the front door. As he unlocked the door, he noticed none of the lights were on inside his house. *Maybe Charlotte is still out*, he wondered.

Jack entered and switched on the light in the hallway, locking the door behind him. He removed his jacket and placed it on the row of coat hooks on the wall. That's when he noticed Charlotte's coat and handbag, hanging beside his coat. *That's odd*, he thought.

'Honey, are you home?' he called out. 'Charlotte?'

He peered into the living room, but she wasn't there. He then moved into the kitchen diner, but it was too dark to see. Jack flicked the light on. His heart stopped for a slight moment. He began to feel incredibly sick. His wife, his dearly beloved Charlotte was lying dead on the floor surrounded by a pool of blood.

A metal mallet lay beside her body with remnants of her scalp attached. *How could somebody do this?* He fell to the floor, crying his eyes out.

'Charlotte?' he cried out. 'Charlotte? Please wake up.'

Jack felt sick rising up his throat. He had to make a quick dash for it out of the front door and threw up on his driveway. *I need to call the police*, he told himself as he wiped the sick from his lips.

He pulled his mobile phone from his pocket and dialled 999.

'Hello,' a voice spoke on the other end of the phone.

'I need the police,' Jack shouted down the phone hysterically. 'My wife's been murdered.'

'Okay, sir.' the operator replied. 'What's your address?'

'Number 8, The Russells, Birmingham. Oh God, I think she's dead,' he informed them.

'Officers will be with you shortly as well as an ambulance crew. Please, sir, try not to enter the house until the paramedics and police arrive.'

'Okay,' he sobbed.

Minutes later the ambulance arrived, followed by a squad of police cars. Jack sat on his porch, crying hysterically as the ambulance crew approached him.

'Hello, sir,' one of the paramedics greeted him. 'My name's Becky. Can you tell me where your wife is?'

Jack lifted his head, removing his eyes from the ground and focused on the paramedic. His eyes covered in tears. He wiped them away before replying.

'She's in the kitchen.'

Both paramedics rushed through the house towards his wife's lifeless corpse once they were given the go-ahead by the officer on the door. Jack was then approached by a couple of detectives.

'Hello. Are you Mr Roberts?'

'Yes,' he continued to sob.

'I'm Detective Inspector Ally Miller and this is my partner Detective Sergeant Jacob Wright,' she introduced themselves. 'I'm so sorry for your loss. Are we able to talk?'

'I don't understand why anybody would want to do this?'

'Do you know of anyone who would've wanted to harm your wife?' Ally asked.

'Charlotte. Her name is Charlotte,' he corrected her.

'I'm sorry.'

'And no, I don't know anyone who would want to do this to her.' Jack thought for a moment about the stalker who had been following him since his time in the woods. 'This might sound odd, but there has been someone following me for the last few weeks. I didn't think anything of it but I saw him earlier today at the office.'

'Did you contact the police?' Jacob asked him while taking notes.

'No. I don't know why I didn't. Something has always stopped me.'

'Did you get a good look at this person?' Ally continued questioning him.

'Yes. His face is all deformed,' he informed them.

'Deformed how?' Jacob fired away another question.

'It's all scarred.'

'Thank you for your time, Mr Roberts. An officer will be with you shortly. And once again, my condolences on your loss,' Ally said softly.

Jacob and Ally moved into the house where they crossed paths with the paramedics in the hallway.

'She's deceased. We couldn't find a pulse on her,' Julie informed the detectives.

'Okay, thank you,' replied Ally as the two paramedics left the house.

The pair of them carried on through to the kitchen where they found the ungodly sight of Charlotte Roberts, dead on the floor. Both Ally and Jacob covered their mouths with their hands.

'We're going to need to get forensics in here right away,' Jacob advised Ally.

'Let's get out of here before we contaminate the scene,' she replied.

Twenty minutes had passed before forensics appeared. The crime scene had been cordoned off around the street. Police cars were everywhere, with their lights flashing. Crowds gathered like they usually do, fishing for the next big story.

The forensic team got dressed into their white overalls before entering the premises. Chloe Fisher was among the team, gathering as much evidence as they could.

Jacob and Ally remained within the perimeter of the police tape, interviewing neighbours and potential witnesses who might have any information that could help with the case.

'They were a nice couple,' old Dorothy from across the road was filling them in. 'They've never really been any bother, until the other night.'

Her grey hair was short and curly as if she'd just had a fresh perm.

'What do you mean, the other night?' Ally asked her.

'Well, I was emptying my bins and I heard shouting coming from their house. Then all of a sudden, it went quiet. I mean really quiet.'

'Then what happened?' Jacob asked, writing down notes.

'I went inside and made a cup of tea,' she continued.

Ally and Jacob turned to face one another, and let out a little giggle.

'Is there anything else you remember?' Ally asked.

'No, I don't think there is.'

'Thank you very much for your time, Mrs Thorpe,' Ally politely thanked her and moved on to their next witness.

'Hello. I'm DI Miller and this is my partner, DS Wright,' she introduced themselves once again but to Mr Avi Hussain this time, with both of them taking turns to shake his hand.

Mr Hussain was a valued member of the community. He loved doing charity work within the neighbourhood and was always there to lend a helping hand to whoever needed it.

'We just have a few questions to ask you,' Jacob informed him.

'Do you remember hearing or seeing anything strange?' Ally asked.

'Not really. There was just a lot of shouting,' answered Avil.

'Do you remember where the shouting came from?' Ally continued.

'Yeah,' he pointed, 'from the Roberts household.'

'What were they like?'

'Usually quite quiet, but the last couple of weeks, Jack's been acting very strange.'

'How do you mean?'

'He used to run most nights. I mean, he loved running, but now he stays in the house, peeping through the windows. He's been like that since December.'

'Thank you,' Jacob replied. 'If you remember anything else that could help, could you please give us a call?' Jacob handed him a card with his number on it. 'Thank you for your time.'

Mr Hussain walked away from them and back inside his house. Jacob and Ally were starting to think along the same lines, that the husband could be involved.

'What are your first thoughts?' Ally asked him.

'The husband might be involved,' he replied.

'Exactly what I was thinking,' she passed over her initial thoughts.

'Easy. Case closed,' Jacob joked.

Jacob and Ally strolled over towards Jack Roberts, who was covered in a foil blanket. Tears still streaming down his cheeks and his nose still sniffling.

'Mr Roberts. I'm sorry to bother you, but we need you to come down the station with us to answer a few more questions,' Ally asked him nicely.

'Can I not come tomorrow,' he sobbed. 'I've just lost my wife.'

'I know and we are deeply sorry for your loss, but this cannot wait,' Ally continued.

'Okay,' he replied.

Jacob led Jack to the police car which would be escorting him to the station and placed him gently inside before shutting the door. Jacob then met his partner back at their car and they started their journey back to the station.

Jacob and Ally arrived back at the station just before 9 pm. Jack Roberts had already been processed by the escorting officer and placed inside an interview room. He sat waiting patiently for his lawyer to arrive.

Jack kept processing the night's events. *Why do I get the feeling they are going to arrest me? It's got to be that guy who's been stalking me.* No matter what he thought, he knew it was strange that he was sitting inside a police interview room waiting for his lawyer.

The door opened and Simon Ballard walked in. Simon had been Jack's solicitor for seven years. And in that time, he'd never been sat with Jack inside a police station. Simon had also been Alex Baker's lawyer as well as his friend.

'Simon, thank you for coming,' Jack said, holding his hand out for Simon to shake it.

'What a mess you've gotten yourself into,' replied Simon, as he shook Jack's hand before sitting down beside him. 'So what's going on?'

'My wife was murdered,' he sobbed his answer. 'I believe they think I've killed her.'

'And did you?' he asked.

'Of course I didn't,' he yelled at him, upset that he'd even think that.

'Okay. You know I have to ask to see what I'm dealing with. It's the best way for me to help you.'

'I know. I'm sorry, it's just been a really stressful day.'

Jacob and Ally sat inside the briefing room discussing what questions they were going to ask Mr Roberts. Ally had another investigation board brought into the briefing room to help with the investigation into Charlotte Roberts' death. Two boards sat next to one another. Two open investigations. The team still had to investigate Barnes' disappearance as well as their new case.

Ally was pinning photos of Charlotte's murder onto the new board, listening to what Jacob had to say. Their only real lead was her husband who was currently sitting inside the interview room with his solicitor.

'So, her husband comes back from work and finds her dead on the kitchen floor. Neighbours heard shouting earlier that morning between the pair. Do we have a time of death on our victim yet?' Jacob asked her.

'They suspect she died around 9 am. We need to ask Mr Roberts what time he left for work this morning,' she replied, still pinning information to the board.

Jacob continued writing things on a sheet of paper. Their list of questions was growing, even though they both felt this was going to be an easy case to close.

'What does Mr Roberts do for work?' Ally asked Jacob.

'He's a manager in the car industry or something along those lines.'

'He mentioned a stalker,' she continued. 'We need to ask him more about that. Description, build, stuff like that.'

'Do you think he could have just been making that up, to help with his innocence?'

'Maybe, but we still need to get as much information as possible,' she replied.

'Has his lawyer arrived yet?' he asked.

'Yes, he's currently in the interview room with Mr Roberts.'

Jacob stopped what he was doing for a moment, realising he'd totally forgotten about Barnes the past couple of hours. Barnes had been on his mind the last couple of days. His disappearance hit Jacob hard, especially after the death of his father.

'Ally, we've totally forgotten about Barnes,' he said. 'He's out there somewhere waiting for us to find him, and here we are, pushing his case to one side.'

'It's not like that, Jacob. We haven't forgotten about him, we just have no new leads. As hard as it sounds, we have to continue our jobs otherwise when the time comes, we'll never have the resources to find him,' she tried her best to comfort him, knowing full well, it wasn't working. 'Officers are on full alert, looking for anyone matching Lily and Barnes' descriptions.'

'I know. I just feel incredibly guilty.'

'I know what you mean. I do too.'

'I've got my dad's Will reading tomorrow,' he informed her. 'It's just been a hard couple of months.'

Ally sat beside him and placed her arm around him, pulling him into a hug. The pair of them sat there for a moment, embracing one another. Neither of them wanted to pull away. Jacob felt warmth and happiness from Ally, but every time anything happy flew into his mind, the memory of Lily came flooding back, making it harder for him to get close to anyone.

Jacob pulled away first. His eyes gazed into Ally's. She replied the gaze and her face gradually leaned in closer to his. Their lips were moments away from touching. Ally's eyelids slowly began to close.

Jacob jumped off his seat and grabbed his notes, alerting Ally that he'd moved further away from her. She opened her eyes to see Jacob standing on the other side of the room.

'I think it's time we interviewed Mr Roberts,' he told her.

Ally, all flustered, replied, 'Okay. Let's do this.'

The pair of them left the briefing room and continued their way towards where Jack was being held. Ally didn't know what to say to him. She felt extremely embarrassed about what had just happened. She didn't understand, thinking Jacob felt the same way about her as she did about him.

Jacob opened the door to see Mr Roberts sat next to his solicitor, who he recognised. He remembered Mr Ballard from when they had Alex Baker in custody.

'Mr Ballard,' Jacob held out his hand. 'Nice to see you again, despite the circumstances.'

Simon reached for Jacob's hand and engaged in a handshake. 'Nice to see you too, DS Wright.'

Ally placed a tape inside the recording machine and waited for the loud beep to end before speaking.

'This is Detective Inspector Ally Miller, with Detective Sergeant Jacob Wright on January 3rd at

9.36 pm, interviewing Jack Roberts on the death of Charlotte Roberts. His lawyer, Simon Ballard, is present,' she introduced for the tape. 'Mr Roberts, can you run us through your actions for today?'

'What do you mean by that?' he asked.

'We need an account of your day, from the moment you woke up to the moment we arrived,' Ally answered.

'Well, I woke up around 8, went to the kitchen and boiled the kettle...' He paused.

'And?' Ally noticed he'd zoned out.

Jack's eyes felt as if they had gone elsewhere. His blank expression made Ally, Jacob and even Simon feel scared. It was as if he'd gone somewhere else within his mind. After a few seconds, Jack snapped back to reality.

'I just remember having this excruciating headache. I can't really remember anything after that,' he explained. 'Though I do remember being at work but I can't figure out how I managed to get there.'

His eyes rocked from side to side. His forehead began to dribble with sweat. Jacob noticed how quickly Jack's behaviour had changed.

'Are you okay?' he asked Jack.

Jack didn't answer. He started to pant, gasping for breath. Jack lifted his head and gazed towards the ceiling with his mouth wide open, breathing as hard as he could. He felt as if he was losing air and not being able to breathe.

Jacob turned to Ally, she glanced back at him. She knew something wasn't right.

'Mr Roberts, are you okay? What's wrong?' she asked.

Jack again said nothing.

'We need to get someone in here,' Jacob informed Ally.

But then Jack stopped gasping and panting. He returned his head to look at them. Jacob and Ally were confused about what had just happened. So was Simon. Jack wiped the sweat from his forehead and interlocked his fingers on both his hands, placing them on the table in front of him.

'Are you okay, Jack?' Simon asked him.

'Yes, I'm fine,' he replied calmly.

'Are you sure?' Ally continued to ask. 'You gave us quite a scare.'

'I'm absolutely fine, DI Miller.'

'Are you happy to carry on?'

'As happy as I'll ever be.'

Jacob was noting down the change in Jack's behaviour, beginning to think maybe there was more to Jack Roberts than meets the eye. One moment he couldn't stop crying, mourning the death of his wife, to then having what seemed like a panic attack, and then ending with a strangely calm and blank expression.

'Earlier when we asked you some questions outside your house, you told us you had been followed by someone. Are you able to describe them to us?' Ally continued with the questions.

'A male. About six foot. Disfigured face,' he explained, keeping his eyes looking at the desk while trying to picture him.

'And where had this man been following you?'

'The first time I was out running on my normal route. He stood right in front of me, blocking me from getting past.'

'Then what?'

'I can't remember.'

His facial expression changed again, this time he looked confused. Jack tried his hardest to remember, but he couldn't. The rest of that night was blank like someone had deleted that specific memory from his brain.

'Don't worry, that's fine. You've had a very stressful night. We'll let you get some rest and we'll pick this up another day,' Ally comforted him, knowing she wouldn't get much more out of him at the moment. Ally ended the tape. 'Have you got anyone you can stay with tonight?'

'Don't worry about me. I'll book myself into a hotel for the night,' he replied.

'I'll call you when we're ready to ask you more questions, Mr Roberts,' she informed him while holding her hand out to be shaken.

He nodded and replied the handshake, before leaving the interview room with Simon Ballard. Jacob remained seated until the door closed behind them. He gave a strange gaze at Ally and she knew something was up.

'What is it?' she asked.

'What was that all about?' he answered with another question. 'The strange behaviour in that interview.'

'I know. It was like he was having a panic attack,' she discussed her view.

'I mean the calm and then the sweating after crying and sobbing. He was all over the place,' he explained.

'So you think he's lying? That he's making up the stalker story?'

'I don't know what to believe, but something's not right. If he's innocent, he might know more about who killed his wife than he's saying.'

Barnes was left hanging by his wrists. Unconscious and alone in the dark warehouse, where the only light he had was that from the moon that peeped through the hole in the roof. Dried blood left a trail downwards towards his feet from his wounds.

The electrocution hadn't killed him, but it had definitely weakened him. His body ached from his head to his feet. The cold January air chilled him to the bone.

A dim light from the other end of the warehouse made him open his eyes slightly, seeing the mysterious man and Lily sitting down together eating something in the distance. *I'm starving*, he thought to himself. His stomach rumbled at the thought of food.

He needed to get out of there. His eyes scouted around once more, looking for anything that would help him cut the rope from his wrists. As he tried his best to get closer to the tray of tools, he heard footsteps coming towards him.

'Oh, you're awake,' Lily spoke as she gained closer.

'Just in time to see your gleaming smile,' he continued to joke with her.

'I know you're not going to tell me willingly about where those diamonds are. I've tried to break you, but you're more resilient than I first thought.'

Barnes coughed a laugh before it became uncontrollable. He'd hoped that would have been the last part of the torture, but it was far from it. He caught a glimpse of a tattoo on the man's arm, featuring a horse with a man on top, holding a flag. The man stared back at him with that frown of anger. The same angry frown Barnes had seen earlier that day.

'Tomorrow is a whole new day, and you are going to talk,' Lily continued in a forceful tone.

Barnes decided not to say a word. He knew his luck was about to run out. Lily wanted him dead and he knew it and no matter how long he kept it up, she'd kill him eventually.

Jacob arrived home around 11.30 pm. Tired and drained, he decided to go straight to bed. But as he opened his apartment door, he could see Belle staring right back at him.

'Evening,' she greeted him with a huge grin on her face.

'Why are you so happy?' he asked, forgetting it had been her first day in her new job.

'Are you not even going to ask me how it went?'

'How what went?'

'My new job,' she answered, holding her hands up at her side.

'Oh Belle, I'm so sorry. I totally forgot,' he replied, lowering his head in shame.

'It's okay. You've had a lot going on lately.'

'So how did it go?'

'Brilliant,' she shouted with a massive grin on her face. 'Made new friends, and I love the job. The boss is good too.'

'That's great to hear. I'm glad you enjoyed it.' He smiled at her excitement.

'And soon I'll be out of your hair.'

'What do you mean?' he asked her.

'Well, now I've got a job, I'll be able to find my own place,' she replied.

'You can stay here. You don't have to move out.'

'Come on, Jacob. You've been really nice to let me stay here as long as I have, but it was never going to be forever. Anyway, I think Kate needs a bit more space.'

He moved in closer towards the kitchen where Belle was leaning on the kitchen island. He placed his keys on the side and leaned opposite her.

'You know I meant it when I said you can stay here for as long as possible,' said Jacob.

'I know,' she smiled. 'Thank you, but I need to do this.'

She kissed him on the cheek before strolling off to her bedroom. Jacob began to feel upset. *Why does she want to leave?* Knowing he had an early start at the solicitor's office in the morning, he decided to head to bed.

His bed felt cold and empty since he'd been sleeping in it alone. The hatred he had for Lily was still inside of him. He tried to replace the feelings he had with hatred and anger, but it was hard. He still loved her.

Then his mind wandered to earlier with him and Ally inside the briefing room. He had felt a connection to Ally since she joined the team. *She feels the same way I do. Why did I walk away?* he asked himself.

Jacob asked himself questions all night, keeping himself awake again.

Chapter 6

It was 9.15 am. Jacob, Adam and Kate were all sat inside their father's solicitors office. John had split everything equally between the three of them. One thing that wasn't shared, was a letter to Jacob left by his father.

Jacob was intrigued but at the same time, worried about what he was going to find in that note. Adam and Kate glared at Jacob wanting him to open it. After the Will had been read, the three of them jumped back inside Adam's car.

'Well, are you going to open it?' Adam questioned him.

'I will when the time is right,' he replied, not taking his eyes off the envelope.

'But why did dad leave just you a letter?'

'I don't know,' replied Jacob. 'I'm worried about what's in this envelope.'

'Just open it then!' Adam shouted, wanting to know what it said.

'I don't know why you're so desperate for me to open this damn letter. It means nothing. Dad is gone and he's not coming back.'

'I know, but are you not a little curious about what he's written?' Adam asked.

'A little,' he replied. 'But I'm not ready.'

'Okay, brother. I'll stop pestering you.'

'Thank you.' He turned his head to face out the window.

Ten minutes passed before Adam pulled up outside Jacob's apartment. He jumped out without saying a word, his focus stayed upon the letter he possessed in his hands. Kate thanked her brother for the ride, before following Jacob back to the apartment. *Why's he written me a letter? Why is it just for me?* He kept asking himself.

Both Jacob and Kate entered the apartment to see Belle lifting a spoonful of cereal to her mouth before she stopped and realised she had an audience.

'How'd it go?' she asked.

'Jacob got a letter,' Kate answered before Jacob could, and opened the fridge to see what there was for her to eat.

'Everything went equally between the three of us,' he finally answered.

'So what's this letter?' Belle continued asking questions.

'I don't know. I haven't opened it.'

'What do you mean, you haven't opened it? Are you not a little bit curious as to why your father left only you a letter?'

Kate peeked her head around the fridge, 'He said he would when the time was right.'

'What harm is going to come from opening a letter from your father?' Belle put it simply.

'I think you're right,' he replied.

Jacob entered his bedroom, closed the door behind him, and sat on his bed. He took a few deep breaths before ripping into the envelope to retrieve the paper inside. Nerves flooded his body, creating a sick feeling inside his stomach. Jacob desperately wanted to know what his father had to say, but at the same time, he didn't want to know.

He pushed the paper back inside the envelope and removed his hand from inside. *Now is not the time*, he thought as he lifted himself off his bed. Jacob placed the envelope inside his bedside drawer.

As he left the bedroom, Kate and Belle stood watching him from the kitchen.

'Well?' Kate asked.

Belle's eyes were fixated on him, wanting to know, as well as Kate, what was written in the letter.

'I didn't read it,' he confessed.

'What?' Kate asked with a confused look on her face.

'I didn't read it,' he repeated. 'I couldn't bring myself to read it.'

'Then give it here, I'll read it to you.'

'No. I'll read it when I'm ready,' he started to raise his voice.

'Okay, calm down.'

'I just don't get why you and Adam are being so pushy about this bloody letter,' he shouted, losing himself.

Belle's eyes diverted downwards at her cereal, feeling awkward, while Kate glared at Jacob with an angry face. He grabbed his keys and his coat and left the apartment. *Who do they think they are? Pressuring me like that*. Work was the only thing that would be able to distract him from the letter.

Jacob arrived at the CID and perched at his desk. The rest of the team tapped away on their keyboards. Jacob pulled his drawer open on his desk, revealing to his eyes a bottle of whiskey he'd been keeping there since his father's death. The office was far too busy for him to take a swig, despite his craving for it.

Shutting the drawer, he focused on his computer monitor, not realising another large envelope had been placed on the side of his desk. Minutes passed before he noticed it to his left. His heart sank, knowing the contents of the envelope would be more photos from one of their crime scenes, knowing that somebody had been watching them the entire time.

Once again, Jacob had his hands inside another envelope, ready to remove the contents. It was what he'd feared. *More photos from another crime scene.* The crime scene of Ella Morgan. *What is this bitch trying to gain from this?* he asked himself. *Is it not enough that she's out there with Barnes? I've got to let Ally know.*

He got up from his seat and marched over towards Barnes' office where Ally had taken residence. On one hand, his fist was clenched and the other grasped the envelope and its contents tightly.

He knocked on the door and waited for Ally to invite him inside. Once inside, he threw the photos on the desk.

'Look at this!' he yelled, but not loud enough for people outside of the office to hear. 'Why's she doing this to me? And why now?'

'I have no idea, Jacob,' she replied calmly, examining the photos.

Jacob sat at the desk opposite Ally, placed his head in his hands and began to sob. Ally rose from her seat and leaned in to hug him.

'It's okay, Jacob,' she comforted him. 'I know you're worried about Barnes. I am too, but don't let her get to you.'

'I can't help it, Ally,' he sobbed.

'Whatever I say to you is not going to make any difference, but just know, Jacob...' she placed her hand on his, 'I'm here for you.'

'Thank you,' he replied, smiling at her but nervous at the same time.

Jacob's feelings for Ally were progressing and he knew she felt the same way. But he wasn't ready for a new relationship just yet. The only thing he wanted to focus on was finding their boss. Every day they wasted, was another day Barnes would be at risk of being killed.

As the pair gazed into one another's eyes, Ethan burst in. Jacob pulled his hand away from Ally's before rising to his feet.

'What is it, Ethan?' he asked.

'They've found it,' Ethan replied.

'Found what?'

'Barnes' car. It's been found outside an old run-down warehouse. Patrol cars are on the scene observing. They're waiting for us,' he explained.

Ethan headed out of the room in a hurry, leaving Ally staring at Jacob.

'Jacob. I need to tell you...'

'It's fine, Ally.'

'Please, I need to explain...'

'Ally, I said it doesn't matter,' he snapped. 'We've got work to do.'

He left Ally alone. She understood why he withdrew his hand from hers, but she wanted to confess how she felt about him. Her feelings had grown for him over the last couple of months and she had a burning desire to tell him.

Jacob entered wearing his jacket and car keys held firmly in his hands.

'Are you coming?' he interrupted her from her thoughts.

'I'll meet you at the car.'

The team arrived at the warehouse around 1.30 pm to find the police car that had been keeping watch, parked up all alone in the distance.

'Where are the officers?' Jacob asked.

The team exited their vehicles and strolled over towards the abandoned police car. Jacob placed his face against the window, glaring inside. He pulled the door handle and to his surprise, it was unlocked. Ally made her way to the back of the car and paused. She was about to open up the boot but hesitated. Her hand pressed the button and the door opened revealing nothing but police equipment inside. Ally sighed with relief, fearing what she could've found inside.

They caught up with the others who had made their way to Barnes' car. They searched the entire car and found nothing but bloodstains inside the boot.

They stealthily continued their way towards the warehouse, making sure not to make a sound. Jacob pulled the door handle and was surprised once again to find the door unlocked. Nothing but silence could be heard, as the team set foot inside. Whoever was inside the warehouse was gone. No sign of Lily and no sign of Barnes.

'Damn it!' Jacob yelled in anger.

Brian stepped over towards a pool of blood where Barnes had been hanging. Surrounding the blood was the two officers, dead on the floor with bullet wounds in their chests.

'Over here,' Brian cried out, before covering his nose and mouth with his left hand.

'Shit,' Sarah swore in disbelief as she approached.

'Looks like we've found the missing officers,' said Ally. 'Let's call this in and get forensics here right away.'

No words were spoken. She had gotten away again, with more innocent people losing their lives.

Jacob felt sick to his stomach as did everyone else. *Who is this woman?* he asked himself. Jacob thought he knew the real Lily, but she had been hiding her true self from everyone she knew.

'Forensics will be here within the hour,' Ally announced. 'When back up arrives we need to secure the perimeter. Let's assume the local news crews will know by now, so please keep them at bay.'

Fifteen minutes passed and the backup officers had arrived and set a perimeter around the warehouse. Another half an hour passed before the forensics team arrived on the scene. Chloe Fisher stepped out of the van and walked over towards Jacob and his team, while the rest of her crew were getting changed into their white suits.

'Did you get her?' she asked without even greeting them.

'No,' Jacob replied, not giving her eye contact. 'She got away again.'

'What about Barnes?'

'He's still missing,' Ally answered.

'You'll get him back.' Chloe placed her hand on his shoulder, before heading back towards her team.

Jacob felt extremely guilty. They were so close but Lily had just gotten away so quickly. It could be days, even months before they could have any scrap of information on Barnes if they get any at all.

'I'm going to call it a day,' Jacob informed the team.

'Are you okay?' Ally seemed concerned about him.

'No, but I'll be fine. I'm just disappointed we missed them,' he admitted. 'I'm tired, Ally. I'm tired of this bitch and her plans. I want my life back the way it was, before all of this.' He started to cry.

Ally moved him outside, back to his car and comforted him. 'I don't know what you're going through right now, and I'm not going to pretend to know, but I'm here if you need to talk,' she hugged him. 'You need someone to lean on, always know, I'm here.'

'Thanks, Ally.'

Jacob got into his car and began his journey home. He wiped the tears from his face, knowing he was not alone in all of this. Ally was a great woman and felt strong feelings towards him, and he wanted to act on his, but couldn't. He needed to trust again before he could get into another relationship.

Chapter 7

10.17 am the next morning, Jacob and Adam were trawling through their father's house. They were trying to organise all of John and Maria's possessions, ready to sell the house. Jacob couldn't bear to enter his father's office, but it needed to be done. The letter his father left him sat firmly inside his jacket pocket, still waiting to be read.

'I'm just nipping out to get breakfast. Do you want anything?' Adam offered.

'No, thank you. I don't think I can stomach any food right now.'

'Okay. I'll be back soon.'

Adam left Jacob all alone in the house. Now was a better time than any, he thought while removing the letter from his jacket pocket, and his eyes began to feast upon the words written.

"*My son.*
If you're reading this, then you know I'm gone. You have made me the proudest father in the world along with your brother and sister. There are parts of my life that I have kept secret from you all of these years. You and Adam, my 2 boys. Since your mother died, I am so proud of how you two adapted to carrying the weight of my depression, and helping me and Maria when your little sister arrived. The 3 of you are the best children a father could ask for.

My secret life I tried to keep well hidden from you, but I fear you will soon learn the truth. Barnes will fill you in. He's 1 of the only people I truly trust.
I love all 3 of you very much.
Dad."

Jacob didn't know what to think. His father had a secret life, one he'd kept hidden from his family, one that could have been partially responsible for his mother's death. Jacob continued to sit on the sofa, re-reading his father's letter, before finding the courage to burst into his father's office.

The carpet was still stained beneath him. He felt incredibly sick just staring at it. The office was a mess with paperwork and files all over the place. Jacob needed answers and this would be the only place he'd get some until they found Barnes.

Jacob rummaged through John's desk drawers, looking for anything that would explain what his father had written in the letter. He came to a locked drawer that required a key, but there was no sign of any key within the messy room.

'You've got to be kidding me,' he yelled and sighed loudly before placing his head in his hands.

He rummaged some more until he came across a file with receipts from a storage locker his father had been renting. The payments had been made yearly.

Why yearly instalments? he pondered. *This must have something to do with his secret life.* He looked down and analysed the receipts and noticed the address of the storage locker. *The same place Lily had her lock up. This better be a coincidence.*

Jacob stood still, processing all the information he had discovered in the last few minutes before his brother entered the house with his hands full of food.

'Jacob, I'm back,' he yelled out to him.

Jacob left the office shutting the door quietly behind him, making sure Adam couldn't see that he'd been in there.

'Surely you're not going to eat all of that?' Jacob said with a look of shock upon his face.

'No, I thought you could do with some food even though you said you weren't hungry.'

'Well, I think you made the right decision. I think my appetite has suddenly come back,' he replied, before ushering his brother towards the kitchen.

Once they demolished the food, it was back to sorting out their father's things. Adam moved upstairs, giving Jacob time to slip back inside the office. He had so many unanswered questions that were eating away at him, and he thought maybe they were hiding in the locked drawer.

Jacob searched again for the key but came up short and figured the only thing left he could do was break it. He crept into the hallway, opened the cupboard under the stairs, and searched through the toolbox for a screwdriver.

A look of delight swept across his face and he quickly tip-toed back into the office, closing the door quietly behind him. It took him no longer than five minutes to break into the drawer. He pulled the drawer out of the desk and dropped it to the floor.

He didn't understand why his father would have wanted the contents locked away. No valuables, just full of letters addressed to Maria. *What have they been hiding? And why lock it away?* Jacob opened the envelope, removed the letter and drew his eyes over it. He couldn't believe what he'd just read.

Jacob heard Adam moving up above him and then his stamping footsteps coming down the stairs. It was too late for Jacob to bolt out of the room, but he was beyond caring now. He couldn't care less if Adam caught him. They had promised to go through this room together, but Jacob's curiosity got the better of him like it always did.

'What are you doing in here?' he asked after finding Jacob sat at their father's desk. 'I thought we were going to wait to...' Adam caught sight of the tears forming from Jacob's eyes. 'What's wrong?'

Jacob said nothing. He looked up, focused his teary eyes upon his brother and handed him the letter. The silence was unnerving, but Adam glanced his eyes down and read what was now in front of him. Jacob analysed his face as he continued reading and then Adam's face turned from confused to shocked within seconds.

'What does this mean?' he asked Jacob.

'It means they've been lying to us this whole time,' he replied.

'What are we going to do?'

'We're going to carry on as normal as if we hadn't read it.'

'What if she finds out?'

Jacob took the letter out of Adam's hand, ripped it up in front of him and placed it inside the bin by the desk.

'The only way she'll find out is if one of us tell her, and that's not going to happen,' Jacob explained.

'What if he finds her?'

'Then we'll deal with it. She doesn't need any more heartbreak, especially now.'

It was almost closing time when Belle discovered the young man still sat inside the cafe. Belle had noticed him earlier that day, mainly because she felt an attraction towards him. His slick blonde hair was just as perfect to her as his flawlessly crafted face.

'I'm really sorry,' Belle apologised as she approached him, 'but we're closing now.'

The young man, in his late teens, lifted his head and smiled at her. Belle's knees went weak and butterflies appeared in her stomach.

'No problem,' he continued smiling. Belle returned the smile before turning around to head back to the counter. 'Aren't you going to ask me why I'm still here?'

Belle turned back to answer him but instead gave him a flirtatious smile before writing down her phone number. It was now or never and Belle thought it was a risk worth taking.

'What's this?' he asked.

'What you've been waiting all day for,' she flirted, before heading back to the counter.

'What's your name?' he shouted his question.

'Belle. My name's Belle.'

He smiled. 'Hi, Belle. I'm Ben.'

Just at that moment, the bell on the cafe door rang as somebody entered. The smartly dressed man walked up to the counter.

'So this is where you work?' Jacob asked.

'Beautiful, isn't it?' she replied.

'What are you doing here anyway?'

'Can I not visit you while you're at work?'

'You're a busy man. You've not got time to visit a cafe,' she joked.

Belle's eyes drifted from Jacob and on to Ben, who had finally decided to leave. Her heart sank slightly, but the hope he'd call her made her perk back up.

'So, fancy getting some food on the way home?' Jacob offered.

'I'll be finished in a few minutes,' she replied excitedly.

'I'll wait in the car.'

Jacob walked back to his car and sat inside, thinking about what he'd read inside both the letters he'd read earlier. *How could my father have kept all those secrets?* Thoughts kept rolling around inside his head, and then Barnes sprung back again. *He's still out there, probably dead or dying, and we have no leads no nothing.*

Jacob checked his phone for any messages but there was nothing new. His finger placed on the phone book icon and pressed Ally's name until the phone started ringing.

'Hello,' she answered on the other end.

'Hi, Ally. It's Jacob. Do we know anything new? Has Ethan found anything in relation to Barnes' disappearance?'

'He's trawling through CCTV. We'll let you know if we find anything.'

'Thanks, Ally,' he replied before hanging up.

His feelings towards Ally were growing. She was constantly on his mind along with finding Barnes, but he knew he couldn't have a relationship right now. He needed to solve their case, find Lily and rescue Barnes.

Belle opened the door and jumped in beside him. She could see Jacob was lost in thought, knowing what was probably spinning around inside his head.

'Jacob, what's wrong?' she asked.

He turned his head towards her, staring into her eyes. 'Nothing,' he lied.

'I know it's not nothing, but if you don't want to tell me, you don't have to.'

'There's just so much going on right now. I don't want to bring you down. You're doing so well at the moment with your new job and all.'

'You can tell me anything, Jacob. Not right now, but whenever you're ready,' she said.

Jacob nodded, unsure about what to say. He was glad Belle was a part of his life. She really helped cheer him up after everything that had happened. But he was afraid he'd lose her when she moved out. She was like a little sister to him.

Jacob started the engine and the car roared down the street. Between them, they couldn't decide what to have for dinner. Chinese food was their top choice, and Jacob knew Kate liked it too.

All Jack Roberts could think about was Charlotte. *Why did I leave her alone when I knew that man had been in the garden?* Questions flew around inside his mind.

He continued to lay on his bed processing everything that had happened, but it hurt him too much to think about. Jack pulled himself off his bed, headed downstairs towards the kitchen, and made a sandwich. He hadn't even buttered one slice of bread before he heard a knock at the door.

When the door opened, Jack lay eyes upon Mr Hussain standing in front of him.

'What are you doing here, Avi?' asked Jack.

'I know it was you!' Avi Hussain started to raise his voice so the entire neighbourhood could hear.

'I don't know what you are talking about.'

'You know exactly what I'm talking about,' he quietly threatened him through his teeth.

'You think I killed Charlotte?' Jack asked in shock.

'We all do,' he answered while pointing back to their neighbour's homes.

'Well, do they all know what you and my wife got up to while I went out running?'

There was a slight pause. Avi had no idea Jack knew about his little fling with Charlotte. Jack had a slight smile in the corner of his mouth, and Avi noticed which made him very afraid of Jack.

'And I'm guessing by your silence, you didn't know I knew about it?' he continued, laughing in Avi's face.

'So is that why you killed her?'

'What makes you believe I killed her?'

'Because she was having an affair with me.'

'Don't think so highly of yourself,' Jack continued to laugh. 'I couldn't care less if she was having an affair. The fact that you think you were special to her is hilarious. Charlotte was constantly sleeping around, she was a whore, but you didn't know that, did you?'

Avi felt humiliated. This wasn't how he expected the conversation to go. Jack laughed before slamming the door in Avi's face and continued making his sandwich. He noticed the garden light was on as he glanced through the window. He felt a presence watching him, but there was nobody in his eyesight.

Jack leaned in closer to the window to get a better vantage point of his garden. *It's probably just a cat*, he thought. But then something caught his eye. The mystery man was back, hiding almost out of sight, down the bottom of the garden.

Jack took a step back out of shock, as the man laughed deeply. The light in the garden turned off sharply, leaving Jack with nothing but the thought of the man continuing to stare at him. He quickly darted for the back door and made sure it was locked, before rolling down the kitchen blind.

Jack fell to the kitchen floor, terrified and panicking. *Who is this guy? And what does he want?*

Jacob and Belle arrived home with their arms full of Chinese food. Kate rushed over to help lighten the load and carried it through to the kitchen. All three of their stomachs growled as the smell from the food became unbearable.

'Let's hurry up and eat this grub,' Jacob announced.

As the three of them tucked into their dinner, Jacob's phone began to ring and he began to sigh while placing his head in his hands. He picked his phone up off the kitchen counter and headed for his bedroom before answering.

'DS Wright,' he announced.

'Jacob, we've got another body,' Ally informed him.

'Where?'

'The same place our last vic was found,' she enlightened him.

'Okay, I'll be there within the hour.'

Jacob hung up, headed to the kitchen and scoffed some more of his food, before picking his coat up.

'Where you going?' Belle asked.

'Got another crime scene.'

'But you've only just got home,' Kate sighed.

'I know. I'm really sorry,' Jacob apologised before jogging for the door. 'I'll see you both later.'

Jacob shut the door behind him and ran towards the elevator. Once he reached the ground floor, he sprinted to his car and raced towards the crime scene, with his police lights flashing brightly throughout the Birmingham streets.

Barnes awoke again, with a pounding headache, laying on a cold, damp floor. Confused and dazed about his surroundings, he realised he'd been moved. *But when?* he thought. *I don't remember being anywhere other than the warehouse.* He suddenly noticed a slight pain in the crease of his arm, like he'd been injected with a needle.

As he rubbed where the pain resided, his eyes locked on to a little red spot. So they did inject me with something. He noticed his wrists weren't tied together and as he moved his body to pull himself off

81

the floor, his legs jangled with the sound of a metal chain. The chain, attached to ankle bracelets, connected to the wall beside him.

'Where the hell am I?' he asked himself out loud.

Barnes tried to shuffle to get a better look at his surroundings. He felt like the floor was tilting from side to side. *That's some crazy stuff they gave me.* His vision was blurry and his head was still pounding.

The room was extremely dark, and the tiny square windows were blacked out. A noise made itself known to Barnes' ears. The sound of people laughing in the distance, chuckling away, enjoying themselves. *I must be near to a road*, he thought.

Barnes roared out loud at the top of his lungs, 'Help!'

He could still hear laughing as it gained closer, but Barnes' voice was too raspy from the injection he'd received.

He tried again, opening his airwaves, 'Help! I'm in here!'

Then he heard nothing but silence. *Maybe they've heard me*, he rejoiced. But then he heard footsteps, not coming from the other side of the wall, but coming towards the room, behind the door. *Shit*, he panicked. *They've heard me.*

The door opened, blinding Barnes with a bright light, shining from behind the silhouette in front.

'So, you're awake,' the voice said.

Barnes knew exactly who it was. His captor was still nearby and had been the entire time. She must have heard his cries for help and come to silence him.

They both heard the sound of people outside talking and laughing again, as Lily placed a finger over her lips, telling him to be quiet.

Barnes had no idea whether to listen to her or risk it, to try and save himself. He took the option that would be less painful and hopefully keep him alive slightly longer.

'Good boy,' she mocked him. 'You know what's best for you.'

'Where are we?' he asked, unsure of their location.

'Like I'm going to tell you that. If I hear any more from you, I'll have no choice but to gag you. Do you understand?'

Barnes said nothing, just nodded, informing her that he understood her command. She slammed the door, shutting the light out from the dark, bitter room. He managed to get a good look at the size and appearance of the room before the light went out. The room wasn't very big but was straight and long. He was worried that because they'd moved, Jacob and the team wouldn't be able to rescue him and capture Lily and her associate. He felt truly alone and terrified of what might happen to him.

As Jacob arrived on the scene, he took a glance at the time. *Is it really past nine already?* He pulled himself out of the car, shut the door behind him and braced himself for what he was about to witness. He'd seen enough death and destruction these last couple of months. He worked so hard for this job, he couldn't quit now, so he decided to carry on. Jacob knew before he could think about quitting, he needed to find Barnes and have Lily behind bars.

She ruined his life. The perfect life they'd built together came crumbling down the day her true identity and motive had been revealed. She was the love of his life and she killed him, not physically but mentally.

As Jacob approached the tape, he could see Ally waiting for him just beyond. She stood with authority and pride but showed sorrow across her face. It suddenly brightened up with a smile as she locked sight upon Jacob. He returned the smile as he got closer.

'Only an hour late,' she joked.

'Sorry. So what's happened?' He noticed the forensic team coming out of Avi Hussain's house.

'Mr Hussain was found dead this evening with extensive head trauma.'

'Do we have a suspect yet?'

'Can you guess?' she asked while looking across at Jack Roberts' house. 'The two had an altercation earlier this evening. Mr Hussain confronted Mr Roberts at his home. Nobody could tell us what it was about.'

'Have you asked old Dorothy if she heard anything while emptying her bins?' he joked.

'Already ticked that off the list,' she laughed, joining in with the joke. 'She didn't hear anything.'

'Has anybody questioned Mr Roberts yet?' Jacob asked.

'Not yet. I've been waiting for you.'

'Did anybody see Mr Roberts approach Mr Hussain's house?'

'Nobody,' she replied.

'Let's bring him back to the station. I think we're best to get it on tape.'

The two of them started to make their way towards Jack's front door. Jacob reached for the knocker and made three loud bangs.

Jack trembled inside. His forehead covered in sweat, knowing the knocking on his door was the police here to arrest him. He'd been peering outside through his curtains the last hour. He knew something terrible had happened and they were going to accuse him.

'Go away,' he yelled.

'Mr Roberts, it's DS Wright. Can you open the door please?' Jacob announced through the letterbox.

'What, so you can arrest me? No chance.'

'We just want to ask you a few questions,' Ally interrupted.

'Who is this?' He was shocked to hear another voice.

'DI Miller,' she announced herself.

'Well, DI Miller, whatever it is you want to ask, you can ask it from there.'

'We need you to come to the station,' Jacob continued.

'No way. You're just going to arrest me as soon as I open the door.'

Jacob tried to reason with him. 'Look Mr Roberts, we need you to come with us and answer a few questions down at the station. There's no cause to arrest you. Nobody has seen you leave your house since your altercation with Mr Hussain, so if...'

'What altercation?'

'We have multiple witnesses confirming yourself and Mr Hussain had a disagreement outside your house earlier today.'

'He slept with my wife and has been for months. He came over to confront me and accuse me of killing my wife,' he explained.

Jacob and Ally took a second to look at one another. They had just heard what the disagreement was about.

'Then you should come to the station so we can record your statement on tape to help with our investigation.'

It went silent. Jacob took a glance at Ally, unsure of what Jack was doing inside his house when they heard the door unlock and their suspect stood in front of them.

'I'm coming to answer a few questions and then I can come home, right?' Jack asked.

'Absolutely,' Jacob said, unsure of what the forensics would find.

Ally and Jacob escorted Jack to the police car, with the whole neighbourhood watching. Jack walked with his head down, embarrassed about what was happening for the second day in the same week. As they crossed the police tape, news reporters pushed their cameras in their faces, while the paparazzi were taking photos with the flash blinding them.

'Stand back please,' Jacob yelled while putting his hand out to cover the cameras in front of them.

Reporters yelled out questions about who the suspect was and what had happened on that street, but Jacob and Ally ignored them and carried on back to the car. Jack was going to be all over the news and he'll be labelled as a killer for the rest of his life.

Chapter 8

Jack sat quietly inside the interview room, listening once again to Simon Ballard blabbering, awaiting the two detectives. His hand tapped nervously on the table while all he could think about was the fact his wife and her lover had both been murdered. The mystery man was the only person Jack could think would be behind it, but he didn't know why. *Why would this man want them dead? Why does he keep following me and want to kill people around me?* He had no idea.

'Jack, you need to realise that you've been here twice within a week over two different murders,' Simon explained to him.

Jack just carried on tapping his fingers on the table, before moving them towards his mouth and nervously biting his fingernails. Ally and Jacob entered the room. Jacob entered the tape into the machine while Ally informed the recording of all the usual relevant information.

'So, Mr Roberts. Could you please explain for the tape what your altercation was with Mr Hussain earlier today?' Ally asked.

'He came over to my house and started accusing me of murdering my wife,' he explained.

'Why would he do that?' Ally continued questioning him.

'I don't know why.'

'Some of the neighbours heard shouting coming from your house the day before your wife's murder. Could that be the reason why he thought it?'

'Possibly, but...'

'But what?'

'He and my wife were having an affair while I went out running,' he continued to explain.

'How long would you be out running?' Jacob asked.

'Probably about an hour or more,' Jack replied.

'How many times a week would you go running?'

'Pretty much every day, until...' he paused.

'What is it? What's wrong?' Ally asked him.

'Until I came across that man, the one with the disfigured face. Then I stopped going out.'

'And is this man still following you?' Jacob threw a question at him, already knowing the answer, but he wanted Jack to answer honestly for the tape.

'Yes. I saw him earlier today. I think he's the one doing all of this, but I don't know why.' He started to cry.

'Do you have any cameras in your garden or around your property?' Ally asked.

'No.'

'What about your neighbours?'

'I don't know,' he replied.

Jacob started to write down a few notes. One was to make sure they check any of the surrounding houses for cameras. Ally announced to the tape the end of the interview with the current time, before standing up to shake Jack's hand.

'Thank you, Mr Roberts. We'll be in touch as soon as we know more, though we might need you to help one of our sketch artists with the description of our suspect.'

'No problem,' he agreed while shaking her hand.

Ally showed both Jack and Simon out of the room while Jacob remained seated, thinking about what Jack had just said. Ally glared at him.

'Are you coming or what?'

'Yeah, I'm just thinking.'

'Oh yeah, about what?'

'This mystery man. Who is he to Jack?'

'That's what we're going to try and find out,' she replied.

'I just don't believe him,' he admitted.

'Why?'

'It just seems like whenever he's questioned he brings up this man from out of the blue. It just doesn't seem right, that's all.'

'Come on,' she laughed at him, before ushering him out of the room.

The next morning arrived, and Jacob couldn't help but think about the letter his father had left for him. Something didn't add up. He sat inside his car, pondering about the letter. *Why did Dad write numbers in words and digits?* He read the note again, trying to make sense of it.

"*My son.*
If you're reading this, then you know I'm gone. You have made me the proudest father in the world along with your brother and sister. There are parts of my life that I have kept secret from you all of these years.
You and Adam, my 2 boys. Since your mother died, I am so proud of how you two adapted to carrying the weight of my depression, and helping me and Maria when your little sister arrived. The 3 of you are the best children a father could ask for.
My secret life I tried to keep well hidden from you, but I fear you will soon learn the truth. Barnes will fill you in. He's 1 of the only people I truly trust.
I love all 3 of you very much.
Dad."

Then Jacob remembered the receipt he found in his father's office. An annual payment for a storage locker. He rummaged through his coat pocket for the receipt. *Maybe he's giving me clues to something.*

Jacob put his foot on the accelerator and drove to the storage locker. He phoned Ally.

'Ally, it's Jacob. I need your help with something. Meet me at the storage lock-up facility on Clyde Street,' he requested.

'Isn't that where Lily's locker was? What's going on, Jacob?' she asked.

'I'll let you know when you arrive. Don't bring anybody else, this is important.'

He hung up the phone and carried on his journey. He wasn't too far now, and he hoped to get some answers about his father's secret life.

Ally pulled into the car park not long after Jacob and approached him standing by his car.

'So, what's so important?' she questioned him while folding her arms.

He showed Ally the receipt. 'I found this in my fathers home office.'

'So, he has a storage locker. That's not so odd.'

'It is when Lily had one in the same building,' he explained. 'I need your help. I want to search my dad's locker, but I don't want anyone to know about what we might find. My father has been keeping secrets about his family's history, that only he and Barnes knew.'

'Barnes?'

'My dad said he's the only one he trusts,' he said while showing Ally the letter.

She took a few minutes to read over the letter. 'What do you think you'll find in here?'

'Hopefully some answers.'

The pair of them entered the building, and a familiar face stood before them.

'Oh, hello detectives,' said Billy, the lock-up's manager.

Both Ally and Jacob had met Billy about a month ago when they investigated Lily's locker. Billy had no idea why the pair of them were stood in front of him.

'Hello, Billy,' Jacob greeted him, holding his hand out for it to be shaken. 'Good to see you again.'

'So, what brings you both here?' he asked.

'I need your help. My father had a locker here,' Jacob said, handing him the receipt. 'He recently passed away. While I was clearing out his house, I came across this receipt. He pays annually for a locker here, and I've come to clear it out.'

'Okay, give me a minute and I'll find out what number locker he had.' Billy clicked away on the computer.

'Thank you, Billy. I really appreciate your help,' Jacob replied.

After a few minutes, Billy had found John's locker. But he gave Jacob a worried look like he was about to disappoint him.

'Good news, I've found your father's locker,' he informed them while bowing his head.

'What's the bad news?' Ally asked.

'Do you remember when you came here last month?'

'How could I forget,' replied Jacob with a sorrowful tone.

'Well, her locker was...'

'249,' he interrupted.

'Your father's locker is 250, right next door.'

Jacob's mouth opened wide in shock. Lily had been spying on my father this whole time, but why? Ally placed her hand on his shoulder.

'Are you alright?' she asked.

'I'm just a little confused and shocked,' he answered. 'Can you take us to it?' he requested.

'Of course. Follow me,' said Billy.

The three of them reached the floor where John's locker had been. A four-digit combination lock kept the locker safe from prying eyes and thieving hands.

Billy spoke up, 'I'll leave you both to it.'

Jacob stared at the lock. *What could the number be?* He tried his birthday, but the lock didn't release. So he tried his siblings birthdays and when they didn't work, he tried his mother and Maria's. Again, the lock didn't release.

'I give up,' he announced defeat.

'There's got to be something you're not thinking of. Did your father not leave a combination in his office?' Ally tried to get him thinking.

Then something appeared in his thoughts. *The letter. That's probably why he added both numbers and letters. He must have known I'd figure it out.*

'Let me try something else,' he announced to her while removing the letter from his coat pocket. 'Two, three, one, three,' he spoke out loud while entering the numbers into the combination.

The lock released and Jacob's stomach started to turn. This was the moment he'd waited for. The secrets were about to be revealed. A deafening ringing could be heard as the fire alarms rang throughout the building.

'Jacob, come on. We need to leave,' she shouted at him.

Jacob hesitated, peeping into the locker. He shut the locker and made sure it was completely locked before he accompanied Ally out of the building.

'This isn't a coincidence,' he shared his thoughts with her as they exited the building.

'What do you mean?'

'We finally get into the locker and get to find out what my father had been hiding, then the fire alarm goes off. I don't buy it.'

'I think everything that's happened has made you paranoid,' she joked. 'We'll come back later when we're allowed back inside.'

Jacob wanted to resist but agreed to go with her, knowing she was right, but also worried in case somebody broke in and took what was inside.

When they arrived back at the station, Jacob returned to his desk. He craved an alcoholic drink. He'd become dependent on it since his father's death, and the cravings grew stronger the more he felt the pain and hurt he was feeling inside.

Jacob opened his desk draw. His eyes gazed down at a small bottle of whiskey he had placed in there for the hard times. He placed his coffee cup inside his drawer, unscrewed the lid on the whiskey bottle, and poured it into the cup. He kept peeking around making sure nobody could see what he was doing.

The drink made him feel slightly better. It numbed the pain he was constantly feeling day-to-day. The loss of his father and the life of lies he'd lived with Lily had taken its toll on him. He still had his friends and family by his side, but being alone and having nothing but his thoughts, reminded Jacob of everything that had happened in the past month.

He had the feeling he was being watched by his colleagues. Their beady eyes looking up from their computers, people tip-toeing around him constantly, too afraid to ask him anything, in case he'd get upset or have another breakdown.

He got up from his seat and left the CID. He couldn't cope with everyone gazing at him, and he needed fresh air. Once he got to the car park, he pulled out his keys and got into his car. He peered out of each window, making sure no one was around, before making a move to his glove box.

Inside was another bottle, this time it was vodka. He unscrewed the lid and took a swig. It calmed his nerves. Jacob needed to get out of the office for a while, so he started the ignition and started to drive.

Thoughts of Lily swam around inside his mind. Tears started to stream down his cheeks which he couldn't control. He pulled over by a local pub, craving another drink. He wiped his tears before pulling himself out of the car and walked into the pub. It was dim and smelt like stale booze. He sat at the bar and ordered a pint of lager, hoping it would do the trick, but it didn't. It didn't even touch the sides on making him feel any better.

The TV was tuned in to a news report featuring his current case with Jack Roberts. *That's all I need now,'* he thought. *I can't be doing with listening to this right now.*

Jacob yelled at the bartender, 'Can you turn this off, please?'

The grumpy bartender grunted, before switching the channel to sports. Jacob drank his pint and kept himself to himself. He sat there thinking about his father and the visions. The visions had gone once the recent string of murders had stopped. He kept telling himself the visions were due to lack of sleep and stress, but deep down, Jacob knew it was something else. His father had even told him, he'd experienced the same thing when he was a detective.

Stumbling out of his seat, Jacob headed back to his car. Outside he scrambled for his keys inside his pocket, almost falling over. He'd hit rock bottom and he knew it, though he didn't care. He had lost everything. His whole family had been torn to shreds.

Jacob looked over the road and caught a glimpse of a man, standing and staring directly at him. He recognised the man very well and thought he'd never see him again. That man was his father, John Wright. *Is this another hallucination?* he thought.

'Hey,' he yelled at the man. 'Wait.'

Jacob pushed his way through the crowd of people in front of him and tried to cross the street. He stepped off the curb in a hurry, making cars swerve to avoid hitting him. Car horns beeped ferociously, with drivers yelling obscene words towards him. But Jacob didn't care, he just focused on the man who resembled his father, who was currently walking away.

Once Jacob reached the other side, he continued to tail the man, not taking his eyes off him, until he bumped into a lady.

'Watch where you're going,' she yelled angrily at him, making him lose sight of the man.

'Sorry,' he apologised, giving her direct eye contact.

By the time Jacob looked back towards the man, he was gone. *Was it my father? Did he cause the distraction earlier with the fire alarm?* Jacob stood motionless for an instant, before making his way back towards his car.

Jacob arrived back at the CID and aimed straight for Ally, who was inside Barnes' office. He shut the door behind him, making sure his colleagues couldn't hear the conversation that was about to take place.

'Ally, I've got to talk to you,' he stuttered.

She noticed his head was sweating and he seemed panicked. 'Jacob, is everything alright?'

'No.' He started pacing. 'I've seen him. I reckon it was him who set the fire alarm off in the lock-up earlier.'

'Who? Barnes?' she questioned him.

'No, my father.'

Ally was shocked and worried that Jacob was having a mental breakdown. Then she caught a whiff of alcohol on his breath.

'Jacob, have you been drinking?' she asked quietly, trying not to have prying ears hear what was being said.

'Yes, well, a little.' he admitted.

'What are you playing at? You know you can't be drinking on the job, especially driving. I'm going to have to send you home, you can't stay here.'

'But you need to listen,' he tried to explain, but she was having none of it.

'No. You need to listen to me,' she tried to show her frustration quietly. 'You need to go home and sleep it off, then I'll come and pick you up in the morning. Now come on, let's get you home.'

The pair of them left the office and headed for the exit, as the team stared at them. Jacob's head was spinning and he had no idea how he'd made it to the CID safely.

Out in the car park, Ally held the door open for him to enter. His drunk body dropped in the passenger seat and she shut the door. The pain he was feeling, felt like he'd been ripped apart, and now everybody he worked with, knew he was an alcoholic mess.

Back inside the CID, Brian and Sarah were chatting about their dating life. Brian had confessed he'd gone on a date the night before after Sarah and Ethan had dragged it out of him.

'What about you then, Sarah? Is there a new lucky man in your life yet?' he asked.

'Man? Who's to say I'm interested in men, Brian?'

Brian blushed, not knowing how to reply and stayed quiet at his desk. Ethan just laughed along with Sarah.

'What about you, Ethan? How's it going with Ruby?' She turned her attention to him.

'Good, actually. We're planning a holiday for the summer.'

The double doors flew open as a woman entered the office. Brian stood on his feet immediately.

'Who's that?' Sarah asked him.

'That would be Barnes' ex-wife, Vanessa,' he informed them, as he walked over to her. 'Vanessa, how are you?'

She was in hysterics, tears streaming down her face. 'Brian, where is he?'

'Look, Vanessa...'

'Something's happened, hasn't it?' she interrupted.

'Come with me and I'll explain,' he said while ushering her into Barnes' office. 'Take a seat.' He shut the door.

'What's happened to Joe? I know some things happened. He usually calls the girls every couple of days, but he hasn't.'

Brian sighed. 'Look, Vanessa, I'm going to tell it to you straight. He's been kidnapped.'

'Kidnapped?'

He nodded and continued, 'We are trying our best to find him.'

'Do you know who's kidnapped him?'

'We have an idea, but no evidence to prove it.'

She burst into tears. She still loved him but felt increasingly left second best to his job, which was the main reason for their split. But she still had feelings for him.

'Will you keep me informed?' she asked Brian kindly.

'Of course I will,' he promised as he lifted his heavy, weighted body off the seat and towards the door.

'Thank you,' she said as she left the CID.

Brian headed back towards his desk and plumped himself down. Sarah's eager eyes focused on Brian, wanting information from him.

'What did she want?' she questioned.

'She knew something had happened to Barnes, so came to confirm it,' he explained.

Ethan strolled back over to his desk. He'd been flicking through CCTV images of the surrounding area of the warehouse, where Barnes had been held hostage. He sat perched, glaring at his monitor, when he locked onto a blue transit van, entering the warehouse premises.

'Hey, guys,' he shouted.

Sarah and Brian rushed over to Ethan's desk, to see what he'd found.

'This van entered the premises a few hours before we arrived. They left not long after arriving and I'm going to track it with the other surveillance cameras to see where it ended up. I'm also running the plates. Hopefully, we'll have a match soon.'

'Good work, Ethan,' Sarah congratulated him on a job well done.

Ethan's computer pinged back information on the owner of the van.

'I've got a name and an address for the owner of the van. Mr Douglas Chambers. It's also been reported as stolen,' Ethan continued to inform them.

'Right, Ethan, I need you to carry on going through the CCTV. Me and Brian are going to pay Mr Chambers a visit and see if he has any information on our van thief,' she barked her orders, as the highest commanding officer in the office, before her and Brian left the CID.

Jacob stirred from his sleep, not knowing how he'd got home. The light outside started to fade. He had no idea what time it was, as he stumbled out of his bed and over to his en-suite. His head was thumping, his vision was blurry, and the feeling of wanting to throw up came with no warning as he leant over the toilet.

He knew he'd hit rock bottom. Once he'd stopped being sick, Jacob carried himself over to his kitchen and poured himself a glass of water, gulping it down as fast as he could.

Belle and Kate were sitting eating snacks but paused when Jacob made his entrance, keeping their eyes fixated on him.

'Rough day?' Belle asked, keeping her eyes locked on him while cramming her mouth full of food.

He just kept his head down, facing the sink. The thought of them eating made me want to puke. He checked the time.

'Damn. It's quarter past five,' he yelled in a panic.

'Chill. Ally dropped you off and told you to rest,' Kate informed him.

'I can't remember anything.' He rubbed his head.

'She told us to keep an eye on you. She said you'd been drinking?' Belle spoke up.

Jacob turned around to face them. 'Look, it's been a rough couple of weeks and I'm just having a rough time.'

'We're here for you if you need us,' Belle consoled him.

'Thank you both. I love you guys.'

They both smiled as Jacob wandered off back to his bed, and the pair of them continued their conversation.

'I'll ask my boss if they've got anything for you at weekends,' said Belle.

'Would you?' Kate replied ecstatically. 'I'd appreciate it.'

'No problem, we could do with the help.'

'Anyway, have you heard any more from Ben?' Kate inquired, wanting to hear some girly gossip.

'He phoned me earlier. We've got a date next week,' she replied with a smile.

Belle's life had turned around since she'd ran away from her parents, not that they noticed she was gone. They were probably too out of their faces to care. They weren't the best parents and as Belle started to get older, they became abusive. So Belle decided to run away.

She lived on the streets until she found an empty apartment that was unlocked from a police raid. She'd been staying there a while before she met Alex Baker, the owner of the apartment. He showed her kindness she hadn't experienced for a very long time.

But once again, destruction followed, when Alex was brutally murdered in the room next door to her. That's when Jacob came into her life. He'd become a big brother to her and her life was gradually getting better.

Memories of her life flooded her mind for a while, but instead of dwelling on the bad, she looked to the recent happiness she'd felt. For once in her horrible life, she was happy.

Sarah and Brian arrived at Douglas Chambers' house. It was a pretty average house for the Birmingham area, in a busy little street. Young children riding bikes in the road, while others were on the field nearby playing football.

As they approached the house, Sarah noticed the door was slightly ajar. She pushed it open a bit wider, trying to get a look further inside.

'Hello,' she shouted. 'Mr Chambers, it's the police. Is it alright for us to come in?'

But there was no reply, making Sarah feel uneasy. She turned to Brian worried, as they were unarmed, and somebody could be waiting to attack them inside.

'What do you think?' She asked Brian for advice.

'I'll take the back, you go in through the front,' he gave his option.

'Coward,' she muttered, as Brian took off around the house.

She entered, slowly and steadily, making sure not to make a sound. As Sarah came to the doorway into the living room, she placed her back against the wall and took a quick peep inside the room. She couldn't see anybody, so carried on straight ahead, towards the kitchen.

That's when she found him, Mr Chambers, dead on the kitchen floor, surrounded by a pool of blood. His throat had been slashed like he'd been taken by surprise from behind. He was a middle-aged man, with longish grey hair and a slight goatee. He was quite muscular and if he hadn't been taken by surprise, he might have stood a chance against the killer.

Brian popped his head up by the kitchen window and saw Sarah stood over Douglas Chambers' body. She called it in. Knowing she was contaminating the crime scene, she decided to leave the house. Her stomach churned and she threw up in the street, for all the children to see.

Brian came running around the corner, panting for breath. 'What happened in there?'

Sarah wiped the sick from her mouth before answering, 'He's been murdered, you idiot. What do you think has happened?' she asked a rhetorical question.

The children slowly approached the house with curiosity, wanting to know what had happened. One child came riding up close to Sarah, wanting to be the first one to find out. His lack of hair showed his mother couldn't afford a barber, so used a number one clipper all over his head. The boy's trousers were also too small for him as was his coat.

'Excuse me, Miss. What's happened?' he asked.

'A police matter. Now run along home,' she said rudely, before turning her back on him.

'Fuck off,' the boy yelled back at her, wanting to show he was the toughest kid in the street.

Sarah turned around in shock at what the boy had just said to her, but he'd ridden off on his bike. She phoned Ally to update her on their progress.

'Hey, boss, we've located the owner of the transit van. Unfortunately, he's dead.'

'Okay, I'll grab the address off Ethan and be there soon. Keep people away until forensics gets there,' she ordered.

Sarah knew that was going to be harder than she thought, as the crowd started to get larger. Everyone started yelling at her and Brian to find out what had happened inside the house. *All I need now is for the reporters to show up*, she sighed.

Chapter 9

Ally arrived on scene an hour later. Forensics had already started working on the house, gathering as much evidence as they could find. She could see news crews standing outside the border of police tape, waiting to get a statement. Families had also congested every possible entrance of her getting through the police tape.

'Excuse me,' she shouted as she pushed her way through the crowd.

She flashed her badge to the officer guarding the perimeter, before getting past the border and to the house, where Sarah and Brian were located.

'So, what happened?' she asked them.

'We arrived, noticed the door was open. Brian went around the back and I entered through the front and made my way through until I found him on the kitchen floor,' Sarah recalled their actions.

'How'd he die?'

'Looks like a knife wound to the throat. I think the assailant took Mr Chambers by surprise and slit his throat,' she explained her theory.

'Could it be our kidnapper?' Ally pointed the finger towards Lily.

'I'm not sure,' Sarah voiced her opinion. 'Mr Chambers has quite a good physique, and wouldn't have been so easy to take down. There's no way Lily could have done this. She must have help.'

'Good point, DS Taylor,' Ally congratulated her.

Sarah became smug and smiled profusely at Brian as if she was the star pupil. Ally got dressed into a forensic overall and entered the house to witness the murder scene for herself.

Inside she was greeted by Chloe Fisher, not that Ally could tell, as everyone inside the house looked the same in their white suits. Chloe continued gathering evidence and taking photos, while Ally grabbed a peek at Douglas Chambers' recently deceased corpse.

Moments later, Brian and Sarah watched as Ally exited the house, and stripped out of the white overalls.

'I see what you mean now, Sarah. About him not being easy to take down,' said Ally.

Ally's phone began to ring. She removed it from her pocket, glanced at it to see Ethan's name, before answering it.

'Hello, Ethan.'

'I've got a location for the van. I ran the plates through ANPR and it entered the Arena car park, off St. Vincent Street, and it hasn't left,' he explained.

'Good work, Ethan. You might have just helped us find Barnes,' she cheered.

She hung up the phone and informed the others of the news. 'Ethan's ran the plates of the van through ANPR and it's stationed at the Arena car park off St. Vincent Street.'

The three of them walked away from the crime scene and back to their cars. They stopped before entering, and Ally gave her orders.

'Brian, I need you to call for armed backup. When we arrive, I want you to pull up outside the car park. I want no police lights to give us away. We'll wait for the AFO, and then search the car park for the van. This is our last hope in finding Barnes. Let's bring him home.'

They entered their cars and sped towards the Arena car park. Ally hoped this would finally be an end to the search for their DCI. She wanted to bring Jacob in on the search but knew he wasn't in the right frame of mind and needed to get himself better.

I can do this, she gave herself courage.

The door inside the room unlocked, lighting up the room Barnes was being held in. He was unsure of what was about to happen. Lily slowly entered the room clutching a plate with both hands. She sat on a chair that hid in the dark corner of the room.

'You hungry?' she asked him.

'Starving,' he replied, his mouth-watering from looking at the sandwich.

Lily took a bite. 'This is good,' she said with a mouth full of food.

Disappointment filled up inside of him, knowing this was another cruel torture of hers. She never intended to give him the sandwich. She just wanted to push him for the information she needed.

'If you want some, all you have to do is tell me what I want to know.'

'Oh, I should have known,' he laughed. 'You're persistent, aren't you?'

'I like to finish my plans. You know that.'

Barnes knew that. She killed his friend and old partner, as well as having orchestrated other murders. He also knew that he was included in the final part of her plan, dead.

'So what are you going to do with me, because you know I'm never going to tell you?' he smiled.

'But you will eventually,' she smirked back at him.

The man Barnes knew only as Cain, entered the room, clutching something in his hand, before passing it to Lily. He then left the room, as she approached Barnes, who was sat uneasy and anxiously on the floor.

'You're going to tell me what I want to know, otherwise, your family are going to get worse than you,' she spoke calmly and softly while showing him recent photos of his ex-wife and two daughters.

'You bitch!' he yelled. 'I'll kill you!'

'Not before I kill them, and you,' she threatened. 'You're running out of time, Joe.'

Tears started to form in his eyes. 'I'll kill you,' he repeated quietly, sobbing his heart out.

'You've got twelve hours to make up your mind.'

Lily walked out of the room and shut the door, locking out the light from the room. Barnes sat in the darkness with nothing but the possibility of what could happen, and it would all be his fault. He did nothing but cry.

They were a mile away from the Arena car park. Ally silenced her sirens and flicked off her lights as she approached. She noticed in her rearview mirror, the other officers did the same as she instructed.

Ally parked her car outside the entrance. Sarah and Brian pulled alongside her, as she departed her car. The Authorised Firearms Officers perched themselves with the car park within the sights of their guns.

'Right,' Ally rounded them up to hear her plan. 'Somewhere in there is this van.' She showed them a photo. 'We're looking to apprehend the suspects alive. We need to know where they're keeping Barnes. Now let's get moving.'

The team took a few minutes to arm up with Kevlar vests and a handgun each. They were taking no chances since they knew how dangerous Lily could be. As soon as they were ready, armed police stormed the building first, before the three of them entered.

The armed police split into three teams and took different access points. Ally went with the team who went left, Sarah straight ahead and Brian to the right.

Once the first floor was clear, they moved further up to the second. Ally checked every inch of the floor before moving up to the next with the rest of the team. Brian began to sweat. He wasn't used to how dangerous this case had become. In all his years on the force, rescuing Barnes was one of the scariest, most intense case of them all. His urgency to find his friend was top of his list, but he wasn't sure they were even going to find him, let alone alive.

As they reached the third floor, Ally's phone began to ring quietly in her pocket, but loud enough for her to hear.

She stopped still to answer it. 'Ethan, what is it?'

'I've just gone through some of our dead victim's accounts, the one with the van...'

'Get to the point, Ethan,' she cut him off.

'Well, it turns out he also owns a canal boat.'

'Does this boat have a name?' she asked with urgency.

'The Queen Rose,' he replied.

'Thanks, Ethan.' She hung up the phone.

As the armed police moved off towards the next floor, Ally hesitated and thought twice about what she was going to do, before finally deciding. She darted off back down the parking garage, towards the entrance. Officers stood guarding, making sure no civilians were able to gain access.

Ally flew past them, running as fast as her feet could take her, turning left around the corner and heading towards the canal. When she made it close to the water's edge, she slowed down, making sure not to give herself away. The light was beginning to fade from the sky, making it nearly impossible to find the canal boat where she assumed Lily was keeping Barnes captive.

Couples and friends sat beside the canal at nearby restaurants, eating their meals, accompanied by fun and laughter. Ally glanced around, checking every canal boat that sat on top of the water, but she kept coming up short until she spotted it a few metres down by the water's edge.

'We've found the van,' she heard Sarah whisper down the earpiece.

She heard the shouts of the armed police before they opened the van. There was silence before she heard the word, clear. There was nothing inside the van.

'It's empty,' she heard Sarah speak again with disappointment.

'Guys, I've got a lead. I need back-up,' Ally informed them.

'Where are you, Ally?' Brian asked.

'Down by the canal. I need you here quickly. I think I'm about to make contact with Lily.'

'What are you doing out there?' Sarah questioned her actions, wondering why she wasn't with them inside the car park.

'No time for explanations, just get here.'

People chatting loudly nearby and slight screams could be heard coming from behind her. She turned her head to see the armed police, followed by Sarah and Brian, marching stealthily. Ally started to move quickly towards the canal boat, removing her holster handgun and aiming it in the direction of her target.

As Ally approached the boat, the armed police moved either side, covering all entry and exit points, in case the assailants made a run for it.

'On my orders,' Ally whispered her command.

Barnes' stomach growled, but the worry was the only thing he could think about. Food didn't seem so important to him now. His family was in danger and it was his fault. If he just gave her the information she needed, they wouldn't have brought his family into it.

He could hear chatting faintly in the distance. *What are they discussing? Hopefully, they're not talking about my family*. Then it went silent. He could see the shadows of Lily and Cain, under the bottom of the door. They were still as if something had spooked them.

Barnes listened carefully and heard a tapping of footsteps outside. He crawled closer to the blacked-out window. *Is there someone out there?* he thought.

He heard a couple of footsteps above him. He had no idea where he was being held, but he had hopes that the movement above, was a rescue team coming to free him.

Watching the shadows beneath the door, he waited to observe what was about to happen. Lily and

Cain stayed still and had been the entire time until he noticed Cain's shadow move slightly. Barnes waited.

A creaky door echoed. Lily and Cain still in their positions, unmoved. It was still quiet and unnerving. Barnes' heart began to race and beat faster and faster with every silent second. Then he heard something.

'Police,' a familiar voice appeared throughout the boat. 'Is anybody down here?'

Barnes hesitated. He knew Lily would harm his family if he spoke and on the other hand, Ally could die if he didn't. He didn't have long to decide what to do, and with every moment he wasted, Ally was a little closer to danger. The shadows of Lily and Cain disappeared into the dark as the light vanished.

Ally was in. Nobody answered her call, making her uneasy and anxious. She took another step down the stairs and into the pit of the boat. Her gun aimed in front of her, pointing the barrel where she faced.

She was scared but she didn't want to show it. If Barnes wasn't here, she didn't know if they'd ever find him. She glanced around the room, not being able to see much other than where she was walking. The canal boat was run down, dusty and needed a lick of paint. *A good place to stash someone*, she thought.

Her heart began to race, her mind wandering all over the place, thinking about who was lurking in the dark. Ally moved slowly through the darkness, taking one step at a time, her gun still protecting her.

She heard a creak from a floorboard. Someone was approaching her.

'Hello,' she called out. 'This is the police. Come out with your hands above your head.'

Still, nothing but silence. Sarah crept down the stairs behind her, making Ally jump with fright, removing her eyes from the darkness which lay in front of her.

'Jesus, Sarah,' she whispered.

'Sorry,' Sarah apologised, before she noticed a six-foot man, charging towards Ally. 'Ally, look out!' she cried.

Ally turned around to see Cain running at her from within the shadows. She dodged his fist, which flew at her with haste. She fell backwards onto the floor below Sarah's feet. Sarah aimed her gun at him.

'Don't move another fuckin' muscle!' Sarah yelled at him.

But that didn't stop Cain. He knew Sarah was just as frightened, as he quickly approached her, knocking her gun out of her hands and dropping it to the floor. Sarah took a step backwards, terrified and worried about what was about to happen to her and Ally. Cain laughed with a deep, frightening roar.

'Armed police! Don't move!' their backup shouted throughout the boat.

The game was over for Cain. He'd been caught.

'Who's laughing now?' Sarah said smugly.

The officers moved into the boat, cuffed Cain and dragged him outside, while Ally, Sarah and the other AFOs searched the rest of the boat. There was no sign of anyone else lurking in the dark, just a locked door at the far end.

'Is anyone else in here?' Ally shouted.

'Ally,' a man's voice shouted from the other side of the locked door.

'Barnes, is that you?' she shouted back, relieved that they'd actually found him alive.

'Yes.' He cried, knowing it was all over.

Ally started to kick the door down but realised it was no good. Sarah called for an officer to come forward. The pair of them moved out of the way as the officer used the end of his weapon to smash the lock on the door.

Ally and Sarah burst through the door to see Barnes on his knees, covered in blood, with an ankle bracelet around his leg which was chained to the wall. His face was unrecognisable it had been beaten so much. Barnes was crying tears of joy. The pain and suffering was over.

'I'm so glad to see you both,' he rejoiced.

Ally helped him to his feet, while Sarah sought after the keys to his ankle bracelet.

'You're okay now,' Ally told him.

Barnes cried as he hobbled out of the canal boat. Paramedics rushed over to assist Ally with helping Barnes to walk. He perched on a side platform while the paramedics checked him over.

'I'm so glad you've got them. I hope they spend eternity behind...'

Ally cut him off. Something bothered her about what he'd just said.

'They?' she asked.

'Lily and Cain,' Barnes answered.

'We only caught the one guy. There was no sign of Lily. Are you sure she was in there?'

'I'm positive,' he continued, starting to cry again.

He panicked, knowing how dangerous she was and she was back on the loose. The danger was real, and it terrified him. Then he thought of the threat she made towards his family.

'Are you sure she's not in there?' he asked again, confirming the reality of the situation.

'Yes, Barnes. I'm positive,' Ally repeated for the second time.

'Then we need a patrol car outside my ex-wife's house,' he yelled.

Ally was shocked. *What has she done to him to terrify him this much?*

'Okay.' She called Sarah over and asked her to send officers over to Vanessa Barnes' home. 'I need you to explain to me what happened, boss,' she demanded, placing both her hands on his shoulders.

'She wanted information from me. I don't know what she was asking me about,' he lied, 'but she threatened my family if I didn't tell her what she wanted to know.'

'It's okay. Your family will be alright,' she consoled him.

Vanessa Barnes' evening was just like any other; cooking her daughters dinners, cleaning up around the house before she put the girls to bed. Once they'd settled down for the night, she chilled on the sofa with a glass of red wine. She wasn't an avid wine drinker, just an average bottle from the supermarket did her just fine.

But somebody interrupted her night with a knock on the door. Reluctantly, she removed herself from her comfy, slumped posture and answered the door, to see two policemen standing in front of her.

'Good evening...' one officer greeted before Vanessa cut him short.

'What is it? What's wrong,' she began to panic, seeing the officers at her door. 'Is it my husband?'

'Your husband is fine. We've been asked to keep guard over your house,' the officer continued to inform her.

'You've found him?'

'Yes, but he believes you and your daughters are in danger. We'll be right outside if you need us.'

'Thank you,' she replied, before closing the doors as the officers returned to their vehicle.

Nervous and worried, Vanessa strolled back over to her sofa and wine. She couldn't relax knowing her ex-husband thought she was in danger, was putting her on edge. *His kidnapper must have gotten away, that's why he's sent the officers*, she wondered.

Vanessa couldn't relax and wanted to check on her daughters as her mind raced through multiple thoughts. One-step, two-step. Before she knew it, she was at the top. As she pushed their bedroom door open, she sighed with relief, seeing them calmly asleep in their beds.

She stood there for what seemed like minutes, watching them sleep. It was an incredible feeling, seeing them laying there while danger was on the loose. But another knock on the door interrupted her moment.

As she walked down the stairs, she thought for a moment. *What happens if it's the kidnapper?* She peeped through the spy hole, to see a female officer stood in uniform.

'Hello,' Vanessa greeted as she opened the door.

'Hi. Just to let you know, Mrs Barnes, we've just had a report that the kidnapper is in the area,' the officer informed her while looking over her own shoulder.

The female officer seemed nervous and on edge. She kept checking behind her and around the street.

'Do you want to come in?' Vanessa asked her.

'I'll check the house, just to make sure, if that's okay?' she replied.

Vanessa caught a glimpse of the officer's badge as she entered. Sam Wilson. As she walked over to check the windows and doors throughout the ground floor of the house, Vanessa offered her a drink.

'No, thank you,' she replied, continuing through the house.

The phone in the hallway began to ring. As Vanessa checked the caller I.D, she noticed it had Brian's name.

'Hello, Brian,' she answered.

'Hi, Vanessa. I'm just checking up to see if the police unit we sent over has arrived?'

'Yes, they're here. Officer Wilson is inside checking the windows and doors. She's just checking upstairs and then she's finished.'

'Officer Wilson?' he asked.

'Yes, that's what I said. Sam Wilson.'

'Vanessa, I need you to listen carefully,' he replied anxiously.

'Why? What's wrong?'

'I need you to tell me the description of this officer,' he asked, still nervous about who was in her house.

'Who is in my house?' she queried with a whisper as she was becoming scared.

'What does she look like?' he repeated, wanting her to give him an answer.

'She's slim, blonde...'

'Get out of the house! Sam Wilson is a man,' he yelled at her.

But before she could even move, she heard steps coming from behind her.

'Put the phone down, Mrs Barnes,' the officer demanded.

Vanessa turned around to see the woman aiming a gun towards her. She placed the phone down by her side, leaving the call open so Brian could hear every minute of their conversation.

'Where are my girls?' she cried, knowing this woman was dangerous.

'Don't worry they're still asleep, and they will stay that way, as long as you do as I say,' she ordered.

Chapter 10

The flashing lights were on, the cars were roaring, blasting across the Birmingham streets. Lily was about to cause more chaos and mayhem. Shattering the lives of the people who took her's from her was all she had left. It was ride or die for her now. To kill or be killed.

She wanted information from Barnes, knowing he was the only one who could tell her what she needed to know. It was the only reason she'd kept him alive. She needed a new approach and going after his family would be her last option.

Barnes was still bleeding from his wounds but didn't want to get stitched up until he knew his family was safe, and Lily was in cuffs. Ally hightailed her way to Vanessa's house, pushing her car to its limit.

It wasn't long before they pulled up outside, to see a police perimeter, with armed police trying to get a vantage point on their suspect.

'What have we got?' Ally asked the officer in charge.

'All we know is the suspect is inside holding Mrs Barnes hostage and is armed,' Richard Banks informed her.

Richard had been in charge of the armed response team for as little as five months. It wasn't the first time he'd been in charge of a tactical operation like this.

'I'm going in,' Barnes demanded, pushing his way through everyone.

'DCI Barnes, this is my operation and you'll do as I say!' Richard shouted at him.

'And that's my family, Richard! So keep out of my way!' Barnes yelled back before storming towards his ex-wife's front door.

He slowly pushed the door open, before hearing a familiar, yet to him, terrifying voice call out to him.

'Come on in, Joe. We've been waiting for you.'

Barnes stepped inside, slowly closing the door behind him. Vanessa sat opposite Lily, crying her eyes out, focusing on her ex-husband, who had a horrifying appearance.

'Joe, I'm so sorry,' she apologised for letting Lily into the house.

'It's okay, Honey,' he calmly responded.

'Do you like my handy work?' Lily asked Vanessa, discussing Barnes' horrific appearance.

Barnes noticed the gun pointed at Vanessa. He stopped moving, trying not to make any sudden moves. This situation could go very badly at any moment, and Barnes knew that.

'It's going to be okay, V,' he tried to calm his ex-wife down.

Jacob couldn't sit still. The craving was back and stronger than ever, as the thoughts of Lily kidnapping Barnes, and killing his father, never left his mind. He decided food was probably the best course of action to remove alcohol from his thoughts.

Belle and Kate were sat watching TV on the sofa, discussing work, gossip and love lives. Jacob finished making his dinner before joining them.

'Where's ours?' Kate joked.

'There's some more in the kitchen,' he replied with a mouth full of food.

The food wasn't enough for him. The craving grew stronger. He turned his head over towards the kitchen counter, where he'd left half a bottle of whiskey. His eyes were drawn to it as well as his thoughts. He needed it. *Maybe it will calm me down*, he thought.

He placed his plate of food on the coffee table, then strolled over to the bottle. After he grabbed a glass from the cupboard, he opened the bottle and poured the liquid. His hand began to shake as he lifted the glass closer to his lips. The smooth whiskey dribbled down, warming his throat. It felt incredibly good.

'Slow down, Jacob,' Belle said. 'You'll be drunk after that one glass.' She laughed.

He chuckled along with her, feeling more relaxed now. He wondered about Barnes; where he was; if he was okay. His thoughts began to drift as he focused on his mobile phone, ringing in his pocket.

'DS Wright,' he answered.

'Jacob, it's Harry Wong, from the forensic lab. Just to inform you that we've lifted prints from the crime scenes, both Mr Roberts' and Mr Hussain's homes.

We've run it through the database and have come up with no matches,' he explained.

'Does that mean Mr Roberts is innocent?' he asked.

'It means we have no evidence on him having killed either his wife or his neighbour.'

'Thank you, Harry,' he said disappointedly.

'One other thing, Jacob. If you speak to Ally, will you let her know? I couldn't get through to either of your team,' he informed him.

'Okay, no problem.'

He hung up the phone, worried about what Harry had just told him. He tried to call Ally, but no answer. Then he tried Sarah, then Brian, but still, no one answered. *Why aren't they answering?* He called Ethan, his last hope.

'Hello,' Ethan greeted.

'Finally,' he praised. 'Where is everyone?'

Ethan didn't know what to say. He was instructed by Ally not to tell Jacob what was happening, due to his current state of mind.

'They're following up on a lead,' he lied.

'Okay. I need you to meet me at The Russells right away. I want to ask Mr Roberts a few more questions about this mystery man.' He explained, wanting a partner to work with.

'Jacob, I've been told not to let you work anything until Ally gives the go-ahead. I'm sorry mate. Can it wait till tomorrow?'

'Yes, I'm sure it can. I'll see you tomorrow then,' he said before hanging up the phone.

Jacob couldn't wait. He needed something to take his mind off Barnes, Lily and his father. He grabbed his keys, coat and phone, then headed for the door.

'Don't wait up,' he told the girls.

'Why? Where are you going?' Belle questioned him.

'Work,' he replied, shutting the door behind him.

Jack Roberts was frightened, peeping out of the windows, scanning the neighbourhood for the mystery man. He couldn't relax, knowing this man was out there, committing murders around him.

Jack shifted from room to room, window to window. Nothing could calm him down. It was just him inside the house now, all alone. He missed his wife every minute of the day. His hands were shaking, his legs like jelly. He couldn't stop shaking. He sensed the stranger was outside of his house, so Jack went to the window, peeped through the curtains once again, to see the man in his back garden.

Jack stepped away from the window and gasped, covering his mouth with his hands. His heart raced, faster than it ever had. He had no idea what action to take now. *Is this it? Has he come for me now?*

There was a knock at Jack's door, making him leap with fright. He didn't know what to do. Creeping towards his front door, he peered through the spy hole, locking his eyes upon DS Wright.

Jack opened the door without hesitation and greeted the detective with delight.

'DS Wright. You've got to help me,' he yelled at him, surprising Jacob.

'What's going on? What's wrong?' Jacob asked him with urgency.

'The man, the one who killed my wife, he's in the garden,' he continued shouting.

Jacob pushed past Jack and ran straight through the house until he reached the back door, but it was locked and the key was nowhere in sight.

'Where's the key?' Jacob demanded.

Jack reached into one of the kitchen cupboards, removed the key, and walked back into the hallway, placing the key in Jacob's hand. He placed it in the lock as fast as he could and dashed into the garden. Jacob inspected the entire garden, but there was no one there, nor was there evidence anybody had been.

'Mr Roberts, there's no one here,' he informed him.

'But he was right there,' he pointed to a section of the garden, where he'd seen the man.

Jacob was concerned, thinking Jack might have paranoia. The pair of them went back inside the house, locked the door behind them and set foot in the living room. Jack was still pacing around the room, terrified of the mystery man that only he had seen.

'Mr Roberts, the forensics have come back on Mr Hussain's home and yours. They've found matching fingerprints at both scenes,' Jacob informed him.

'Do you have a match?' he asked, concerned.

'Not yet, but we'll keep you updated. I just wanted to tell you in person.'

Jacob noticed Jack had a strange, gazed look upon his face.

'Mr Roberts, are you alright?' Jacob asked.

But Jack didn't move, he didn't even flinch. His eyelids remained open, gazing straight ahead of him. There was no movement, not one slight bit. Seconds passed before Jack snapped back, changing the way he acted. Jacob noticed the difference between when he arrived, to how he was at that moment.

'Sorry, DS Wright,' he apologised. 'I don't know what came over me.'

'Are you okay?' he repeated, noticing the calmness Jack had upon him now.

'Yes. I think I'll be absolutely fine.'

'Are you sure? You seemed nervous as hell before I arrived,' he recalled.

'You said there was no sign that anyone had been out there, so I think I'll be fine. I'm probably just paranoid,' he joked and laughed.

'You can come back to the station with me if you want?'

Jacob gave him the option for his safety, even though he wanted to keep a close eye on Jack as his behaviour had become unusual. But Jack just smiled a creep half smile towards him. Jacob felt apprehensive about his change in behaviour. *Maybe this man did kill his wife and her lover?* he began to think.

'Okay, I should be going,' Jacob said while heading for the door fast.

But Jack had other ideas, knowing Jacob had noticed he'd changed and grabbed one of his wife's ornaments. He never liked them, and always thought they took up too much space. With the ornament held tightly in his grasp, he smacked it over the back of Jacob's head, knocking him to the floor.

Jacob lay unconscious. Nobody had any idea where he was. His head slightly cut and bleeding over Jack's carpet. Jacob was now in a dangerous situation, just like his DCI.

Barnes stood in the hallway of his ex-wife's house, glancing between Vanessa and Lily, worried about the gun Lily held tight in her grasp. Vanessa's eyes were watery from the tears which streamed down her cheeks. Barnes was in agony but held back the pain, trying to remain strong. His knees were getting weaker, but he needed Lily to see he was still able to fight.

'So, I know what you want, Lily, as we've been over it a few times. But what do you think's going to happen to you after you leave this house? You think you're just going to walk out of here?'

She laughed, but she didn't have an answer.

'Just let my wife and kids go, Lily. They are not part of this,' he begged.

'What have I told you, Joe? Don't beg, it doesn't suit you.'

'What do you want me to do?' he yelled. 'You want the answer to something I don't know. You've held me hostage for days and now you're holding my family hostage. I'm begging you, Lily. Just let them go.'

Barnes started to cry. He had become physically and mentally broken and was at his lowest, just the way Lily wanted him to be. She began to get impatient and wanted the answer to her question.

'Well, none of this would be happening to your family right now, if you left what wasn't yours. You would be dead and your wife and kids would have moved on, and I would have what was mine,' she stood up shouting, approaching and pointing the gun at Barnes.

Joe suddenly heard a noise coming from the stairs to the right of him. His two daughters had awoken from their slumber.

'Daddy,' April said, rubbing her eyes. 'What's going on?'

April and Bonnie turned six just before Christmas. They were identical twins with the same personalities, but their curiosity they inherited from their father.

'Nothing sweetie. You and your sister go back upstairs to bed,' he told her, with tears in his eyes.

April and Bonnie held hands as they turned around and took themselves back to bed. Barnes couldn't help but think of Jacob and Adam when they were younger, in the same circumstance that his daughters were in now.

'Is this how it went with your sister and John's wife and children?' he demanded her to answer, raising his voice slightly. 'Jacob and his mother? Were you there to witness his mother's murder? You know, the man you promised to spend your life with before you killed his father,' he explained.

Vanessa stared at Barnes shocked, not knowing any information on who this woman was until Barnes revealed her true identity.

'Oh my God! You're Lily!' she shouted.

'Live in the flesh,' Lily giggled, pointing the gun back in Vanessa's direction. 'No, I wasn't there, Joe. I spent most of my time alone while my sister took care of her plans.'

'Why don't you just get out of here, Lily,' he pleaded. 'Just sneak out the back and disappear.'

'Do you really think I'm that stupid? I'm in the endgame now. The only way I'm leaving here is in a body bag or in handcuffs.'

'But if you really do love Jacob, like you say you do, then you'd surrender yourself.'

'Not till I get what's mine!' she shouted back at him.

Lily knew there was no way out of the house. She was trapped. There was no escape other than captured or dead, but she wouldn't surrender until he told her where the diamonds were.

133

'It doesn't matter. You'll never get to them either way,' Barnes admitted he knew where they were. 'You'll be dead or arrested before you can get anywhere near them.'

'So you know where they are? This whole time you could have just told me and spared yourself and your family so much pain. Did you ever think why I just came after you? I knew you took them and I know they're not where they are supposed to be.'

'Lily, I'm begging you, just let my wife and daughters go and I'll tell you where they are,' he continued to beg.

'You had your chance.'

Before Barnes could move, Lily stared Vanessa dead in the eyes before pulling the trigger, blasting a bullet straight in her stomach. She hit the floor with a thud with blood pouring everywhere on the floor. Barnes rushed to snatch the gun out of Lily's hands before she could take a shot at him, but she was quicker than him and pointed it in his direction.

'No sudden movements, Joe,' she demanded calmly.

'Let her get some help,' he pleaded. Lily said nothing, making Joe shout, 'She's gonna die! She needs to go to the hospital.'

'Nobody's leaving,' Lily yelled back, still pointing the gun at him.

The twins had come back to the stairway after hearing the gunshot, to see their mother bleeding on the floor beneath them.

'Mummy,' Bonnie cried out, her tears streaming down her cheeks.

April came running down the stairs and towards her mother before Barnes stopped her from getting any closer to Lily. Bonnie remained on the stairs, too afraid to move. Her eyes focused on the gun Lily had pointed at her father.

'Stay back,' Barnes said to April, as he pushed her behind him, shielding her from Lily.

'This is all your fault, Joe,' she yelled once again.

'Aren't you going to do anything?' Ally yelled at the armed response officer.

'We can't ma'am. We can't get a clear enough view. The curtains are drawn and we can't get a shot on the suspect,' he explained.

She stormed off and approached the front of Vanessa's house, despite the officers shouting at her to return to a safe distance. She could hear shouting coming from what she thought was Lily's voice. Children crying was the next thing Ally could hear, before hearing her boss pleading and begging.

Ally quietly rushed back behind the tape and informed the armed officers of what she heard.

'Someone's been shot, which I believe is Vanessa Barnes. Our suspect, Lily Black, seems to be inside and armed.'

The officer responded with just a nod while keeping his sights on the house in case of any activity. The rest of her team made their way across the street and reconnected with Ally.

'Pretty ballsy, boss,' Brian joked.

'Lily has Barnes' wife and kids hostage,' she explained to them. 'I'm gonna go round the back and find a way inside.'

'But you can't. They won't let you enter there alone,' said Sarah, talking about the armed response unit.

'I don't care. There are two little girls inside that house and one mother, who is bleeding out from a gunshot wound, and the most they are doing is aiming at a house with no target in sight,' she explained with frustration.

Ally opened the boot of her car, put on her Kevlar vest, and gave her gun the once over before moving towards the house. She ran around the back while the officers once again shouted at her to stand down, but Ally wasn't waiting any longer. Barnes and his family were in there and in danger.

Once she made it into the garden, she checked the back door to see if it was open. That's when she noticed one of the glass panels in the door had been smashed. The door was still slightly open, making it easier for Ally to enter.

Her foot avoided the smashed shards of glass currently laying on the floor and made her way through the kitchen and to the hallway. Sounds of shouting could still be heard, echoing throughout the house.

Lily sounded panicked as if she had no idea how to remove herself from the current situation she was trapped in.

'Lily, please just calm down. You're scaring my daughters. Just let them and my wife go,' he begged once again.

'I've told you, no one is leaving,' she replied, with her hands on her head pacing around the floor, trying to think of a way out of the house alive.

Vanessa was unconscious and losing blood. Barnes heard a noise to his left, like a squeaky floorboard, coming from his right. He took a quick glance and caught sight of Ally, peeking from behind the door frame.

Ally moved stealthily across the hallway to the room opposite which would give her another vantage point at Lily. Barnes moved his focus back on Lily. He could see Ally hiding by the door frame from the dining room next door to the lounge area. Both Barnes and Ally now had Lily cornered with nowhere to go.

'Lily, just walk out of here, before you end up dead,' Barnes instructed.

'What makes you think I'll end up dead?' she questioned with a smirk.

'Because you're cornered,' Ally informed her, aiming her gun at Lily.

Lily took a quick shot at Ally, missing, before moving her gun back at Barnes and pulling the trigger. But Barnes calculated her next move and jumped behind the wall to the hallway with April.

'You and your sister go upstairs and don't come out of your room till you hear me, okay?' he told April, giving her clear instructions, before removing his gun from the back of his trousers.

Ally fired back, also missing Lily as she ducked behind one of the sofas, getting out of the line of fire from both Ally and Barnes.

'Is that the best you've got?' Lily called out to Ally, taunting her.

Barnes peeked around the corner, looking to get a clear aim of Lily, but no joy. He could hear the sound of footsteps approaching the door to the left of him before the door flung open and an army of police stormed through the house.

'Armed police!' the first officer shouted. 'Put your weapon down and surrender yourself.'

All Barnes could see in the lounge, was two arms held in the air with empty hands. Lily removed herself slowly from behind the sofa and into the open area of the lounge.

'Get down on the floor with your arms above your head,' the officer continued to shout his instructions.

Lily did as she was instructed and lay on the floor as the officer cuffed her hands together and removed her from the house. Barnes rushed over to his ex-wife who lay unconscious on the floor.

'I'm so sorry,' he sobbed.

Two paramedics came rushing in and moved Barnes out of the way, before trying to save her life.

Ally hugged Barnes, not knowing what to say. Once they released from their hug, Joe ran upstairs to his daughter's room.

'You can both come out now, my brave little soldiers,' he said softly with his arms wide open.

April and Bonnie came rushing out of their closet and into their father's open arms. The three of them stayed hugging for minutes, crying their hearts out.

'It's okay now girls. Daddy's here.'

It had been a long and hard night for the team, but finally, they had Lily in custody, and it was all over.

Chapter 11

Belle ate her breakfast like she did most mornings before leaving for work. The weather was slightly chilly, but the sun peeped out from behind the clouds on occasion.

She couldn't help but think about Ben. They spent the whole night texting one another, staying up until the early hours of the morning. She felt incredibly happy. Her life was back on track. No more worrying about where she was going to be sleeping each night or where her next meal was coming from. Her life had changed for the better.

On the commute to work, she noticed a strange man had been following her from outside the apartment. She had never seen the man before and wondered what he wanted from her. She picked up the pace, trying to speed up, not being that far from her destination. But he was gaining on her. She turned the corner but as she did, she noticed the man began to jog before placing his hand on her shoulder.

'Hey, I need to talk to you.'

Belle gasped out of fright, pulling herself away from the strange man. He took a step back as he noticed the scared look upon her face.

'It's okay, I'm not going to hurt you. I just want to talk to you, Kate,' he explained, not realising he was talking to the wrong person.

'My names not Kate. I think you've got the wrong person.'

The man looked shocked. 'I'm so sorry. I just seen you come out of the same building.'

'That's okay,' she replied, wanting to get away.

'You don't know Kate Wright, do you?' he asked.

Not knowing what the man wanted from Kate, she decided to lie. 'No, I don't. Sorry.'

Belle scurried away as fast as she could. *What does he want with Kate? Who is this man?* She had arrived at work. Another long day ahead of her before she could get any answers about the mystery man.

The light shone through Jacob's eyelids. He opened his eyes slowly, trying his best to get a glimpse of his surroundings, but the light was too strong. He tried to move his arms to cover his eyes, but couldn't. Something was restraining them tight. His head was pounding from the smack he received from Jack Roberts.

After a few minutes, his eyes were completely open and inspecting his surroundings. Jacob was strapped to a chair with duct tape and rope, trapped inside the same room he asked Mr Roberts questions in the night before.

No sounds could be heard, not even quiet footsteps pacing the room next door. It was dead silent. Only the sound of the early morning birds tweeting in the trees outside could be heard. Jacob tried to call for help, but his throat was dry and his voice raspy from the lack of fluids.

Where is Jack Roberts? he asked himself. *I need to get out of here.* Jacob tried to pull at the duct tape surrounding his wrists. The robe hugged his chest and the remaining duct tape cuffed his ankles to the chair legs. Glancing around trying to find anything that could help him escape, he noticed a piece of folded paper on the cabinet beside him.

He continued trying to tear the tape that bound his wrists the best he could. Jacob knew he was in trouble and if Jack didn't come back, he'd be stranded here with no one knowing where he'd gone. He cried for help again, this time his voice was clear and vocal. He yelled at the top of his lungs, just enough for a neighbour to hear.

Ally arrived at the station after a long night. The place was quiet and untouched since the night. Lily was taken to a holding cell awaiting her interview of questions. Ally needed to prepare, but this was the part where she needed her partner in on the interview. She couldn't involve him now. He was too involved in this case along with Barnes, so she was on her own and in need of a new partner to help.

Sarah suddenly burst through the doors as if she had a feeling Ally needed her help. Ally was inside the briefing room staring at the photos on the investigation board. Everything they had on Lily was hanging right in front of her and now they had her in custody. She took them off, picture by picture when Sarah entered.

'Need any help?' she asked.

Ally turned around, seeing Sarah lent against the door frame. 'I'm just taking down the investigation board on Lily. I can't believe we've finally got her.'

'I know. It's a relief knowing she's locked up. Do you need help with the interview?' she cut straight to the point.

'With Barnes and Jacob not being here, I think I'm going to need you,' Ally smiled.

'Have you told Jacob yet?'

'No. I don't know how to. He'll be happy we've found Barnes alive, but how do I explain what Lily had done to him. He'll want to see her, maybe even kill her, and I don't want him to lose himself.'

'I think Jacob can handle her.'

'I don't think he can. You should have seen him yesterday. He's taking it hard. She killed people, including his father and lied about her entire life. He's not himself anymore,' Ally explained to her.

'But think about how annoyed he'll be if he finds out you've hidden this from him.'

'You're right,' she agreed. 'I'll call him.'

Ally left the room and headed to Barnes' office where she called Jacob. There was no answer, so she tried a second time. Still no answer. She walked back to Sarah in the briefing room.

'Have you heard from Jacob since yesterday?' she asked.

'No, why? What's wrong?'

'I tried calling him, but no answer.'

'Maybe he's sleeping.'

Ally sighed. 'Maybe.'

The two of them continued planning the interview of Lily. She was finally in a cell and this time she wouldn't escape from their grasp. Ally couldn't help but think about how this was going to set Jacob spiralling back into depression. She worried about the drinking and his mental health the past month. *I love him, but if I act on my feelings now, it's either gonna push him away or bring him close to me.*

Jacob had been awake in the chair for over an hour, trying to find something close that would help him escape the clutches of the duct tape. The tape hadn't ripped as much as he'd hoped and he was in for a long day, hoping and praying someone would find him soon.

That's when Doris, the nosy neighbour from across the road, approached the Roberts' house and peeked through the window. She noticed DS Wright strapped to a chair with rope and duct tape and decided to call the police.

'Hello, is this the police?' she asked. 'He's at it again. My neighbour. He has one of your detectives. He is being held hostage in his house in The Russells, just off Russell Street. Come quickly.'

She hung up the phone and glared at Jacob through the window trying to signal she had notified the police. Jacob thanked her before she sneaked back over the road to her house, afraid that Jack was still in the house.

Ten minutes later the police arrived outside. Doris filled the officers in on the situation before the AFOs showed up. A perimeter had been set up around the house, with the armed police trying to get a view inside the house and of their suspect.

Ally and Sarah were ready for the interview of their career. Lily Black was the most horrific case they'd ever worked on and she showed no remorse for what she had done or who she had killed.

'Are you ready, Ally?' Sarah asked.

Ally took a few deep breaths. 'It's now or never,' she responded.

The pair of them grabbed their notes and made their way towards the interview room when the officer guarding the door approached them.

'She didn't want her lawyer present.'

'What do you mean?' Sarah asked the officer.

'She told me there's no point. She said she knows the game is over for her now,' she explained.

Ally sniggered. 'Game? Does she think this has all been a game? She's disgusting.'

Ally moved past the officer and opened the door to the interview room. Her eyes set upon Lily's which appeared black and tired. *She mustn't have slept well*, Ally thought. *I'm glad*. She smiled as she sat down, Lily not taking her eyes off Ally. Sarah followed before shutting the door behind her, then sat down beside Ally.

'Are you sure you don't want your solicitor present?' Ally asked her politely, though she didn't want to be.

'No. Like I told your colleague, I know what I've done, who I've hurt,' she replied, looking Ally dead in the eye. 'I'm going down, either way, lawyer or no lawyer.'

'Okay then,' Ally replied, trying not to smile, placing the tape in the recorder. 'This is DI Ally Miller with DS Sarah Taylor interviewing Lily Black on the 7th of January at 10.47 am. Lily, for the tape can you confirm you didn't want your solicitor present for this interview.'

'Yes,' she mumbled.

As they were about to begin the interview, someone knocked on the door. All three of them jumped with fright. Ally paused the tape, lifted herself up and answered the door to see Ethan standing on the other side, silent and keeping his head down.

'Come on, Ethan. Spit it out. What is it?' she questioned him, frustrated that she had to pause the interview.

'It's Jacob.'

'What's wrong?' she asked, starting to worry about what he was going to say.

'He's at the Roberts' house. He's in a hostage situation,' he explained.

'Is he okay?' Ally started to panic and Lily noticed the feelings she had for her ex-fiancee. 'I've got to go.'

Sarah followed her out of the room and informed the guard to send Lily back to her cell. The three of them ran through the station and jumped into Ally's car and sped towards The Russells. Ally's mind was uncontrollable. *Not again. Not another hostage situation. Not today.*

Chapter 12

Ally dashed through red lights; her siren blaring and echoing throughout the streets. Sarah sat beside her, holding on to the passenger handle for dear life. Ethan was being thrown about in the back seats wanting to puke from being travel sick.

'Any chance you could slow down?' Sarah freaked out.

'Why? What's the problem?' Ally glanced at her surprised, taking her eyes off the road momentarily.

'I just don't think I'm ready to die yet,' she replied with sheer panic as Ally manoeuvred her way through the traffic.

'We're almost there. Just hold on a bit longer.'

Minutes later they arrived at The Russells, pulling up on the busy street full of police cars and vans. News reporters had beaten them here and already getting the low down on the situation, interviewing neighbours and trying their best to get a statement from the police.

Ally rushed over to where the ranking officer on scene was prepping a scenario to rescue Jacob.

'What's going on? Have you had any contact with the perp yet?' she threw her questions at him.

'DI Miller, I presume?' He held out his hand for her to shake.

'Yes,' she grabbed his hand.

'We haven't seen or heard from anyone inside the house. The lady from across the street called it in after she heard shouting coming from the house. She took a peep through the window and saw DS Wright tied to a chair and that's when she called it in.'

'Do we even know if Mr Roberts is inside?'

'We have no confirmation on that yet,' he answered.

Sarah and Ethan finally caught up to her and she filled them in. This seemed like it was becoming a regular thing in their team. They had seen two hostage situations in the last twenty-four hours. Everyone's emotions were on high alert.

Moments later, Brian turned up alongside Barnes. Ally was shocked and couldn't believe Barnes was standing in front of her after everything he'd been through.

'Boss, what are you doing here? You should be resting,' she looked concerned.

'One of ours is in danger. I can't sit back and leave everyone else to it. Besides, I owe it to his father,' he replied, showing her his compassion towards his team.

'How's Vanessa doing?' asked Sarah.

'She's doing fine. The doctors think she'll recover. The bullet didn't hit any major arteries or organs so she'll be just fine.'

'What about your daughters?' Ally fired another question of concern at him.

'They're with Vanessa's mother. So, what's going on?'

Ally informed him of what was happening. He sat down on the curb and placed his head in his hands.

'Are you alright, boss?' Brian asked with concern for his friend.

'Yeah, it's just been a long couple of days. Do we know how long this guy's had Jacob?'

'I spoke to him last night. He was trying to get me to come with him, but I told him we'd do it this morning. He agreed and that was that. I didn't think he'd come here alone,' Ethan informed the team.

'It's okay,' Sarah comforted him, placing her hand on his shoulder after seeing the tear in his eye. 'He's gonna be fine.'

Ethan nodded in response. Then the team noticed the armed police unit sneaking towards the house, ready to burst through the front door. They broke the front door down with one push of the metal ram and entered while yelling out their presence inside the house.

Barnes and the others could hear each officer shout clear as they entered each room, and within minutes Jacob was being carried out by two officers under each of his arms.

Ally ran straight up to him, placed both her arms around his neck and squeezed tight. His embrace comforted her as much as it did him. They held each other tight, forgetting about the crowd which surrounded them. Ally had shown her true feelings to more than just Jacob, but she didn't care. She had fallen for him in such a short amount of time.

'I'm glad you're okay,' she whispered in his ear.

Sarah and Ethan joined them, each giving him a hug once Ally removed herself off him. Brian then followed before Jacob laid his eyes on Barnes, who smiled at him from down the path before he approached.

'Oh my god, Barnes,' he greeted him, surprised to see Barnes stood in front of him. 'How'd you get away? You look like shit,' he joked.

'You don't look too good yourself, son,' Barnes replied the compliment and laughed back at him.

The pair of them laughed before they gave one another a hug. It had been a difficult few days for the pair of them, but it was all over.

Paramedics rushed over to Jacob and checked him over inside the ambulance. He smiled, staring at his team and thinking how happy he was to see them all together. He could finally take a sigh of relief after all the panic and trauma they'd experienced after the last month.

Ally strutted over to the ambulance and lent against the frame, while Jacob remained seated on the steps.

'So, how are you feeling?' she asked him.

'Better now I've seen you,' he smiled.

'Such the charmer, aren't you?' She replied with a smile. 'Look, Jacob. I know you're not looking for a relationship right now, but I want to get it off my chest. I have feelings for you and I can't just ignore them. What I'm trying to say is, when you're ready, I'll be waiting.'

'Look, Ally...'

'It's fine, Jacob. You don't have to say anything.' She smiled at him again before walking away from the ambulance and back to the rest of the team.

Barnes noticed Jacob sat on his own and went to speak to him, knowing they had loads of catching up to do.

'So, are you going to tell me what happened here?' Barnes questioned him, arms folded with a stern look upon his face.

'Are you going to tell me what happened at the cemetery?' he threw a question back at him.

The both of them smiled before Barnes came up with an idea.

'You buy me a drink and I'll tell you all about it.'

'Tonight?' said Jacob.

'Okay, I'll let the guys know. We could all do with a distraction.'

Jacob arrived home early that evening, thinking he'd beat both Belle and Kate home. He threw his keys on the kitchen side, grabbed a glass from the cupboard and poured himself a glass of water. Once the water touched his lips, he could feel the liquid making its way down his throat. He chugged the entire glass before pouring another one.

'Hey, slow down,' he heard a voice say from across the apartment. 'Must have been a good night, you dirty stop out,' Belle laughed.

'You don't know the half of it,' he smiled at her as he turned around from the kitchen sink.

Belle gasped as she caught sight of his bruised face, from hitting the floor.

'My god. What happened to you?'

'You know, the usual kidnapping and being tied to a chair scenario.'

Belle didn't know whether to laugh, thinking he was telling a joke or to worry as if something serious had happened to him.

'Looks like you went ten rounds with Mike Tyson.'

'It looks worse than it is.'

'Are you going to tell me what happened?' she continued to ask.

'Got hit, then tied up overnight. Nothing more than that.'

'Crap night then,' she chuckled. 'At least you can say your life is never boring.'

'Indeed,' he agreed with a smile. 'Enough about me, how's your day been?'

'Actually, there's something I've been meaning to tell you,' she said with concern.

'Oh yeah, what's that?'

'A man followed me to work earlier. I'm fine, but there's something you should know. He thought I was Kate,' she informed him.

'What did he want with Kate?' he asked, knowing already who this man was and what he wanted.

'He didn't say. To be honest I didn't give him time to explain. I was too frightened and rushed off to work as quick as I could.'

'You did the right thing, Belle. You let me know if you see this man again.'

'Who is he?'

'I don't know,' he lied. 'But I'll find out.'

'Thanks, Jacob. I had to tell you.'

'And I'm glad you did.' Belle started to walk into her bedroom, before Jacob continued, 'Not a word to Kate. I don't want her worried about this.'

Belle nodded, agreeing with him and entered her bedroom. Jacob let out a long and hard sigh before picking up his phone and dialling Adam's number.

'Hi, brother,' he greeted. 'He's found Kate. I don't know what to do.'

Kate entered the apartment as Adam began to speak on the other end, but Jacob didn't want to discuss it with their sister in the room.

'Adam, she's just walked in,' he whispered. 'I'll talk to you soon.'

He hung up the phone as Kate approached the kitchen, glaring at the bruise on her brother's face.

'Wow, what happened to you?' She questioned him too.

'Nothing to worry about,' he replied, wanting to take the attention off of him. 'How was school?'

'Same old. People are still tip-toeing around me,' she confided in him.

'I know. I still get it at work,' he confessed. 'It will take a while before things go back to normal.'

'I guess,' she said with a saddened voice.

'Well, I've got to get ready. I'm off out with the team. Me and Barnes are going to have a catch-up.'

'You've found Barnes?'

'Oh yeah, I forgot to tell you. They found Barnes late last night and Lily is in custody,' he explained.

'Damn. I was hoping you'd say she was six feet under,' Kate announced her thoughts about Lily.

'I know what she did was vicious, but...'

'But nothing, Jacob. That bitch killed my mother and our father. I know she was your fiancee but you can't feel sympathetic for her.'

'I don't,' he replied.

'Well, it seems like you are. I get you have memories and had a life together but she's a cold-blooded killer and always will be,' she shouted before storming off to her room.

Jacob remained in the kitchen with his head in his hands again. He and Barnes were out of danger but the list of problems kept on growing. He did love Lily but knew Kate was right. He needed to stop being sympathetic. She was a killer.

Jacob scurried off to his bedroom to get ready. He showered quickly, then got dressed after deciding which shirt would be more suitable for a night out after kidnappings. He sneaked out of the apartment and made his way to the bar they all agreed to meet at.

Barnes found himself a table and sat alone while waiting for the others, clutching a beer in his hand. He stared around the bar, people laughing, joking and enjoying themselves. *This is what life is about*, he thought. Barnes' perspective on life had changed since his ordeal. Knowing how much he still cared for his ex-wife, he wanted to try to work things out. He now realised what life was about.

Barnes checked up on his daughters, before phoning Vanessa to see how she was doing. He still had feelings for her and was ecstatic that she was going to recover.

'I'm glad you're going to be fine. If you need anything, just let me know,' he said before hanging up the phone.

Ally entered the bar next and her eyes immediately locked onto Barnes.

'Hey. How long have you been here?'

'Not long,' he replied, slipping his phone back into his pocket. 'You look lovely. Definitely gonna turn a few heads.'

Ally just smiled. 'How are you?'

'I'm getting there. Just a strange week.'

'How're the girls doing? It must have been hard for them after what they witnessed.'

'They're a little shaken, but I think they will be fine. They've seen Vanessa and know their mum is getting better. How's Jacob been since the funeral?' he asked, knowing Ally would discuss her true opinion.

'I don't think he's taken any of this well. He came to work in a drunken state. I took him home before anyone realised.'

'We need to monitor him and keep it between ourselves for now. Hopefully, it was a one-off but I expected as much with all he's been through, to be honest.'

'I need to talk to you about something in confidence before the others get here,' Ally was nervous about what he'd say.

'Go ahead, the floor is yours.'

'I have feelings for him. Strong feelings. I've told him how I feel but we haven't taken it any further. If you want me off the team, I wouldn't blame you,' she admitted.

'So neither of you have acted on your feelings?'

'No.'

'Then why would I need to take you off the team? You are one of us now, Ally, and you're a damn good DI. I appreciate you telling me, but you're not going anywhere,' he smiled.

Ally felt relieved knowing she wouldn't have to leave, but she knew sometime soon her feelings for Jacob would have a reaction. She'd have to make the decision to either be with Jacob or leave the team she also grew to love.

Sarah and Brian arrived at the table, just as Barnes and Ally had finished discussing private matters.

'Hey, hope we're not too late,' Sarah greeted them.

'No, just in time. Sit down,' Barnes invited.

The four of them discussed recent events, told jokes and even told old stories from their pasts before Jacob entered half an hour later.

'Have I missed anything?' he asked as he approached the laughter.

'Just a few funny stories,' Brian replied, still laughing from the story Sarah had just told.

'Come, sit down, Jacob,' Ally patted the seat next to her.

As he joined the group, Ally flirtatiously smiled at him, even though she realised it would be him or her job. But she couldn't hold back on the feelings she had for him. He was worth the risk.

Hours had passed before everyone decided to disperse. Ally, Sarah and Jacob caught a cab together, mainly because Jacob was too intoxicated to make his own way home and also because he could barely stand on his feet. Barnes left the bar and headed straight home to his empty house, filled with piles of dirty dishes.

Jacob passed out inside the taxi while they stopped outside of Sarah's place. She jumped out, paid her share and headed inside. Once the taxi pulled up outside Jacob's apartment building, Ally tried lifting him to his feet, not wanting to drag his heavy carcass inside alone. He was extremely heavy.

'Come on, Jacob. I need you to help me get you inside,' she huffed while trying to carry him.

As she dragged him through the building with his arm wrapped around her neck, he mumbled some words drunkenly. Ally had made it to his apartment door. She rummaged through his coat pockets, trying to find his keys, when his apartment door opened with Belle stood chuckling at him.

Ally smiled at her. 'He's drank a tad too much,' she giggled.

'Doesn't look like he's the only one,' Belle smirked at Ally, before moving aside to invite the pair of them inside.

Ally continued to tow him until she reached the sofa and hurled him on top. Jacob's eyes were sealed and his lips began to release a wail of a snore.

'That'll be him for the night,' Belle enlightened Ally. 'Would you like a cup of coffee or tea?'

'Coffee, if you don't mind.'

Ally glanced down at Jacob, taking in the sight of his drunken mess, thinking about how much she didn't care how bad he looked at this moment, he looked perfect to her. She took a seat on the armchair across from the sofa, while Belle made the coffee.

'Do you take sugar?' she shouted across to Ally.

'No, thank you,' she replied. 'I've never really asked this, but how did you and Jacob meet?' Ally inquired, curious as she was never really told the full story.

'Do you really want to hear the full story?' she asked while carrying their drinks into the lounge area.

'Yeah. I've heard dribs and drabs but never heard the full story. Jacob has been distracted since I've worked with him, so I've never really heard it.'

'Well, I ran away from home. My parents weren't the best and it was safer for me to leave. I lived on the streets a while before I heard about an apartment that had been raided by the police,' she started.

'Alex Baker's?' Ally questioned.

'Yes,' she confirmed. 'Well when Alex was released from prison, he arrived back to find me squatting in his apartment. He took me out for dinner and told me all about what happened. Then we arrived back at the apartment and he was murdered. I saw the lady who killed him and she heard me. She came looking for me, so I hid and that's when I called Jacob's number. He spoke to me the entire time, keeping me calm until they arrived. He saved my life.'

Ally took her eyes off Belle and placed them on Jacob, who had dribble sliding out of his mouth. Not the most attractive look. A moment had passed before Ally wanted to change the subject to something happier.

'So, I hear you've got yourself a job down at the local cafe?'

'It's about time, hey?' Belle said, before lifting her mug to her lips.

Barnes phoned his mother-in-law to check on the girls. Barnes and Vanessa's mother never really got on, but they had no choice but to speak to one another as she was taking care of his girls. Once he got off the phone, Barnes started to pick up the dirty plates and rubbish that surrounded him. It was time for a clean.

On entering the kitchen, he noticed half a bottle of whiskey on his table. *Maybe just a sip*, he convinced himself. Once the bottleneck touched his lips and the whiskey poured down his throat, he craved more. With each swig, the traumatic few days flooded his thoughts, making him take bigger sips. The focus then changed from the trauma to his and Vanessa's wedding day, then to when the twins were born. Placing the whiskey bottle back on the table and wiping his lips with his sleeve, he realised drinking wouldn't make him any happier nor solve the situation.

Once he cleaned around the house, he glanced at the clock, noticing it was the early hours of the morning. Barnes took himself to bed. Laying there, he thought about his ex-wife and how happy they once were. He would still put himself in danger to save her life, knowing deep down despite their arguments and disagreements, he still cared deeply for her.

They were once a happy family, but it came to an end when Vanessa realised she would always be second best and Joe's job would always come first. He wanted to change, for them to give their relationship a second chance but he didn't think

Vanessa would feel the same way. Contemplating his failures, he lay awake, staring at his ceiling, wondering what else life would throw his way.

Chapter 13

Barnes arrived at the station the next day to applause from colleagues, welcoming him back, happy to see him alive and well. Each member of the CID approached him, shaking his hand or giving him a hug before Ally walked towards him from inside his office.

'Good to have you back, boss,' she greeted with open arms.

'Glad to be back,' he replied, engaging in her hug.

As Ally ushered him into the office she'd commandeered, she updated him on their current case, but he wasn't listening. He was too busy glancing around at what she'd done to his office while he hadn't been there.

'Oh yeah,' she said, noticing his eyes taking a good look around. 'I'm sorry. I needed a quiet place to work since taking control of the team.'

'It's fine,' he accepted her apology. 'This is the least of my problems. Where are we with interviewing Cain and Lily?'

'Still got it on my list of things to do,' Ally replied.

'Well, let's get to it.'

Half an hour passed before Ally was ready to commence the interviews. Cain was first on the line-up. Barnes relaxed in a room behind the glass mirror, witnessing the interview. Ally wanted Sarah to join her again, and this time there'd be no interruptions.

'So, Cain,' Ally started. 'What ties you to Lily Black?' He remained silent. 'We know your real name

isn't Cain, but Nathan Lawrence, born in London.'
Once again he remained silent. 'What brought you to
Birmingham, Nathan? Was it Lily? Were you both
involved with one another?' Still, nothing but silence
as she continued asking questions. 'You know, this
would be much faster if you started talking.'

Ally began to lose patience with him and it was
showing. Sarah noticed too and started to intervene.

'Nathan, or whatever you wanna be called. All we
know is Lily was calling the shots and you listened like
a good lap dog. Hell, she even did it with Mia and
Ava, but you already know about them, right?'

Cain started to smirk as he folded his arms. Ally
caught sight of his tattoo.

'Did Lily do that for you?' she asked, pointing at it.
'We know she's a good tattoo artist.'

Cain leaned on the table as he edged closer to
them. 'No, she didn't. And I'm not Nathan Lawrence,'
he finally answered in a gritty, deep voice.

'So who are you then? Because you have no last
name and you go by just the name Cain,' Sarah
questioned him.

'I'm Cain, but you might know me by another
name,' he smirked again.

'Oh yeah. And what might that be?' Sarah
continued.

'Conquer. Maybe even War.'

Ally and Sarah started to giggle at his answer,
thinking he was delusional. Cain continued smirking
at them and their ignorance, sitting back in his seat
and folding his arms.

'Let me get this straight,' Sarah started to mock him, 'You're one of the four horsemen of the apocalypse?'

'That's what I said.'

'I think you're as crazy as Lily is,' Sarah laughed.

Ally turned her head towards Sarah, nudging her to stop laughing. Cain didn't change his facial expression. If anything, it had gotten creepier.

'Do you really want to know why I am here?' he asked the pair.

Ally took charge of the interview. 'I thought that's what we had been asking? We want to know why you helped Lily in DCI Joseph Barnes' kidnapping?"

'She released us.'

'Us?' she replied.

'Yes. There are four of us, remember. Nathan Lawrence was kind enough to give me his body.'

Sarah was confused as to why Ally was encouraging him. Barnes had his eyes fixated on Cain's tattoo, trying to search the internet to see if there was any truth to his story.

'What do you want with Mr Lawrence's body?'

'I needed a vessel.'

'You said Lily released you? Released you from where?' Sarah questioned him.

'We were trapped inside the diamonds Lily left at the last crime scene, and that ritual she finished, freed us from our prison,' he explained.

Ally ended the interview and she and Sarah left the room and caught up with Barnes.

'Do you think he's telling the truth?' Ally asked Barnes.

'Do you?'

'I certainly don't,' Sarah piped up. 'It's a load of nonsense just so he can plead insanity and get a lighter sentence. We've seen it a thousand times,' she explained her theory.

'I can't help but think there is some truth to his story,' Ally expressed her concern.

'Me too, no matter how crazy it sounds. He said there were three others out there, but we have no idea who these people are and where they live,' said Barnes. 'They might not even live in the UK. I want to speak to him, off the record.'

'Boss, I don't think we should let you do that. You were part of this case, plus it's against protocol,' Ally expressed her views on the matter.

'I'll be fine. I'll be a few minutes.'

'You've got five minutes,' she informed him.

Barnes entered the room and shut the door behind him. Cain smiled as Barnes turned around and he recognised the man standing in front of him.

'You know who I am and you know why I'm here?' Barnes said.

'You want me to tell you more about myself and my siblings,' Cain guessed. 'Straight to business, DCI Barnes?'

'I haven't got time for idle chit chat. I need you to tell me who these people are,' Barnes raised his voice.

'I don't know. Once we were released, we were split up. Don't forget they are taking the bodies of people, like myself and Nathan here,' he joked.

'Is that why Lily wanted the diamonds? To put you all back inside?'

'Do you think I'd have helped her if that was the reason?' He laughed. 'No. She needed them to help her get her mother back.'

'You both keep saying this but never tell me where her mother actually is.'

'That's because you wouldn't believe us if we told you,' Cain lent forward.

'Try me.' Barnes lowered his voice and smirked, 'I know where the diamonds are.'

'Then why didn't you tell her? You'd have saved yourself a lot of pain.'

'She'd have killed me either way. I'd rather the world be a safer place with me dead.'

The door opened and Ally stood in the doorway, eyes glancing between Barnes and Cain.

'Time's up,' she told him.

Barnes left the room, but before they shut the door, Cain had something to say.

'I hope your wife's okay?'

Barnes took one angry look back at Cain before shutting the door on him.

Jacob lay in his bed, glaring at the ceiling, wondering what was happening at work without him. The winter sun made an appearance, peeping through his bedroom blinds. He didn't want to move from his bed. Between the blinding light in his eyes and his pounding hangover headache, Jacob couldn't focus on removing himself.

Clanging noises rang throughout the apartment as if somebody was banging pots and pans. Rolling over, he felt his stomach turn, sick rising to his throat. The room was spinning with every movement, more than it did before. Jacob drunkenly stumbled to the bedroom door and twisted the handle. A burst of light shone through the open gap of the door as he covered his eyes with his hand.

A smell of pancakes drifted up his nose as he extended the door wider. His eyes caught Belle flipping the pancakes on the frying pan. A bright happy smile glowed on her face while she sang.

'Somebody's happy this morning,' he observed as he entered the room.

Belle smiled at him. 'You want some pancakes?'

'Maybe just one,' he answered, knowing if he ate too much he'd risk being sick.

'You look like shit. You must've had a good night,' she continued flipping pancakes.

'Yeah, I think it was a good night, from what I can remember,' he rubbed his head. 'When did you learn to make pancakes, anyway?'

'Work. Don't forget I work in a cafe.'

Belle plated a pancake and slid it in front of him. It looked so appealing but Jacob's stomach was still rotating, but he was hungry. He took a mouthful before he decided to surrender and admit defeat.

'You don't like it?' she asked him with a sad appearance.

'It's amazing. I'm just so hungover.'

'It's okay. Are you going to work today?'

'I think I'll give it a miss for today,' he laughed while trying to keep the vomit down.

Jacob moved his body away from the breakfast bar and jumped in the shower. His head still pounding, he sat on the tiled shower floor, trying to not make any sudden movements. Trying to keep his mind off his hangover, recent events flooded his thoughts again. From the happy years he spent with Lily, to the events that led up to his father's death.

Jacob couldn't sit and reminisce on the good and bad memories of his past anymore. Knowing he needed to pull himself together, he lifted himself off the floor. Once out of the shower, he grabbed some clean, smart clothes and grabbed his police badge. Wanting to go to work, he stopped and realised he wouldn't be able to drive. So he grabbed his phone and called the only person he could trust to pick him up and have complete confidentiality of his situation.

'Hi, Ally. It's Jacob. I'm just wondering if you'd be able to come and get me?' he asked.

'Jacob, I don't think you should even think about coming to work at the moment. You should take a few days off.'

'With all due respect, Ally. I can't sit here anymore. I just keep thinking of everything that's happened lately. I need a distraction,' he confessed.

'Are you still drinking?' Ally interrogated.

'What do you mean by that?' he turned defensive and sharp.

'I know you've been drinking while on the job, Jacob. I've been trying to hide it from everybody, but someone is bound to notice soon. I can get you some help...'

Jacob cut her off. 'I don't need any help!' he shouted. 'Forget about it. I'll make my own way in.'

Jacob hung up the call and grabbed his coat and keys. As he left the apartment, he ordered an Uber to come and collect him. He was furious with Ally, but deep down, knew she was right. He had been drinking, more than usual, all because of Lily and her actions. He started to sob as he made his way to the bottom floor of his apartment building, thinking of Lily, her double life and his father.

Barnes sat inside his office, searching for any information he could on Nathan Lawrence's background. He was clean, not one single shred of criminal activity to his name. He couldn't help but think that Cain might be another persona. A split personality. It was the only other explanation for what he had been describing to them.

Barnes spent half an hour researching Dissociative Identity Disorder. Something was eating away at him, but a phone call from Vanessa distracted him from his thought. She phoned to make sure the twins were alright and to thank Joe for saving her life.

'I'm glad you're okay,' he replied. 'Have they gave you an estimate of when you'll be able to go home?'

'In about a week hopefully.'

'Let me know when and I'll pick you up.'

'Thank you, Joe. Not just for that, but for being there and saving my life. I... I just want to say...'

Barnes interrupted, 'Just get some rest. I'll talk to you soon.'

He knew what she was about to say next, but didn't want her to say something just because of what she'd been through. Barnes carried on researching before there was a knock at his door. It was Jacob. He waved at him through the glass window, telling him to enter.

'Hi, boss. How're you doing?'

'I'm alright. Just a little banged up still, but I'll heal,' Barnes answered.

'Have we discovered the whereabouts of Jack Roberts yet?' Jacob enquired.

'Not yet, but we've got officers on the lookout for him.'

'Okay. I'm going to do some work since I'm here,' Jacob announced, knowing Barnes wouldn't allow it, but his head was stuck in his computer.

Jacob walked to his desk and plumped himself down. His desk was full of paperwork he should have completed a while ago, so he got stuck in. Ally stomped over to his desk, with anger written all over her face.

'What do you think you're doing here?' she asked quietly, looking around, making sure people weren't listening.

'Nice to see you too,' he joked, not removing his eyes off the paperwork.

'I mean it, Jacob. I told you not to come in.'

'I can't just sit at home when Jack Roberts is on the loose.'

'Have you had a drink today?'

'No, I haven't,' he replied with anger starting to show.

Ally pulled open his desk drawer and saw the bottles of spirits inside. Her head turned to look at him.

'Before you go home, these need to be gone,' she whispered.

'Sure,' Jacob replied, still keeping his focus on the paperwork in front of him.

He was furious with her but understood she was only looking out for him. Ally cared a lot for him and tried her best to stop him from losing his job. Knowing Lily was only a few metres away from him and his team, was the main reason for his anger. But he couldn't face her, no matter how much he wanted to.

Barnes sat inside the interview room with Ally and Lily. Just like her co-conspirators, Lily didn't want a solicitor as she knew the game was over.

'What's your connection with Nathan Lawrence?' Barnes started questioning her.

'With who?' She looked confused.

'The man who helped you.'

'Oh, you mean Cain,' she smiled. 'Where's Jacob?' She tried changing the subject.

'He doesn't want to see you,' Ally interrupted.

Lily turned her attention to Ally and smiled before turning back to Barnes.

'I think someone else has the hots for him.'

Ally's face clenched. She really wanted to jump across the table and plough her fist in Lily's face, but she realised it wasn't worth her job. Instead, she folded her arms and sat quietly, leaving Barnes to ask the questions.

'Lily, we don't need much else from you as we've already got enough evidence to convict you for the murders of John and Maria Wright as well as my kidnapping and the attempted murder of my ex-wife. You're going away for a long time, so you might as well tell us what we want to know,' Barnes continued with the interview.

'I will only speak to Jacob,' she answered. 'If you want your answers, let me speak to him.'

'No deal,' Barnes replied to her demand. 'He doesn't want to speak to you.'

'Well I guess you don't want your answers then,' she smiled, sitting back in her chair with her arms folded.

Ally stopped the interview tape and both she and Barnes removed themselves from the room, leaving her alone. They both strolled back to the CID discussing their options.

'What do you think we should do?' Barnes asked Ally.

'I'm not sure. She'll be going away anyway for what she's done.'

'But we won't get the answers on Cain that we want.'

Barnes thought about it. They had the people involved and the case would be officially closed, but he couldn't help but think about what if Cain was telling the truth or maybe he did have another personality. His mind couldn't rest on the matter.

Jacob lifted a file and his eyes noticed an envelope underneath, one which resembled the others he'd received. As he picked it up, Ally and Barnes returned. He approached them with the envelope tight within his grasp.

'Look what I've just found,' he announced quietly with a whisper.

'In the office, now,' Ally ushered the two of them.

Once the door was shut, Ally released the blinds from prying eyes, before Barnes insisted Jacob opened the envelope. More pictures appeared as Jacob slid his hand out from inside the envelope. It was filled with photos taken from the distance of another crime scene. It was from when they found Freya, murdered in the car park. Someone had been watching them during the entire case. They knew where and when to take the photos.

'It's got to be Lily,' he shouted hysterically.

'Jacob, we need to talk,' Barnes said, looking at Ally's face for her reaction.

Ally glanced back at Barnes with a serious stare as she didn't want him to tell Jacob about what Lily asked. But that didn't stop Barnes.

'Okay,' Jacob replied. 'But what is this about?'

'We've just been trying to interview Lily, but she won't talk to us. She wants to talk to you.'

Jacob's head lowered as he stared at the floor. His elbows rested on his legs, while his hands came together and interlocked his fingers.

'Why does she want to see me?' he asked.

'We don't know. Our best guess is she just wants to see you, maybe to explain why she did what she did,' Barnes explained his theory.

'You don't have to see her, Jacob. Not if you don't want to,' Ally tried to reassure him that he does have options available.

Jacob lifted his head and rose from his seat. 'I don't want anything more to do with that woman. I'm sorry,' he said before leaving the room.

It was too emotional for him and it would open old wounds he'd tried so hard to seal. He'd tried his best to shut that vile person out of his life and feared that seeing her would be too painful and undo everything he'd done to forget about her.

Chapter 14

Jack Roberts had been on the run for over a week, ever since he'd knocked Jacob out and tied him to a chair in his living room. His pounding headache was becoming more and more intermittent. Not to mention, the pain was becoming increasingly worse with each passing day. Jack hadn't seen the mysterious man since being on the run, but the whispers still surrounded him, no matter where he was. *Am I going insane?*

'What do you want?' he yelled out, hoping the whispers would answer back, but they spoke quietly, enough for him to be unable to hear. 'Stop. Just stop whispering. You're driving me insane. I can't cope anymore,' he continued, before breaking down with his head in his hands, sobbing as many tears as he could let out.

'Stop resisting, Jack,' a voice spoke.

The voice was sinister, scratchy, and freaked Jack out, making him panic, not knowing who or where the voice was coming from.

'Who are you?' Jack asked.

'Look deep down and you'll find the answer you seek,' the voice replied.

He thought about what the voice had just said and took a moment to clear his mind. Jack spun around to take a look at his surroundings. *How did I get here?* He was in a rundown hotel room, with ripped wallpaper and damp seeping through the ceiling. The bed had seen better days, as well as the en-suite bathroom. As he rushed in there, he glanced at himself in the mirror. His eyes were black and bloodshot from the tiredness, but he couldn't recall where he'd been or what day it was.

Jack cupped his hands under the tap and collected a handful of water, pushing his face into it. The cold water on his face was refreshing and it cooled him down. For a moment he'd forgot about everything, but the voice spoke again.

'That's better, isn't it?'

Jack started to panic again, turning his head from side to side to see nothing. He was alone in the bathroom. He closed his eyes.

'It's all in my head. It's all in my head,' he kept repeating.

'You're half right,' said the scratchy voice.

Jack opened his eyes and saw the reflection in the mirror talking back to him. The image was of him but his face was disfigured. He jumped with fright and closed his eyes.

'It's not real. None of this is real.'

'You know it is, Jack. You know I've been looking out for you. You've just chosen not to believe it.'

'What do you want?' Jack asked the voice in his head.

'For you to stop resisting. I need you, but not in the driver's seat.'

'This is my body and my mind, I'm not going to just give it so you can continue wreaking havoc,' Jack explained.

'Your wife was having it off with that man across the road. Not to mention, she was poisoning you. Now they've paid for what they did to you, all thanks to me,' the voice confessed.

'So you did that? With my body?' Jack started to wake up and realise that the police would know it was him.

'Yes. Then that detective got in the way...'

'What did you do to him?' Jack interrupted.

'I didn't kill him, don't worry.'

'So every time I blacked out, was that when you...'

'You're becoming quite the detective, Jack. Yes. Every time you fazed out, that's when I struck,' he laughed.

'Oh my god,' he cried out. 'The police are going to be all over me.'

Jack sprinted out of the bathroom, flicked open the blinds that hung over the window, and glanced down at the street below. He was nervous and unsure of when the police would show up to arrest him. It was quiet, not a sound could be heard, not a person in sight. He was safe for now.

Jacob had been helping with the search for Jack Roberts, but ran out of luck. Nobody had seen him for days. Jack had last been spotted withdrawing money from an ATM in the Birmingham city centre. Since then, he'd vanished into thin air and Jacob and the team had trouble trying to locate him.

Barnes and Ally were sat inside the briefing room with Jacob, updating each other on the very little information they had finding Jack.

'Have you got any new leads on our friend?' Barnes inquired.

'Nothing since the withdrawal. We've tried tracing his phone, but it's coming back empty,' Jacob updated him.

'Officers are keeping an eye out for anyone matching his description. I've also contacted other county police and shared with them his description,' Ally voiced her input.

'It's just frustrating that this guy has done a runner and we can't find him,' Barnes shook his head.

'It's okay, boss,' Jacob replied. 'We found you and caught Lily. We'll find Jack Roberts too.'

Ally's phone started to ring from inside her pocket. Her eyes caught sight of the screen, displaying a name in which she never expected to see again.

'Sorry,' she said to them both as she left the briefing room to answer it.

'You're right, Jacob.'

'I know,' he smirked at Barnes.

'Have you had any more envelopes?' Barnes asked him.

'Nothing yet. I thought it was Lily, but when I received that last lot of photos, she was in custody.'

'Maybe she posted it just before and it took a while to get here,' he told Jacob his theory.

'Maybe she did.'

Ally suddenly returned to the room as the pair turned to face her. She carried on while the pair of them, being nosy, waited for an explanation on her phone call.

'What?' she replied to their stares.

'What was the phone call about?' Barnes questioned her.

'Can't a girl keep anything private around here?'

'I think that's too much to ask. Nothing stays private, look at our investigations for example,' Jacob laughed.

'I think you may be right there, Jacob,' Barnes joked along with him.

Ally got fed up with the laughter, 'If you must know, that was an old...,' she paused. '... a friend of mine. He wants me to join his new team.'

Jacob's heart sank. He couldn't believe what he'd just heard. *Does Ally really hate it here that much, that she'll leave the team?* Barnes' face was just as shocked as Jacob's.

'What new team?' Barnes demanded answers. 'Are you thinking of leaving us already?'

'I told him I'd have to think about it. I'm not ready to leave the team yet. As you said, I've not long joined you guy's but it's a fantastic opportunity,' she explained in not too much detail.

'Is it in Birmingham? Or will you be leaving the city too?' Jacob started to raise more questions.

'It's in Hawaii,' she answered.

'Hawaii,' both Jacob and Barnes yelled at precisely the same time.

'There's a lot to consider before I make a decision anyway.'

She turned her attention to Jacob, trying to see what his reaction was like. Her feelings for him were the main contributor to her answer, knowing she'd be leaving him behind.

'I think you should do what your heart tells you,' Jacob advised her.

She didn't know if he meant he wanted her to stay, or that the opportunity was too good to miss. After all, the weather was much nicer in Hawaii.

'Does that mean you'll have to go back to school to learn how different the policing is over there?' Barnes seemed interested but also disappointed that she was considering leaving.

'More than likely. Look, I'd prefer it if we could keep this between us three for the moment until I've made a decision.'

They both agreed and the three of them left the briefing room. Ethan approached them eagerly with new information as they came out of the room.

'I've just had a phone call. Someone has seen our social media post and have called to say they've seen Jack Roberts at the Premier Inn by the airport.'

'That's a good half-hour drive from here,' Jacob raised his concern. 'He might be gone before we even get there.'

'You're right,' Barnes said, thinking of what else he could do before they arrived. 'Send the closest police cars in the area to that location and tell them to make sure he doesn't leave until we get there,' he barked his orders at Ethan.

'Yes, boss,' he responded before heading back to his desk and picking up the phone.

Barnes, Ally and Jacob grabbed their coats and ran to the car park. The three of them leapt into Barnes' car and sped off towards the airport.

Kate had been working since she'd finished school for the day. It had been the same shift as it had been for the last few days. The same man had been sitting at the same table every day, as usual, for hours. He gave Kate the creeps so much she hated going over to the table to ask if he wanted anything else, even though she knew the answer.

'No, thank you.'

Kate scurried back to the counter as quick as she could, letting Belle know her thoughts on the man. Belle kept quiet about her encounter with the man, knowing the reason he was sat inside the cafe was to see Kate.

When Kate's back was turned, Belle whacked out her phone and text Jacob one sentence;

"*He's here.*"

Kate was getting impatient as the man still slurped away at his coffee, unaware of their closing time. Her face began to blow up like a red balloon before she chose to confront him.

'Excuse me, mate. We're closing soon. Can you hurry up and finish your two-hour long coffee.'

He chuckled while raising the mug up to his lips, angering Kate even more.

'What's so funny?' she shouted.

Belle ran up to her, trying to pull her away. 'Kate, come on.'

'You've got a fiery temper, Kate,' he continued laughing. 'You are so much like your mother.'

Belle stopped pulling at Kate's arm. Kate stood still when Belle noticed she'd started to restrain less.

'What do you mean by that?' she demanded answers.

'Kate, come on,' Belle pulled at her arm again.

'No, Belle,' she replied, pulling her arm out of Belle's grasp. 'What did you mean? Who are you?'

The man turned his attention off his cup of coffee and on to Kate.

'Did your mother never tell you about me?' he asked.

'Who are you?' she continued demanding he answered.

'If you haven't figured it out already, I'm your father,' he finally answered her questions.

Kate felt a mix of emotions. She wanted to cry, refusing that her parents had lied to her all along, and she also wanted to smash the man's face in with her fist.

184

'Get out of here,' she calmly asked, pointing to the door.

'Come on...'

'I said get out!' she shouted in his face.

The man rose to his feet slowly, looking Kate directly in the eyes, before having the last word.

'I'll be seeing you soon, Kate.'

Kate watched as the man, who claimed to be her father, strolled out of the cafe. She sighed as she collapsed, gripping the back of a chair. Silence flooded the room before Belle placed her hand on Kate's back.

'Kate, are you...'

Kate brushed Belle's hand off her back and pushed her away.

'You knew, didn't you?' she cut Belle off. 'You kept trying to pull me away from him. It's like you knew what he was going to say.'

'Kate, I'm sorry...'

'Don't you talk to me. I don't want to hear your excuses,' she yelled as she stormed out of the cafe, leaving Belle to lock up on her own.

I can't believe she knew all along! Kate continued on her journey home, making sure he wasn't following her. Her pocket began to buzz and as she removed the phone from her pocket, she saw Belle's name. She ignored the call and continued onward.

Jack Roberts awoke on the floor of his hotel room covered in blood. His t-shirt was stained. He checked himself over, making sure it wasn't his blood. *What happened?* But deep down he realised what had happened.

'What have you done?' he demanded the voice answer.

But it stayed silent. Panic set in, as Jack frantically ripped off his t-shirt and jumped in the shower to rid himself of the blood he was covered in. As the water poured down his body, the shower floor turned red. His body started to shake, not from being cold, but from fear. He was terrified. Jack knew nothing of what his counterpart had done, who he had killed.

Once he turned her shower off, Jack put on a fresh set of clothes and tried to figure a way of disposing of his blood-drenched clothes. The voice inside his head was still quiet, making him believe he'd gone insane. He tried to provoke it.

'Who's blood is this?'

But still no answer. He grabbed a bin sack and chucked his dirty clothes inside, sealing it by tying the handles together. Jack lifted the bag, opened the hotel door and stuck out his head, peering from left to right, making sure nobody was about. Once he thought the coast was clear, Jack flew out and down the corridor, running towards the exit.

Once he found an industrial bin, he swung the bag over his head and launched it inside. Running back to his room, he packed his belongings into his bag. He needed to get out of Birmingham. Knowing he'd be the police's number one priority, he wanted to skip out of the country but knew he'd be blacklisted as a flight risk.

Jack exited the hotel and tried to catch a bus from the National Exhibition Centre. As he sat at the bus stop, he could hear sirens roaring in the distance. *They've come for me.*

Barnes' car raced around the roundabout and straight into the car park of the Premier Inn. The three of them shot out of the car, along with the other officers who'd arrived at the same time. The building was surrounded as they made their way inside. *There's no way he's getting out of here*, Jacob thought.

Barnes entered first, followed by Jacob and Ally. It was nearly impossible for the officers outside to distinguish the appearance of the hotel's guests. Barnes informed the staff at reception about one of their guests and asked which room he'd been staying in.

'So, I spoke to the lady at reception and nobody under Jack Roberts had booked a room here. I showed her the photo and she told me he'd been staying in room nineteen,' Barnes repeated to Ally and Jacob.

The three of them stealthily made their way across the hallway until they came to room nineteen.

'Mr Roberts, this is DS Wright. Open the door, we need to talk,' Jacob shouted, making his presence known.

But there was no answer, nobody was home. Barnes placed the spare key card into the door's locking system and opened the door, revealing nothing but a ransacked room.

'Looks like our guy's made a quick getaway,' Barnes observed the mess surrounding them.

Cupboard doors wide open, hangers on the floor. The room was a mess and it looked as if someone was in a hurry to leave.

'He was definitely here,' Jacob said while investigating the room.

'No doubt about that,' Ally agreed.

'We've got officers patrolling the area. He can't have gone far,' said Barnes.

Ally rushed out of the room to give orders to the police officers outside. She widened the search area, hoping they weren't too late and he hadn't gotten away.

'I've called forensics,' Jacob notified her as she returned to the room.

'Good. I've widened the search. He's been gone a while, that gives him enough time to get a bus or find a new hiding spot,' she informed them.

Barnes was still snooping, trying to get a little more information from the scene as he could. Then he entered the en-suite, before realising something.

'He's not long left.'

'What makes you say that?' Jacob asked.

'The steam on the bathroom mirror. The humidity of the room. He's recently showered. I'd say he's been gone about ten to fifteen minutes. We need to get out there. I want every bus that's been in this area around that time, grounded.'

'What if he'd taken a taxi?' Ally threw her question out there.

'Good point, but he's trying to lay low. He knows his face is plastered everywhere and a taxi driver would notice him right away as it's up close and personal. A bus has more of a way to hide in plain sight,' Barnes explained.

The three of them joined the search along with their colleagues, traipsing throughout the busy Resorts World area. Sarah, Brian and Ethan arrived tackling all the grounded buses and their passengers, making sure Jack Roberts wasn't hiding among them. Each bus had been searched and each one had no sign of Jack on board.

'That was Sarah,' Barnes informed them while removing the phone from his ear. 'They've checked the last of the buses and he's not on board.'

'So that means he's gotta be close by,' said Jacob.

The three of them started to turn their heads, trying to get a better glimpse of the crowd that surrounded them. There were too many people and too much ground to cover. None of them knew what he was wearing or where he was hiding.

'I think we're going to need to split up,' Barnes insisted. 'The area's too big for us to cover as a group. If you find him, don't approach, just call and we'll meet as a team and take him. Do you both understand?'

Ally and Jacob nodded and they all split up. Barnes took the NEC, Ally took the surrounding grassland, while Jacob took the Resorts World building. Something stood out to Jacob about the building. *If he was going to hide anywhere, it would be inside a small building full of people.*

Shops, restaurants, another hotel, even a cinema. There were plenty of places for Jack to hide in there. As Jacob entered the building he could already see crowds gathered all over the place. He needed to reach higher ground if he was to get a good view of their suspect.

Jacob ran up the stairs, running out of breath as he neared the top. People were everywhere and he found it nearly impossible to spot his target, also having no clue of what he was wearing. The only thing Jacob could do was lookout for someone acting strange and erratic. Then he caught sight of him.

On the bottom floor was Jack Roberts, flicking his head side to side, making sure nobody was following him. Jacob flew down the stairs while dialling Barnes' number.

'Boss, I'm in pursuit,' he puffed as he jumped down the stairs. 'He's inside the complex, wearing blue jeans and a red t-shirt.'

'We're on our way.'

Jacob reached the bottom floor and tried to remain out of Jack's sight, but keeping a close watch on him. He watched as Jack started to move out of the open area and towards the toilets. Barnes and Ally burst through the entrance, and Jacob waved them over to him.

'He's just gone in the toilets,' Jacob informed them.

Barnes and Ally stood either side of the toilet door, while Jacob prepped himself to enter, unsure of the situation he'd find himself in. Ally began to alert the rest of the officers of Jack's whereabouts, in case the situation escalated. Jacob breathed deep breaths before entering the toilet.

Upon entry, he discovered the room to be empty. Jacob scouted around and looked underneath the cubicle doors to see any feet standing inside. One of the doors opened, revealing a man staring directly at him on the floor. The man gave a concerning glare before Jacob put his finger to his lip, signalling the man to be silent. He moved past Jacob, washed his hands and left. Silence entered the toilet once more. Jacob remained on the floor, even though he couldn't see any more feet, but he remained silent, hoping Jack would think he was safe.

A minute had passed since the toilet door had been closed, and Jack slowly placed his feet on the floor after standing on top of the toilet. The door slowly creaked open, and Jacob caught sight of a red t-shirt. Picking himself off the floor, Jacob quickly moved out of sight of Jack, wanting to take him down stealthily. Jack left the cubicle, unaware that Jacob was standing a few centimetres away from him.

'Jack Roberts. You're under arrest,' he announced his presence.

Jack hesitated before running for the exit, not realising Jacob wasn't here on his own. Barnes stuck his arm out from around the corner as Jack flew out of the toilet door, knocking him to the floor.

Barnes smiled at him on the floor. 'Don't bother getting up. Guessing you had trouble hearing my colleague in there. You're under arrest.'

Belle arrived at their apartment building. She grabbed the post from their lockup on the ground floor, before heading upstairs. Once she arrived inside the apartment, she flicked on the lights, placed the post of the kitchen counter and called out for Kate. But there was no answer. She knew Kate would still be upset, remembering she didn't want to talk to her, so she entered their bedroom.

It was dark and no sign of Kate. *Where is she?* Belle phoned Jacob, but it went straight to voicemail.

'Jacob. I need you to call me as soon as you can. It's urgent,' she left a message.

She tried phoning Kate, but it didn't even ring. She must have turned it off. Belle didn't know what to do. She was all alone in the apartment and had nobody to ask for help. Then a thought crossed her mind. She picked up her phone for the third time and gave Adam a call.

'Hi, Adam. Kate's missing. I need your help,' she pleaded.

'Okay, Belle. I'll be over soon,' replied Adam.

She waited patiently, pacing the apartment for an hour before there was a knock on the door. She rushed over to see Adam standing there.

'Tell me what happened?' he asked as he entered.

'We were at work and she confronted this guy who'd been at the cafe all week. It was closing time and she'd gotten into a heated argument with him,' she began to explain, leaving out the important part.

'Then what happened?'

'He said he was her father,' she continued.

Adam rubbed his hands down his face and exhaled. Belle figured by the appearance on his face, he knew that Kate wasn't their sister.

'How long have you known?' Belle asked.

'Since Jacob found the letters inside my father's office. Did you know?'

'Not until tonight. I think Kate thought I knew,' she explained to him.

'We need to get out there and find her. God knows what's going through her mind right now.'

The pair of them ran out of the apartment and jumped into his car, driving the streets searching for Kate. *Where could she be? Where would she go?* Belle asked herself.

Chapter 15

Jack Roberts, dragged in handcuffs, entered the police station, was booked in and thrown in a cell until they were ready to interview him. The cell was cold and empty, leaving him alone to ponder in his thoughts. *How'd my life end up like this?* Simon Ballard was on his way, but that didn't put Jack's mind at ease. He continued to pace his cell with thoughts of what was going to happen.

The team arrived back at the CID not long after. Everyone else dispersed to their desks while Jacob, Barnes and Ally prepped in the briefing room for the interview. Barnes' phone began to ring. An officer informed him they'd discovered another body not far from where they'd apprehended Jack Roberts.

'Right, we've got to press pause on the interview. Another body has been discovered on the grounds of the NEC,' he informed them.

Barnes stepped out of the briefing room and called over to Sarah. 'Can you call Mr Ballard and tell him we're stepping out for a while.'

'Sure thing, boss,' she yelled back across the office. 'Where you all going?' she asked.

'They've found another body.'

The three of them grabbed their belongings before running out of the CID. Sarah hung up the phone and moved over to Brian, who was making himself a cup of coffee in the break area.

'I can't believe they're leaving us out of the investigation again,' she released her frustration. 'Some things never change.'

Brian just carried on making his coffee, trying his best to ignore the comments Sarah kept making. She followed him as he strolled back towards his desk, spurting more anger in his ears.

'Sarah, if you have something to say, please discuss it with Barnes when he gets back. I can't sit here and listen to this all night,' he calmly gave his thoughts on the matter.

Sarah stormed off, flicking her red locks as she turned. She grabbed her coat and keys and left for the night. Entering her car, she phoned her date, who she had cancelled on because of work.

'I'm sorry about tonight. It's just been a busy one. Are you free now? I'm just leaving work.'

Ethan also had a phone call to make, telling her that he won't be home for another hour or so. Brian lived alone and felt envious of people contacting their loved ones when he knew he was going home to an empty house.

The office was quiet apart from him and Ethan being there. Everyone else had gone home for the night, but Brian stayed as long as he could, trying to remain busy to take his mind away from his lonely life.

Barnes raced through the very little traffic that was on the road. Jacob's face turned green, sick rising to his throat.

'Do you have to drive like this?' he asked, wanting to release his vomit in the car.

'He's like this when I'm driving,' Ally added, laughing at the sight of him from the back seat.

Barnes just laughed and carried on speeding to their destination. Jacob hung onto the handle above his head for dear life. They arrived five minutes later to police lights and tape surrounding the crime scene. As they exited the vehicle and approached the crime scene, Barnes questioned the officer in charge.

'What do we have?'

'Staff members found the body of our victim while nipping out for a cigarette around ten,' he started to explain as he took Barnes to the scene of the crime.

They approached a dark area opposite the lake, next to the Resorts World complex they had recently visited that night. The body of a female had been propped up against the wall as if she was sat down. Barnes caught sight of Julia Higgins examining the body.

'Evening, Julia,' he greeted her.

'Evening, Joe,' she replied the greeting.

'Do we know what happened to her?'

She pointed to the victim's neck. 'The bruising across her throat, suggests she was strangled,' she explained.

'Do you think that was the main cause of death?' he asked.

'I wouldn't rule it out, but once I've performed the autopsy, I'll let you know.'

Ally's phone started to ring and she moved away slightly, to hear the voice on the other end more clearly.

'Have forensics managed to get any DNA or fingerprints off of her yet?'

'Yeah, they've done their sweep and are heading back to the lab. Weren't you guys here not that long ago?'

'Yeah, about one, maybe two hours ago,' Jacob piped up.

'Do you think this is somehow linked to your case?' she continued asking questions.

'We think so, but until we get the results back on the DNA, we can't be sure,' Barnes informed her.

Ally strolled back to them with some new information.

'Forensics have found a black bag full of bloodstained clothes back at the Premier Inn where Jack Roberts had been staying. They're taking them back to the lab. Hopefully, if the blood matches our victim here, we've got her killer.'

Barnes turned his attention back to Julia. 'Did our victim have any I.D on her?'

'Yes, she had a driving license. Her name's Hannah Jones. She's only twenty-three.'

Barnes turned to Jacob and Ally. 'Can you two inform her parents?'

They both nodded and Barnes flicked his keys in the air and Jacob caught them.

'You're letting me have the Jag?' he said with surprise.

'Just take care of her,' he joked as both of them walked away.

Ally pushed Jacob out of the way of the driver's side door.

'What was that for?' he asked, smiling at her.

'I'm driving,' she laughed.

'In your dreams,' he replied, still laughing. 'I've been sick enough for one night.'

The pair of them chuckled as they entered the car. Jacob noticed a notification of a missed call from Belle. *What does she want?* he wondered. He listened to the panicked voicemail she'd left in his inbox.

'I need to go to mine first,' he told Ally.

'Why? What's wrong?' she asked.

'Kate's gone missing,' he explained.

'Okay, we'll go find her first. I'll let Barnes know.'

Adam had been driving around for a couple of hours with no luck in finding Kate. Belle began to sob in the passengers seat.

'What's wrong?' he asked Belle.

'It's my fault. If I had just told her...'

Adam interrupted her. 'Hey, this isn't your fault. Stop blaming yourself. The only people to blame here are her mother and my father for keeping this from us all. It makes no difference about her finding out now, she'll always be our sister, no matter what,' he tried to console her.

'I know, but if I had just told her about the man approaching me...' She began to cry again.

'Then that's mine and Jacob's fault. You are not to blame for any of this. I think we need to head home and see if she's back,' he said while turning the car back around.

As they arrived outside the building, Adam sat silent for a minute.

'I wanted to tell her, you know,' he began to explain. 'Jacob thought it would be best not to. I knew he'd come looking for her eventually.'

'Where's he been this entire time?' Belle asked.

'Prison. He killed someone from what we've discovered.'

'Do you think she's in danger?'

'I don't know. I think it's best we find her and watch this guy around her.'

Walking into the building, Belle received a phone call from Jacob as they entered the elevator.

'I'm on my way,' he explained.

'Me and Adam have been out searching for her. We've just arrived back at the apartment to see if she's come back home,' she informed him of the situation on the search.

'Okay,' he replied. 'Keep me updated.'

The pair of them entered the apartment after reaching their floor, to find Kate sat in the dark, sobbing her heart out. Belle ran over and sat beside her, pulling her into her embrace.

'Where have you been?' she asked.

Kate could barely string two words together. 'I went for a walk,' she sobbed. 'Why would they lie to me?'

'Who?'

'My parents. Why would they keep this from me?'

'They probably had a good reason,' Belle tried to console her but also hiding something else from her.

Kate just sat crying hysterically in Belle's arms as Jacob and Ally burst in. Adam turned towards them both with sadness on his face.

'She was here when we arrived,' he explained to them. 'She's distraught, Jacob. We should have told her.'

'I thought...' Jacob lowered his head.

'That's the problem, you thought,' Adam rudely replied before storming out of the apartment.

Jacob chased after him and confronted him in the hallway. 'What's that supposed to mean?'

'I wanted to tell her, but you told me not to. We always do as you say and now look at our sister. She's sat in there crying her eyes out.'

'And you think this wouldn't have happened if we'd have told her?'

'She wouldn't have been mad with us and have a stranger tell her that he's her father,' he shouted, walking away from him and to the elevator.

Jacob shook his head and returned to the apartment, witnessing his sister's heartbreak.

'I'd better go,' Ally said to him. 'I'll inform Hannah's parents. You just stay here with your family. I'll be fine.'

'I don't know if she'll want me around, to be honest.'

'You're her brother, no matter who her parents were. You've been there her entire life. You are her family,' she explained.

'Thanks, Ally. I'll call you later,' he said as she walked through the door.

'Okay, speak to you soon.'

Jacob shut the door as she proceeded to the elevator. She wanted to be there for him, but this was a family matter, one she didn't want to intrude on. Jacob sat opposite Kate and Belle and tried his best to explain why he kept it from her.

'Kate. I'm really sorry. Me and Adam only found out...'

'Don't talk to me,' she rudely snapped at him. 'I don't want to hear excuses because you feel bad. To have a pure stranger come up to you and tell you he's your father, do you know how that feels?' She rose to her feet.

'I'm sorry.' Jacob had tears in his eyes. 'If I knew he'd show up...'

She cut him off again, 'You'd what? You'd have told me? You should have told me anyway!' she shouted.

'It doesn't change anything. You're still my sister,' he tried to explain.

'But I'm not though, am I? I'm nothing to do with you or Adam. You're not blood relatives.'

'But that changes nothing. We've been there for one another, ever since I can remember,' he continued to try to calm and console her.

'But it does!' she shouted. 'You're not my brother!'

She stormed off to her bedroom and slammed the door shut behind her, leaving Jacob and Belle alone. Jacob's eyes began to leak tears, while Belle moved over towards him and gave him a huge hug.

'She'll calm down,' she embraced him. 'She doesn't mean it.'

'I think she does though. I made the mistake of hiding this from her. I should have just told her.'

Scarlett Thatcher was ravenous. Her hunger had taken over her thoughts, being the only thing on her mind as she tried to get a good look at her surroundings. But it was no good. It was too dark. Her lips were dry, gasping for a slight drop of water. Her throat dry and itchy was unable to say a word to the woman lying next to her.

The woman's body was bone and scrawny like she hadn't eaten for weeks. Even though Scarlett had been trapped for a week, her body was not as bad as the woman next to her. In that time she hadn't even had one meal or fluid.

'Hey. Are you okay,' Scarlett asked the lady.

She didn't answer. Scarlett tried to nudge her with her elbow, but the chains and shackles around her wrist didn't let her reach that far. The woman hadn't moved in hours. The smell of the room was foul, like a vile odour of what she could only imagine dead corpses to smell like.

'Hey, lady,' she called out again, but no answer.

Scarlett pulled on the chains, trying to free herself, but no such luck. She desperately wanted to see her family again, to kiss her girlfriend and feel her warm embracing hug. She started to get teary, before trying again to free herself.

A voice came out from the dark corner. 'I wouldn't do that if I was you.'

'Who said that?' Scarlett asked.

'You won't be able to see me. It's too dark in here,' the female voice replied.

'How long have you been here?'

'I think it's almost been two weeks. Hard to tell in here,' the female voice explained.

'Are you as hungry as me?' Scarlett asked.

'I'm starving,' she replied. 'I think she's starving us to death.'

'She?'

'Yeah, I only ever seen her the once, when I first arrived.'

'How'd you wind up here?'

'I was out with friends, just about to go home when they put a bag over my head and stabbed me with a needle. The next thing I know I woke up here. What about you?'

'Similar situation. Out with friends, bag over my head and an injection of some sort.'

The woman next to Scarlett awoke and started to talk with an itchy voice, but she couldn't understand her. The voice from across the room knew what she was asking.

'She's asking for water. She'll be next.'

'What do you mean, she'll be next?' Scarlett demanded to know what she meant by her comment.

'They'll come and take her. She's on death's door.'

'So, these people enjoy watching us starve to death?'

'We only leave here when we're dead,' the woman explained.

The women could hear the jingle of keys as somebody approached the door to the room, and what sounded like the key turning in the door. Footsteps entered the room as the squeaky door creaked open.

'Anybody dead yet?' the woman shouted and laughed as she walked in.

'Go to hell!' Scarlett shouted.

The woman laughed. 'You first.'

She edged closer to Scarlett and leaned in close. She smelt the air surrounding Scarlett and the lady next to her.

'Somebody's close to death around here,' she chuckled again.

Scarlett mustered as much saliva as she could before launching it into the woman's face.

'You little bitch!' she yelled at her, before slapping her across the face, knocking Scarlett's face to the floor.

Chapter 16

The next morning, Barnes arrived at the CID before 7 am, to see Ally in the briefing room. She spent the whole night trying to figure something out that Hannah Jones' parents had told her when Barnes walked in.

'Morning,' he greeted her. 'Early bird catches the worm, hey?'

She chuckled, but he noticed something wasn't right with her.

'Okay, what's wrong?' he asked.

'Just something Hannah's parents said to me last night. They told me she'd been missing for over a week,' she explained.

'Missing? So this can't be linked to Jack Roberts then?' he expressed his thoughts.

'That's what I thought. That means there could be two killers out there. Both struck in the exact same place on the exact same night. That can't be a coincidence.'

'Two separate killers. I'll pass it over to another team to investigate,' he said, removing his phone from his suit jacket.

Seeing that Julia Higgins had left a voicemail, Barnes decided to call her back. It took a few rings before she finally answered.

'Thanks for calling back,' she answered. 'I've completed the post mortem and I've found something strange. Our victim did die of asphyxiation due to the strangulation around her throat, but she also hadn't eaten in days,' she explained her findings.

'Do you think she could've been anorexic?' he asked.

'No. She may have weighed considerably less than what she should, but there are no clear signs that she was suffering from anorexia.'

'So somebody starved the girl, then strangled her to death?'

'The lab has run the DNA found on Hannah's body and it's a match to Jack Roberts,' she informed him.

'That's great!' Barnes shouted with delight.

'But listen, Joe. The blood found on our victim isn't hers, neither is it Jack's.'

'Then whose is it?'

'We don't know. Hopefully, the forensics will be able to tell you, but I'm afraid there might be somebody else out there who starved Hannah Jones.'

'Thank you, Julia. Please keep me updated if you find anything else,' Barnes said, hanging up the phone. He turned his attention onto Ally. 'Julia Higgins has just informed me of what we feared. Jack Roberts' DNA has been found on Hannah's body, problem is, the blood on her body isn't a match to her or Jack,' he explained.

'Then who does it belong to?'

'We don't know. I need to phone the lab myself and find out if the blood on Hannah's body is a match to Jack's clothes we found inside the bins.'

He marched out of the briefing room and into his office, leaving Ally pondering more about the case.

Two killers? Are they working together? Is Jack involved in something bigger than what we thought?

It was nine-thirty in the morning and Jacob hadn't slept a wink, with thoughts about the previous night floating around his mind, keeping him awake. A glass caressed his lips as a touch of whiskey poured down his throat. Jacob had lost count of how many sips of whiskey he'd consumed that night. His vision blurry and the room spinning, Jacob crawled to his bathroom, needing to throw up. He lay against the toilet and let the vomit release itself.

All he could think about was how much he'd hurt Kate, and the words she said. She hated him because he kept his father's secret from her. Saying they were not related hurt Jacob. He cared for her like a sister, she always was, even when he found out his father's lie. *She'll understand one day*. But it was the hurt that drove Jacob back to the drink.

Lifting himself away from the toilet, he stumbled to his bed and dropped his body on top, blacking out into a deep sleep, dreaming of happier times from his childhood. The way his mother read him and Adam stories at bedtime, baking in their kitchen, and the loving, warm embrace, she caressed them with. He missed her deeply and with every passing day, his memory of her began to fade. Then he was surrounded by darkness.

'I'm proud of you, my son,' her voice whispered.

'Mum?' Jacob called out.

His mother came out of the dark, still the image he remembered.

'Hello, Jacob.'

'Mum? I've missed you so much.'

'I miss you too, my boy. But this is still not your time. You are dreaming and you'll soon wake up.'

'But I don't want to,' he cried, staring into her eyes.

She caressed his cheek with her hand. 'You'll get through this. Just like last time. Better days are coming. Just look through the storm and you'll see the sun.'

She started to fade away as Jacob began to wake, knowing he was back to being alone and full of self-pity. Death and misery followed him, clinging like a reaper in the night. Unseen, but causing havoc wherever he goes. Quietness filled the apartment, nobody home to make the place feel lively and warm.

The craving for another drop of alcohol returned. *What am I doing with my life?* Beginning to cry, he lifted his heavy head from his pillow, letting the tears drip from his eyes and down his cheeks. The betrayal of Lily to her murdering his father, Jacob's life wasn't improving, even now. All he wanted was to be happy, but that was turning out impossible.

Ally started calling him, but his phone was across the room, plugged into the charger. His blurry vision made it nearly impossible for him to attempt to reach it as well as his state of mind. He just sat crying silently, thinking about everything he'd been through in his life. Tears flooded down his cheeks, dripping on his legs below as he remained seated on the bed.

A knock on the door surprised him, his hands wiped away the tears as his groggy voice told them to enter. Belle opened the door to see Jacob perched on the edge of his bed, as she grasped a fresh brew of coffee.

'I brought you a fresh cup of coffee,' she said gently.

'Thank you,' Jacob answered, still sobbing slightly.

'Are you okay?'

'I'll be fine.' His head didn't move, just remained looking against the wall.

'You know I'm here if you need me.'

'I know.'

Belle couldn't bear to see the man she admired look so down and depressed. The light barely peered through his blinds, making the room dim and gloomy. She walked over to the window and lifted the blinds up, releasing the sun into the room.

'I'm not going to just let you sit here and be all depressed,' she yelled with a forceful tone. She decided it was time to take action to cheer him up. 'Get up, we're going out.'

'Belle, I don't...'

She stopped him mid-sentence. 'I don't care if you don't want to. I'm not going to let you mope around in this apartment, feeling sorry for yourself. So what if your sister has fallen out with you. She'll come around. I know you've had it hard,' she started to be sympathetic before rising back to being forceful. 'But it's not doing you any favours. Now get dressed and meet me in the kitchen.'

Belle left the room, allowing him the privacy to get ready. Not knowing what Belle had planned, he had no idea what to wear. *Maybe just the usual*, he thought as he picked out jeans and a black t-shirt. Sitting on the bed he placed on his black trainers, hoping he'd appear decent for what she'd planned. Belle's face was full of glee as Jacob stepped out of his bedroom.

'There he is!' she smiled.

'What have you got planned?' he asked without a clue.

'You'll find out when we get there.'

'We'll have to take a taxi,' Jacob told her, not wanting to admit why.

She just smiled, already knowing the reason why. 'Don't worry, I knew and planned ahead.'

Belle's phone began to ring, but she ignored it, but Jacob had noticed her trying to hide it.

'Answer it,' he demanded politely. 'I know it's that boy from the cafe. You have been so happy lately and I'm guessing he's the reason why?'

'We've been talking for a few days. I quite like him,' she confessed. 'But today's our day. You need cheering up.'

'I appreciate everything you're doing for me, but I'm fine. Honestly.'

Belle's phone rang again, this time being the taxi, calling to let them know he was outside waiting. The pair of them left for the day, with Belle hoping this would do the job of making him slightly happier, knowing it wouldn't fix everything that had happened but hopefully it was just enough to take his mind off it.

Ally and Barnes returned to the crime scene where they found Hannah Jones. Barnes kept thinking about what Julia had told him over the phone. *Someone had starved Hannah, but why? And why did Jack strangle her? Did he know this girl? Maybe he's working with someone and his wife found out, and that's what got her killed. But why Mr Hussain? Is it because he told Jack he was having an affair with his wife?* Barnes ran different scenarios in his head, hoping something would click, but it didn't.

Sarah was already looking into any connection between Hannah and Jack when they left the CID. They needed to find who and where Hannah had been held captive, so they could connect the dots.

Barnes studied the area, trying to find anything that might help him uncover where Hannah had come from, before her untimely death. Forensic investigators had found footprints in the mud and sent the measurements and their findings to the lab to try to distinguish the type of shoe worn as well as the size. Ally had just finished her phone call before approaching Barnes.

'Julia has just informed me that they also found manure underneath Hannah's nails.'

'So she was held at a farm nearby, stumbled a few yards till she gets here and is murdered by Jack Roberts. We've got to widen the search. I want nearby farmyards searched. We've got to find out where she came from.'

'Okay, I'm on it, boss,' she walked away, dialling on her phone.

Standing where they'd found Hannah's body, Barnes glanced around to see if he could figure out which direction she came from when a forensic investigator stood beside him.

'Do we have any idea which direction Hannah Jones had come from?' he asked.

The investigator proceeded to explain what they'd found out so far, showing Barnes in a reenactment of her struggle with her killer. Showing Barnes Hannah's footprints in the mud, then the killer's, he assumed Jack followed Hannah from behind until she reached the secluded alleyway. Then grabbed her attention to turn her around before he struck, strangling her and choking her to death.

'But what about the blood?' Barnes asked.

'Could have covered her as he got in closer and moved her body upright against the wall,' he explained.

Barnes thanked him for his time before returning to Ally, who'd just finished on the phone.

'So, there are a few patches of land nearby, but separating us from there, is the M42. There's no easy way across either, which means the first place I'd like to search is less than two miles away.'

'Let's get back up there right away and take a look around. We've got to find out where she came from, Ally. We need to find a connection to Jack Roberts.'

Scarlett's face was hurting as she lifted her head from the floor. She noticed the woman next to her was barely breathing as the sunlight drifted through the open patches of the wooden roof, lighting up the room for her to see. Women all around the room, tied up with metal shackles. About fifteen women in total. She couldn't believe her eyes as some looked as if they hadn't been fed for weeks. All bone and no muscle.

'Good. You're finally awake,' the woman from the night before made herself known. 'I'm guessing you're the one I heard get the smack last night?'

'Yeah,' she replied. 'The bitch almost knocked my bloody teeth out.'

'Just be lucky that's all she did. She's a dangerous woman.'

'We need to get out of here,' Scarlett told her while glancing around.

'I wouldn't bother. I'm Alice by the way,' she introduced herself.

'Scarlett,' she replied, also introducing herself.

All the other women were unconscious, leaving her and Alice talking alone. They discussed a young girl who'd been held there with them but recently escaped and hoped maybe she'd have told the police where they were.

'But nobody's been here to save us. She mustn't remember where we were,' Alice continued.

The strong smell of faeces stuck up Scarlett's nostrils. The sun became dimmer as it hid behind the clouds, shielding light from the room. There was no movement from beyond the door. Scarlett's stomach growled as the thought of food and a drink crossed her mind. Wondering if her family would ever see her again was the next section of thoughts. She forced herself not to give up and tried yanking at the chains once more.

'I'd give up, girl. You'll end up like the rest of us eventually,' Alice tried bringing her down.

'I'm not giving up. I'm getting out of here,' she insisted.

Slowly, the bolt keeping the chains attached to the wall was coming loose. She continued pulling the chains with force, as hard as she could, wanting to free herself and get her fellow prisoners out. *Once more*, she thought to herself, looking at the loose bolt coming away from the wall. Scarlett grasped the chains tight in her tired hands and gave a quick pull with force, pulling the bolt completely out of the wall.

She was free to move away from the wall, but the shackles on her wrists remained, leaving her slightly vulnerable to the crazy woman keeping them captive. Scarlett scouted the room for an exit, but the only way out was through the damaged, worn-out roof, or through the door with the crazy lady on the other side. She'd not signed up to the gym four times a week to not be able to kick down a door when she needed to.

She raised her knee to her stomach and pushed her foot against the door, breaking the padlock on the other side. The door creaked open slightly as the other women watched in horror.

'You're one crazy bitch, Scarlett,' said Alice cheering her on.

'I'm not the only crazy bitch around here,' she replied, not removing her focus from the door.

She slowly pushed the door to, making sure not to make any more noise that would alert their captor. Scarlett didn't just go to the gym four days a week but also took a self-defence class too. She wasn't going to let people like this woman take advantage of her. Scarlett was a fighter and had a strong will to never give up. She'd get out of here one way or the other but as a survivor.

'Stop,' Ally commanded, as Barnes pulled up at a slight distance near an old shack of a house. 'This is it, I'm sure of it.'

'Are you sure?' said Barnes.

'That's what I said, wasn't it?'

'Okay, let's wait for back up to arrive,' he instructed before Ally darted out of the car.

She crept quietly towards the house as Barnes lifted himself out of the driver's seat, slowly creeping towards her. Ally peered through the broken window of the old shack, unsure of what she'd find inside.

'What part of wait for back up, did you not understand?' he whispered with fury.

She continued to ignore him and noticed inside a table with food and drink. *Why would anybody want to live here? This is definitely the right place.* Turning her head and glancing around, Ally picked up a large piece of wood that was situated at the side of the house and grasped it tightly, in case of emergency.

Ally edged closer to the front door, pushed it open quietly, and made her way silently through the house, investigating the room as Barnes followed close behind.

'The food's still quite warm,' she said as she felt the bowl of soup situated on the table.

'They've got to be nearby.'

Ally heard a bang as a door inside the room slowly creaked open and the padlock fell to the floor. Ally gave Barnes the instruction to be quiet and keep an eye on the door. She raised the piece of wood to her shoulder, ready to strike. The door crept open slowly and a dark redheaded girl came running out in shackles. Ally didn't hesitate for a second and smacked Scarlett Thatcher to the floor with the wood she'd grasped so tightly.

'Who are you?' Ally yelled at the girl as she felt the line of blood dribbling on her forehead.

'Scarlett Thatcher,' she said. 'What the fuck do you want with us?'

'What? We're not keeping you here,' she informed Scarlett. 'A girl called Hannah Jones was being held somewhere nearby, which we believe to be here. Do you know where your captors are?'

'No idea. So, who are you people anyway?'

'I'm Detective Inspector Ally Miller and this is my boss, DCI Barnes,' she introduced herself.

'Please, get us out of here,' she pleaded.

Suddenly, the three of them heard chatting from outside, and darted for the prison room, quietly shutting the door behind them. Ally sat down beside Scarlett, while Barnes hid behind the door, holding Ally's piece of wood tightly.

The woman slowly opened the door, wondering why the lock was broken. As she entered she noticed Ally sat on the floor.

'Who the hell are you? she asked, knowing every girl's face in the room, and Ally wasn't one of her girls.

Barnes slammed the piece of wood straight on the top of her head, knocking her to the floor unconscious. Then he removed the handcuffs from his coat pocket and placed them on her wrists. The woman was in her forties with dark blonde hair and a medium build. Barnes called for back up and informed other officers of what they'd discovered, while Ally consoled the other victims, giving them food and drink from what she found from inside the house.

Minutes later backup arrived and Barnes shoved the captor inside the police car, instructing the officers to keep her in holding, ready for them to interview her. Barnes noticed Ally's face was full of thoughts as he approached her.

'What's the matter?' he asked.

'I just thought about something. We heard talking as we hid, but only this woman entered. I don't think this woman was working alone,' she expressed her concern.

'I think you're right,' he said before running outside and telling the remaining officers to search the surrounding area.

Then Ally remembered something. *Hannah Jones had a penetration mark on her skin from something like a needle. She must have been injected with something.* Ally grabbed a pair of latex gloves from her pocket and walked back inside the house, searching all the draws for any needles. She found nothing and she felt frustrated with herself before another search place sprung to mind.

She ran out of the house and searched the bins and black bin bags close by. It was never the nicest of jobs but it needed to be done. She didn't feel comfortable until she'd searched everywhere, knowing the forensic team might not have searched the bins. She wanted to nail the bitch that held these women against their will and to find her accomplice.

Dirty tissues, food waste and stinky food cans were all the things Ally came across before hitting the jackpot. She found a bunch of disposed needles inside a box within a box.

'Gotcha,' she cheered.

'Boss,' she yelled out to get his attention.

'What is it, Ally?'

'Look what I've found.'

Barnes glanced down and peered inside the black bin liner, to see the discovery Ally had made. He turned to the officers who stood on the perimeter of the house.

'Get forensics here, now!' he yelled. 'Good work today, DI Miller,' he congratulated her on a job well done.

Ally loved her job, her team and the work they were doing, but the opportunity of going to work in Hawaii was hanging over her head. She kept the truth from her team, trying not to upset anyone, especially Jacob. The phone call she'd received was from her ex-fiance, who'd broken her heart by leaving to take up a new job in Hawaii. The job she was offered was to do with a case they'd worked together. But she was happy here and didn't want to ruin what she had, for someone who'd left her in a heartbeat without a second thought.

She watched as forensics turned up and started to photograph everything and collecting evidence in front of her. Her mind had wandered. She wanted to phone Jacob and tell him the truth about the job offer. She wanted him to tell her not to go, to tell her that he loves her, but maybe she was just hoping there were mutual feelings there.

She unlocked her phone, opened up the phone book and scrolled to Jacob's name. She hesitated not knowing to phone him or not. Barnes interrupted her as he approached.

'Good news. We've got an I.D on our perp. Her name is Felicity James, clean record, nothing out of the ordinary, other than this.'

'How did you find out her name? I can't imagine she just gave it to you,' she laughed.

Barnes smiled, 'Found her purse when we searched her.'

'So what makes someone with no criminal record want to keep women prisoners?' Ally wondered.

'No idea. I'm sure we'll get the answers we need. We've still got officers searching the area. I think our work here is done.'

'I think you're right,' she agreed, as the pair of them walked back to the car, leaving the forensics and other officers in charge of the crime scene.

Chapter 17

As they strolled into the station they could see officers struggling to place Felicity James into a cell as she frantically screamed at them, crying her eyes out. Two officer's each holding an arm, trying to push her into the cell but her feet resisting against the floor.

'What's going on?' Barnes asked one of the officers.

'She's hysterical, saying she's done nothing wrong and it wasn't her,' the officer replied before giving them a hand getting Felicity in her cell.

'Do you think she's trying to tell them that the other person was the one holding them there?' Ally asked Barnes.

'Maybe, but these are questions we need to ask in the interview,' he told her.

They still had to interview Jack Roberts about his criminal activity. The interviews kept racking up. *Where's the connection between Jack and Felicity?* Barnes thought. He'd already given Ethan Felicity's name for her history, so he was hoping he'd come up with a connection between her and Jack.

Walking into the CID, Barnes and Ally appeared at Ethan's desk, making him look up from his screen.

'Managed to find a connection yet?' Barnes asked him.

'There's nothing, Boss.'

'Nothing?' he repeated, staring at him with an angry appearance.

'I'll keep looking,' he said, placing his head back into his screen to avoid Barnes' glare.

'Ethan, I need anything that can tie Felicity to Jack. There's no way Jack Roberts just stumbled upon Hannah Jones after she'd escaped that farm shack. I just don't believe in it being bad luck or coincidence,' Barnes discussed his thoughts.

'Leave it with me, boss,' he replied, still not giving Barnes eye contact.

Barnes went to his office, tired and exhausted, sat down at his desk and sighed. It had been another tiring day for him. He was still recovering from his ordeal with Lily and Cain. A knock at the door frightened Barnes, making him jump with fright as Ally entered.

'Are you feeling okay?'

'Just fine, DI Miller,' he lied. 'Why do you ask?'

'Well, it's just the way you were with Ethan,' she began to express her concern. 'I think you may need some rest. You've been here all the time since you've been back. You need some rest.'

Barnes knew she was right. Ally always was, but he needed to close this case before he could take the time to rest. There was so much left to do, and the team needed everyone on board.

'I will, once we've solved this case,' he said.

'Now you're starting to sound like Jacob,' she smiled.

'Let's just get the answers we need, then we can all have a day off.'

Belle had pulled it off. Jacob had forgotten all of his worries and they enjoyed mini-golf together. To begin with, Jacob was in the lead until Belle pulled it back around and won with the last few holes. It had been a great day and they'd enjoyed themselves for the first time in a long time.

Once they'd finished, they decided to get some food. They both decided on Pizza Hut after spending five minutes discussing what they fancied. While tucking into their pizzas, Jacob decided to express his appreciation.

'Thank you so much for today, Belle. It's just what I needed.'

'It's nothing, Jacob. I owe you so much for what you've done for me,' she started to express her gratitude.

Belle could see tears forming in his eyes, knowing his thoughts had gone back to the past.

'I'm sorry,' Jacob apologised for crying.

'It's okay. You've had a shit couple of months. I don't know how you've coped with it all. Just don't bottle it up, talk to us. You have family all around you, and we're here for you, day or night,' she consoled him.

'Thank you, Belle. It means a lot. I'm so grateful you came into my life.'

They finished their meal and discussed having dessert when Belle's phone began to ring again. It was Ben, but she didn't want to spoil hers and Jacob's evening, so placed it back in her pocket.

'Answer it,' Jacob insisted. 'He's so desperate to talk to you.'

'Are you sure? You'll be alright?'

'Yes, I'll be fine. Now go and phone him back,' he demanded politely with a smile.

Belle walked outside of the restaurant to make the call, leaving Jacob sat alone at the table. He removed his phone from his pocket and scrolled through it. His home screen featured photos of him and his family, making tears form again in his eyes. Wondering what was happening at work, he scrolled through his contacts, seeing Ally's name at the top.

He stared at it for a minute, not moving an inch. *Has she taken the job?* he pondered. *I hope not. But how do I express my feelings for her? I've just come out of a really bad relationship.* Jacob wanted her to stay. *What if she's already made her mind up and doesn't want to stay?* He called her, putting the fear of rejection at the back of his mind for a change.

'Hi, Ally,' he greeted as she answered. 'How's the case going?'

'We've discovered where Hannah was being held and have one person in custody,' she explained.

'That's great news. Is there any connection to Jack yet?'

'Not yet, but Ethan's checking that out. Did you just call for a check-up or was there something else you wanted, Jacob?' she asked with humour in her tone.

'I wondered if you fancied going for a drink sometime?' he went straight for it, leaving the thought of rejection behind.

'Not even a meal first?' she joked.

'Well... we could go for food first... that is if you wanted to?' he started to stutter.

'I would love to,' she said.

'How about tomorrow night?' he gleamed with excitement.

'Let me just check my calendar.' She paused for a moment leaving the line quiet. 'Yeah, tomorrow seems fine with my busy schedule,' she laughed.

'Good, so it's a date.'

'Well, I wouldn't call it that,' she teased, joking once again.

'I'll see you tomorrow.'

'Take care of yourself, Jacob. Get plenty of rest.'

Jacob had not long hung up the phone before the waitress approached and took his dessert order. Belle walked back in from phoning Ben, to find Jacob munching on his warm cookie with ice cream.

'Started without me?' she said.

'I couldn't wait,' he laughed. 'I've taken your advice on staying positive and phoned Ally to ask her on a date.'

'And what did she say?' she asked before scooping ice cream into her mouth.

'We're going out for dinner tomorrow night,' he smiled.

Jacob felt incredible for a chance, focusing on the good rather than the bad. Kate would come around eventually and they'd be as close as they had been before.

'Wow, check you out. Who's this guy, and what have you done with Jacob?' she laughed.

'So, what did Ben want so badly?'

'We're going out on a date tomorrow too,' she announced.

'I'm really happy for you, Belle. You've done really well. You've escaped your past and made a future for yourself. I'm proud of you,' Jacob said while trying not to cry again.

'Thank you. I'm glad I've got you looking out for me.'

After dinner, Belle and Jacob returned to the apartment. It was pitch black, making it incredibly hard for them to see. Belle flicked the light switch on, brightening up the place. Jacob headed for his bedroom, but before he walked through the door, he turned to face Belle.

'Thanks for a great day.'

'You're welcome. Glad you had fun,' she replied.

He walked into his dark, depressing bedroom and flopped onto his bed. Jacob just kept thinking about Ally, thinking she must feel the same way about him, making him feel ecstatic. Happiness was all he felt, focusing on the happy things in life, just like everyone had told him. Nothing was going to stand in his way between him and happiness.

His tired eyes began to close as he blinked repeatedly, trying his best to keep himself awake, but failing. His vision became blurry with every blink until he eventually fell asleep.

Standing in a dark alley, Jacob was confused about how he ended up here. His vision was blurry, just like before he fell asleep. A woman came from around the corner of the building. She resembled Hannah Jones. *Hannah?* Jacob said to himself. *How is she alive?* His eyes caught sight of a silhouette behind her as she stumbled closer to him. His vision became clearer and could see it was Jack Roberts.

'Excuse me,' Jack said in a deep voice, getting the attention of Hannah.

She turned around just as he edged closer to her.

'No, Hannah. Don't!' Jacob shouted, unable to move, he held out his hand.

But Hannah couldn't hear him, leaving Jacob to hear her choked screams while Jack had his hands around her throat, squeezing the life out of her. Jacob covered his mouth in shock as he watched the life drain from her eyes, as she got lower to the floor. Once her breathing terminated, Jack propped Hannah up against the wall and walked away. Jacob stared at Hannah's corpse in horror, before opening his eyes to a blinding light.

Jacob glanced around, sighing with relief as he realised he was inside his bedroom. *Are the visions back?* he asked himself, not sure what had just happened. He sat up, rubbed his eyes and checked his phone. Nothing, not from Ally and not from Barnes, no missed call or text message. The night had passed and the day had begun, as the sun seeped through his blinds like it usually did.

Lifting himself off the bed, Jacob left his room and the smell of a cooked breakfast hit his nostrils like a smack in the face.

'I made breakfast,' Belle said from the kitchen.

'It smells amazing.'

'It tastes even better,' she laughed. 'Take a seat.'

Jacob sat on the stool by the kitchen counter as Belle plated the food and slid it in front of him. The plate was piled high with scrambled eggs, bacon, sausage and toast, and she watched as Jacob tucked into a huge bite.

'You're right, it's amazing!' he mumbled with a mouth full of food.

'Are you going to work today?' she asked, knowing he couldn't keep away from the station for too long.

'I was thinking about it,' he replied, still cramming food in his mouth like he'd never been fed.

'Me and Kate have both got work this morning so you'd be on your own otherwise.'

'How is she?' he asked with concern.

'She feels betrayed, but she'll come around. She just needs time, Jacob. She knows you're there for her, but she'll talk to you when she's ready. You have to remember, her whole life has been a lie. She thought your dad was hers too.'

'Do you think I did the right thing by not telling her?'

'I honestly don't know. I can see why you did it, but she also has a right to know, and she probably wouldn't have taken it out on you if you told her,' she replied.

Jacob rose from his seat and stepped into his bedroom to get changed before leaving for work, as Belle did the same. She and Kate left moments before him. Grabbing his phone, coat and keys, Jacob left the apartment and headed for the station.

Barnes and Ally sat inside the interview room with Jack Roberts and his solicitor, discussing the evidence they'd found against him. His attitude and behaviour had changed since their last encounter, as he sat with his arms folded with a dark and terrifying grin on his face.

'Mr Roberts, you know why we're all here. We found bloodstained clothes in the bins outside of the Premier Inn where you were arrested. We've had the clothes processed and we've found traces of your DNA,' Barnes informed him.

Jack said nothing. He just stared at the detectives, smiling with his creepy grin. His solicitor seemed as worried to them as they were.

'We also discovered the body of Hannah Jones nearby, not long after arresting you. Did you know Hannah?' Ally said, but Jack remained silent. 'Was she just at the wrong place at the wrong time?' Still, he said nothing. 'Did you know Hannah was being held prisoner at a farm shack before you strangled her to death?'

Ally placed photos of both Hannah Jones' body and the farm shack in front of him in evidence bags. Jack glanced down at the table, scanning his eyes over the photos. Ally could see the enjoyment on his face as he stared at the photo of Hannah.

'Do you like looking at that one?' Ally asked, feeling sick to her stomach at the thought he was getting off on seeing her lifeless body. She snatched the photos off the table, away from his prying eyes. 'We arrested someone at the farmhouse earlier today. Does the name Felicity James ring any bells?'

Jack lent forward, leaning his elbows on the table, looking Ally straight in the eyes. 'What if it does? You can't tie her to me. Jack and Felicity have no connection.'

Ally didn't understand why he'd referred to himself in the third person and it freaked her out. His eyes didn't once remove themselves from hers, making her feel slightly vulnerable, even with two other people in the room.

'We know you killed Hannah, but we don't know why. Another burning question we'd like to ask you, Jack, is whose blood is on your clothes?' Barnes interrupted his staring.

'Now that would be telling,' he answered as he leant back in his chair, smiling profoundly.

'Are they dead?' Barnes asked.

Jack remained quiet once again, not wanting to give them any information.

'Where are they, Jack?' Ally demanded, but he still kept his silence.

'Interview terminated at 9.34 am,' Barnes spoke before stopping the tape recorder and leaving the room with Ally.

'What kind of game do you think he's playing in there?' she asked him.

'I don't know. He doesn't quite seem like the grieving husband I'd have pictured.'

'He's totally changed since that night me and Jacob arrived at his home.'

'I hope Ethan's found a connection between these two,' Barnes hoped.

'And me. Do you think Jack knows we haven't found one yet and that's why he said it in there?' she said.

'Maybe.'

They walked back into the office and saw Ethan still sat at his desk when they made their way over.

'Found anything?' Barnes didn't hesitate to get to the point.

'I might have, but it's probably clutching at straws,' he answered as Ally and Barnes looked more intrigued. 'So the guy you call Cain...'

'Nathan Lawrence,' Barnes interrupted.

'Well, he was admitted to the hospital when he was younger with psychosis. I looked into Felicity's background after that and found out she was admitted a few times due to substance abuse, which would sum up how she knows where to find certain drugs to help capture her victims.'

'I don't see where you're going with this Ethan,' Barnes couldn't work out his logic with his research.

'I'm getting there, just hold on. Have you ever heard of Dissociative Identity Disorder?'

'Isn't that like multiple personalities?' Ally jumped in and answered.

'Correct, DI Miller,' Ethan congratulated her. 'Do you know what could cause someone to exhibit this disorder?'

'Stress from trauma?' Ally answered again, while Barnes stayed confused.

'Correct but there are many different reasons including substance abuse and psychosis.'

'You think both Nathan Lawrence and Felicity James could be experiencing this multiple personality disorder?' Barnes piped up.

'I did tell you I was clutching at straws,' Ethan joked.

'But why would that make them killers?' Ally asked.

'I don't know, I'm a police officer, not a psychiatric doctor,' he laughed.

'Thanks, Ethan,' Ally said as she walked away with Barnes in tow. 'Do you think Ethan could be right about this?'

'I'm not sure, but it does explain an awful lot,' he replied. 'Can you look into Jack Roberts past and see if he fits any of the symptoms of Dissociative Identity Disorder?'

'Sure thing, boss,' she said before leaving Barnes to enter his office alone.

He sat at his desk, his head pounding from an ungodly headache. The doctors told him to rest after his ordeal but thinking he knew better, he ignored their advice and continued with work. It was the only way he'd be able to take his mind off the trauma he experienced, but the quiet moments were when his mind took him back to those moments. Being inside that warehouse and canal boat, the blood pouring out of him, the shock from the electrocution and the pain from the knife wounds. It was all he could think about in those quiet moments. He lost sleep every night because of them.

As he woke from his thoughts, he noticed Jacob entering the CID and walking over to his office. Barnes wiped his face with his hands before the door knocked.

'Come in,' Barnes spoke before the door opened.

'Morning, boss,' Jacob greeted him. 'What's been happening in my absence?'

'Where do I begin?' Barnes said, making Jacob laugh, not meaning for it to be funny. 'Ethan seems to think Felicity James and Nathan Lawrence are suffering from Dissociative Identity Disorder,' he explained to Jacob.

'What is that?'

'It's when someone suffers from multiple personalities.'

'So where's the connection?' Jacob asked.

'We haven't found one.'

'What about Jack Roberts? Do you think he suffers from the same disorder as them? He sure shows symptoms of it.'

'I've got Ally looking into his history. Anyway, how are you? Is everything okay at home?' Barnes asked him.

Jacob sat in the chair, and Barnes noticed tears welling up in his eyes as he explained what had been going on in his own life. He didn't want to seem self-absorbed, knowing what Barnes had been going through in his own life.

'Wow, our lives seem to have taken a toll for the worst lately,' he comforted Jacob. 'Look, I know you want to jump straight back into work, but these past few months have been hard, not just for you, but for all of us, and I think the thing we all need right now is to have a holiday. Once this case is over, I want you to take a break as will the rest of us,' he continued.

'I think that's a good idea, sir,' Jacob agreed.

Before another sentence could be said, Ally came rushing through the door with some new information.

'Boss, I've found something,' she started, before closing the office door behind her. 'When Jack Roberts was younger, he was put into the care system.'

'Right,' Barnes said, wanting her to get to the point.

'The reason for that was because he watched his parents get murdered,' she continued.

'Do you think he had post-traumatic stress disorder which brought on Dissociative Identity Disorder?' Barnes theorised.

'Could be. Maybe sparked up once he saw his wife's body,' she also put her theory out there.

Jacob interrupted the pair of them. 'But if you think this is multiple personalities, he said he'd seen the disfigured man lurking before the incident. How'd you explain that?'

'Maybe something else triggered it, and his brain was showing him the personality before he murdered his wife.' Ally continued.

'I think Mr Roberts is suffering from D.I.D, but I think it's quietly been there since his childhood and suddenly something has caused his secret personality to come out and take over,' Jacob expressed his concern. 'The thing we need to find out is what caused it to come out.'

'There's got to be a connection between these three people. I don't believe it's a coincidence that three people with D.I.D are all in the same city. I also don't think it's a coincidence that Hannah had just escaped from Felicity to be murdered by Jack. There's more to this that we're not seeing,' Barnes started to get frustrated.

'Or that we choose not to see,' Jacob interrupted.

'What do you mean by that, DS Wright?' Barnes questioned him.

'Look, last year we were searching for a cult of witches that were doing sacrificial killings. I'm just saying, let's look at this with an open mind,' he explained his thoughts.

'You think this is supernatural in some way?' Ally asked him seriously.

'I wouldn't rule it out,' he replied.

'Okay,' Barnes said, rubbing his finger across his chin, deep in thought. 'Myself and Ally are going to interview Jack Roberts again and I want you, Jacob, to be listening in. It's better to have more eyes on this,' Barnes ordered.

Chapter 18

Jacob and Ally left the CID for lunch and sat inside a quiet little cafe a couple of miles away from the station to discuss the three cases and their similarities. Jacob ordered a cheeseburger and fries, but Ally wanted to watch her figure and chose a salad.

'Do you think all three of them really are suffering from Dissociative Identity Disorder?' he asked Ally.

'I sure think Jack Roberts is, but I'm unsure of the others. Like Barnes said, how can three people in one city all have this rare disorder? Only seven percent of the world's population suffer from it and three of those people are all in the same city and involved in our case? It doesn't make sense,' she explained.

'What makes you think Jack is suffering from it?'

'Because I saw the pain on that man's face the night we turned up at the scene. He was a broken man and I think he truly loved his wife.'

'What about the murder of Mr Hussain?'

'I don't think it was him. I think it was his other personality,' she said.

The waitress appeared with their food, placing it in front of them. Jacob took a huge bite of his burger as the waitress disappeared back to the counter, leaving them to continue their discussion.

'You need to ask him about the personality in the interview,' Jacob muttered between bites.

'I would but I think the personality is the one who's doing the talking.'

'What do you mean?'

'When we interviewed him this morning, he wasn't the same guy. He showed no remorse for what he had done, he just kept smiling, and I mean it wasn't just an average smile, it was creepy.'

'What about the bloodstained clothes? Did he ever say who he'd hurt?' Jacob asked.

'Nope. No idea and the victim is still out there somewhere. We have no idea who they are or where they are.'

'And the other person involved with Felicity, did they find them?'

'Again, no.'

They were both silent for a moment while Jacob looked out of the window, trying to think of a connection when Jacob noticed a man staring in at him from across the street. Ally noticed Jacob's face change and glanced out of the window.

'Not again,' he said quietly.

'What's the matter?' she asked, turning her attention back to him.

'I just keep seeing my father. I think I'm suffering from some post-traumatic stress myself,' he expressed.

'I don't think you are,' she replied.

'Why?'

'Because if you are talking about the man across the street, I see him too,' she explained.

Jacob jumped off his seat and rushed out of the cafe, running in the man's direction. Ally was close behind him.

'Stop, police!' Jacob shouted. 'Stay where you are!'

The man started to run away and headed for an alleyway close by. Jacob ran so fast, he didn't realise he was leaving Ally behind. As Jacob turned the corner, he saw the man right in front of him, standing completely still with his back to him. Jacob stood still on the spot, gasping for breath, but keeping his focus on the man who resembled his father.

'Dad? Is that really you?' Jacob asked.

The man turned around and stared at Jacob right in the eyes. He realised the man wasn't his father. His eye colour was different, knowing his father's eyes were blue and not green, like this man's.

'Who are you?' Jacob asked the man.

Ally came rushing with panic around the corner. Not knowing what was going on, she just spectated.

'I'm your uncle,' the man explained.

'My uncle?' Jacob seemed confused.

His father had never explained his own past with his son's. As far as they were aware, their father never had any family. His past was kept a secret from them.

'I'm guessing your father was telling me the truth when he said he kept the family history a secret from you and your brother,' he laughed.

'What are you laughing at?' Jacob yelled at him.

'You don't have to be afraid...'

'I'm not!' he interrupted him.

'Good. I'm not going to hurt you.'

'Why am I only just finding out about you now? And what's your name?'

Jacob started to relax slightly, but still keeping up his guard.

'My names Dan and I can explain everything you want to know, just not out here,' he explained, his head turning from side to side like he was worried about something.

'Jacob,' Ally alerted him. 'We've got to get back to the station.'

Dan handed him his number. 'Call me when you're free. I'll explain everything your father kept hidden.'

Jacob never said a word, just stared at his uncle he never knew existed, then turned to follow Ally back out on to the street. He kept wondering, *Why now?*

'I have no idea what's going through your mind right now, but I need you to focus on the interview later,' Ally said as they approached the car.

'Life doesn't seem to be giving me a break lately, does it?' he said as they got inside.

Ally sped back to the station, not wanting to sit in the awkward silence a minute longer. Minutes later they arrived at the station and headed inside the CID. Jacob strolled over to his desk while Ally walked into Barnes' office and shut the door.

'Did you know John Wright had a twin brother?' she asked him.

Barnes lifted his head and looked strangely at her, trying not to reveal the truth. 'I had no idea. I knew the guy for years and he never once told me, and he told me a lot of secrets,' he explained. 'Where's this coming from?'

'We met him earlier when we were on lunch. Jacob saw him from the window and gave chase. He confronted him in an alley and he told him who he was.'

'What was his name?' Barnes asked, grabbing a pen and paper. 'I'll do a background check.'

'He said it was Dan,' she told him.

'Leave it with me,' he said, as she rose to her feet.

Ally left the office and headed for the briefing room to prep for the interview. She wanted to know if their theory about Jack Roberts was true. Barnes began to panic, worried about the lies he was keeping would come back to bite him later.

Jacob remained at his desk, wondering why all of a sudden his uncle wanted to get in contact. *Does he want to meet because my father's not in the way?* he pondered. He began to remove his focus from his thoughts and back onto his work. He researched Dissociative Identity Disorder and the main causes of it. The more he researched, the more he felt they were headed in the right direction about Jack.

Barnes opened his office door and stood glancing around. He then moved over to the briefing room and peeped inside to see Ally writing down notes on a notepad. When he opened the door, Jacob got off his seat and marched over to see what they were discussing.

'Are you ready?' Barnes asked her.

'Almost.'

Jacob entered the room. 'What's going on? Are you about to interview him?'

'You need to get yourself ready, Jacob. We will be soon,' Barnes informed him.

'I've been researching D.I.D, and I believe his trauma may have brought this on,' Jacob explained his thoughts.

'Good. I'm glad we're all on the same page about this. Now let's go and ask Jack or whatever personality he is today, where this unknown victim is,' Barnes demanded, trying not to raise his voice.

Jacob entered a room with a video surveillance screen set up, while Ally and Barnes entered the interview room, to see Jack Roberts alone without Simon Ballard present.

'Mr Roberts, do you not want your solicitor here?' Barnes asked.

'No, thank you,' he replied calmly with a smile.

'Okay then,' Barnes said as he sat down, while Ally placed the tape in the recorder.

Barnes did the usual speech into the tape recorder before they started the interview again.

'Mr Roberts...'

'Call me Jack,' he interrupted.

'Earlier we spoke to you about the bloodstained clothes we found at the Premier Inn you were staying at, and who the victim is? Are you going to tell us now?' Barnes continued.

'Maybe,' Jack replied, still smiling at them.

'Look, Jack,' Ally interrupted, 'Just tell us who and where this person is!' she raised her voice and lifted herself from her seat.

'Detective Inspector Miller, please don't interrupt your senior officer,' he spoke with a calm and well-spoken tone.

'Are you even Jack Roberts?' she asked while placing her bum back on her seat.

'Why do you ask?'

Barnes butted in. 'We think Jack suffers from Dissociative Identity Disorder, triggered by witnessing his mother and father's murders. What we want to understand is why it's taken so long for you to make an appearance?'

'I'd like to say I've always been there, hiding within the shadows, but I'd be lying,' he confessed.

'So how long have you been in Jack's head?' Barnes continued with his line of questions.

'Since December,' he said sharply, remaining in the well-spoken tone.

'What triggered him for you to come out?' Ally desperately wanted to know.

'Do you really think I'm a personality?'

'Because we have two other people who we think have the same disorder, in our custody,' Barnes informed him.

'So you've found my brother and sisters?'

'What do you mean by brother and sisters? What are you?' Ally continued.

'DCI Barnes, I think you must already know. One of them must have told you when you were in their captivity,' he smiled leaning his elbows on the table between them.

Barnes thought about what he said and remembered what Cain had told him in the warehouse about his siblings.

'You know Nathan Lawrence?' Barnes asked him.

'You mean Cain? I don't know Nathan Lawrence,' he answered.

'Is Cain one of your siblings?'

'One of three.'

'Who are you?' Ally asked.

'My name is Damien. You might know me by another name.'

Barnes began to lose patience. 'Oh yeah, and what might that be?'

'Death,' he replied, his smile growing wider.

Nothing but silence filled the room. Barnes and Ally weren't sure how to react to what he'd just said. Barnes was getting frustrated by people claiming to be demons of some kind.

'Are you telling us that you are Death? One of the four horsemen?' Barnes humoured him.

'Yes, DCI Barnes, that is what I'm telling you,' he replied.

'I didn't realise death was a murderer,' Ally began to smirk, knowing her comment would annoy him.

'Are you going to tell us where your last victim is, or are we just wasting our time?' Barnes asked.

Jack just laughed at Barnes, knowing they needed to know where his final victim was. 'If you want to know, I can show you where they are,' he answered.

'Enough of your games. You know that's not going to happen,' Barnes shouted at him.

'Then you'll never know who or where they are,' he leant back in his chair, still keeping the psychotic smile on his face.

Barnes stood up and left the room, while Ally announced what was happening for the tape.

'DCI Barnes has exited the room. Interview terminated at 15.07.' She stopped the tape. 'Mr Roberts, someone will be along shortly to collect you.'

'I'm guessing he's not taking me up on my offer.'

'I guess not,' she smirked at him, before exiting the room.

Barnes was standing outside of the interview room waiting for Ally, his arms were folded and one arm reached to the bottom of his chin, with his index finger rubbing it.

'Please tell me you're not considering taking him up on his offer?' she asked him.

'Hopefully, we don't have to. I'm hoping he realises that he either tells us or doesn't, and thinks we're not giving in,' he explained his plan.

'Let's hope it goes to plan then.'

Jacob came marching down the hallway towards them, his face red with anger.

'You're not going to give him what he wants, are you?' Jacob questioned him.

'What do you think?' Barnes answered with a rhetorical question.

'Good. We don't need another guy like that out on the street.'

The three of them walked back to the CID, contemplating what their next move would be, trying not to get to the conclusion of letting him out for a day trip to find the missing victim.

'If Jack's correct about being one of four horsemen,' Jacob started, 'then we've got one more to find. We've already got three of them in custody.'

'Jack Roberts seems to think he's Death, so we should find out who the other two think they are, and try to create a profile of who our fourth is identifying as, and locate how they'll kill their victims,' Ally expressed.

'You're right. I think we need to interview Felicity James. Do you remember when she was brought in, Ally?' he asked her and she nodded. 'Do you remember what she was screaming?'

'Yes, that it wasn't her that kept all those women prisoner,' she responded.

'Yeah, and now we know what we know, it sums that moment up perfectly,' Barnes smiled with glee.

Kate was due to finish work at 4 pm. She glared at the time, 3.45 pm, as she wiped over the empty tables with disinfectant spray and a cleaning cloth. Belle approached her from the counter.

'Come on, Kate. You haven't spoken to me all day. Talk to me, come on,' she pleaded.

'Please just leave me to get on with work. I don't want to talk about it right now.'

'You never want to talk about it. It could help you once you get your feelings off your chest.'

Kate ignored her and moved over to the next table and repeated her actions. Belle continued following her, despite Kate's warning.

'Will you just leave me alone,' she snapped at her quietly, making sure not to draw attention to them.

'Fine!' Belle replied before storming away to the counter.

Kate continued wiping the tables when she heard the door to the cafe open, making her glance behind her to see who entered. She soon regretted her decision once she locked eyes with the man claiming to be her father. She tried to scurry away but he was already stood next to her.

'Can we talk?' he asked.

'I don't want to talk to you. Not now, not ever,' she said angrily, but quietly once again, trying not to draw in an audience.

'I get you're mad at me, but this isn't my fault. I never hid this from you. Please don't be mad at me. I just want to get to know you and try to figure out why your mother would keep me away from you.'

Kate thought about it for a moment, before she realised his words made a little sense.

'Meet me at the pub across the road. I finish in ten minutes,' she said.

He left the cafe and she watched as he strolled across the road and entered the pub. She finished cleaning the dirty tables and removed the plates, glasses and filthy cutlery, and walked into the kitchen.

Belle confronted her again, demanding to know what was going on.

'What did he want?'

'None of your business,' Kate replied, not giving Belle any more of her time.

'What's happened to us, Kate? We used to be the best of friends.'

'And you went out to cheer Jacob up. What about me, Belle? He kept my father's secret from me. He was the one who should have suffered but you went and chose him over me.' Tears started to well up in her eyes.

'Your brother...'

Kate cut her off short. 'He's not my brother!'

'He is your brother and he always will be! He's done so much for me, and he needed someone to be there for him. So, yes, I did go and try to cheer him up,' she yelled before leaving the kitchen and headed back to the cafe counter.

Kate pulled her apron off in an angry motion, before chucking it on the side. She grabbed her belongings, stormed out of the cafe and marched to the pub. Belle started to hold back the tears, unsure if they would ever be friends again. She sure hoped they would.

Kate entered the pub, scanned her eyes and noticed her father sat at a table with a pint. She wandered to the table and sat opposite him. Her hands were trembling, not knowing what she'd say to this man, but she wanted to hear him out.

'I'm glad you agreed to this,' he said. 'Do you want a drink?'

'No, thank you,' she answered. 'I just want answers.'

He sighed, thinking this was not how he wanted this to go. Kate just stared at him, waiting for him to speak.

'Okay. I've just been released from prison,' he confessed. 'This isn't how I wanted this to go.'

'This isn't how I wanted my life to go either, but here we are,' she replied sarcastically. 'What were you in prison for?'

'Assault,' he said sharply. 'Not my best moment, but I'd like to say I'm a changed man. If you'd give me a chance, I'd like to get to know you?'

'Listen, a week ago I had no idea John Wright wasn't my father. Now I'm here with a strange man who wants to get to know me, claiming he's my father. You have to understand how sudden my life has changed.'

'I don't want to push you. Just know I'm here when you're ready. I know it's been a lot to take in and I can only apologise for that,' he said.

'Thank you. I'm really sorry, but I never asked your name?'

'Craig. Craig Ross,' he answered.

She held out her hand to be shaken. 'It's nice to meet you, Craig Ross.'

Felicity James' hands shook vigorously from fear, not knowing why she was suddenly sat inside a police station. Her solicitor sat beside her, trying to get answers of her crimes before the detectives commenced the interview. She had no clue what had happened. The last few weeks had been a complete blur, just like when she had her blackouts. Her body ached all the time like it had been in fights every day and her head pounded violently.

DI Miller and DS Wright entered the room, placed a tape in the recorder and waited for the loud beep to stop before speaking.

'This is Detective Inspector Ally Miller with Detective Sergeant Jacob Wright, interviewing Felicity James on the 25th of January at 5.07 pm. Felicity James, do you know why you are here today?'

Felicity shook her head in response, too afraid to speak.

'Can you confirm for the tape please, Miss James?' Ally asked.

'No,' she trembled.

'Okay. On January 24th, myself and Detective Chief Inspector Joseph Barnes, entered a premises just outside of the N.E.C grounds, where we discovered at least twenty women locked inside a farm shack. You then approached the farmhouse and entered the room where me and DCI Barnes were hiding with the women. We then arrested you at the scene. Do you not remember any of that?'

'No. That wasn't me,' she cried out.

'Then who was it, if it was not you?' Ally continued with her questions.

'I don't know.'

'Do you know what's going to happen now?' Jacob asked calmly.

'No.'

'You are going to go to prison for abducting these women, one of which escaped, only to be strangled to death,' Jacob continued.

'These women were starved and almost left for dead. Do you enjoy seeing women dying of starvation?' Ally raised her voice.

Felicity just sat there and cried, not knowing what to say. They didn't believe her, and why would they. It would sound crazy to her what she'd have told them.

'Felicity, have you ever heard of D.I.D?' Jacob asked.

'No, what's that?' she asked between sniffles.

'It stands for Dissociative Identity Disorder. It's when a person has another personality they sometimes don't know about which can be brought on by many different reasons. We took a look through your medical records. We know you used drugs, which can cause Dissociative Identity Disorder,' Jacob explained.

'You think I have another personality?' she asked.

'We do, along with two other people who have been involved in our current cases,' Ally informed her.

Felicity burst into tears, unsure of what was going on. *What are they telling me? Am I crazy?*

'Felicity, we need to know if you remember anything about your other personality? Their name? If they met anybody else?' Ally threw questions at her.

'I don't know,' she continued crying.

'I'm sorry, I know it's a lot for you to take in right now, but there is someone else out there, that is going to endanger other people's lives if we don't find them,' Jacob explained.

'I don't know,' Felicity repeated. 'I don't remember anything.'

Jacob didn't want to freak her out anymore than what she already was, but they needed her to remember anything she might have witnessed while her other personality was in control.

'Have you ever heard of the four horsemen of the apocalypse?' he asked.

Her solicitor gave him a funny glance from across the table, wondering where he was going with his questions.

'Yes, from the movies and stuff.'

'Well, one of our suspects seems to think he is one of the horsemen.'

'Which one?'

'Death and we really need to know if your personality has another persona they like to go by?' he braved the question.

Her headache got worse as her hand started to shake more violently. Unsure of what was happening to her, she tried to cry out for help, but her lips wouldn't move. She just stared at Jacob. One tear formed in her eye and trickled down her cheek.

'Miss James,' her solicitor spoke. 'Are you okay?'

'Felicity?' Jacob called out.

'Jacob,' Ally whispered in his ear. 'Do you remember the interview with Jack Roberts?'

'Yes.'

'She's doing something similar. I think we're about to meet personality number two.'

And within a few minutes, Felicity stopped shaking and sat still in the chair. She was calm. The back of her hand wiped the tears from her eyes calmly as she stared blankly, then placed them back by her side. She seemed distant and emotionless.

'Is this Felicity we're speaking to?' Ally asked, hoping for the answer she wanted.

'Felicity is gone,' she answered, remaining calm and still. 'My name is Ruth.'

'Hi, Ruth. It's nice to meet you. I'm...'

'I know who you, DI Miller,' she interrupted. 'I'm always there, listening in the background. What do you want with my siblings?'

'We want to know why you're here?'

'Why we're here? You should know why we're here.'

Jacob remained silent, just observing what Ruth had to say.

'Well I don't, so why don't you fill me in?' Ally remained calm too, folding her arms and leaning back in her chair.

'Have you both even figured out how we got here yet?' Ruth asked.

Felicity's solicitor seemed even more freaked out now than he was before, not knowing what on earth was happening in this tiny interview room. The room filled with silence while Jacob and Ally stared at Ruth waiting for her to answer.

'I'll leave you both to figure that one out,' she continued.

'I'm guessing it was you and not Felicity who held those women prisoner in that run-down shack,' Jacob finally decided to pipe up.

'Oh, you do want to speak to me after all, DS Wright. Yes, it was me who captured all of those women. Have you guessed which one I am yet?' They both kept their eyes on her.

'I'm guessing by starving your victims, you like to think you're Famine?' Jacob announced.

'Correct!' Ruth shouted at the top of Felicity's lungs. 'So, you have me and my brother, Damien. Which means you either have Cain or Esther?'

'Your turn to guess,' Jacob joked.

Ruth smiled. 'I'm guessing you've got Cain? He was always too stupid, thinking he knows better.'

'Just like me, you've guessed right. Which one is he then?' Jacob asked.

'Well he held your DCI against his will, didn't he? So it's got to be obvious as there are only two left to guess from.'

'It was Lily that held him there. Cain was just an accomplice,' Jacob burst out.

'Calm down, DS Wright. Do you really think she'd do it all on her own?'

Jacob sat in silence, not wanting another outburst like he'd just had.

'My guess is Cain is Conquer. Makes sense, him and Lily keeping Barnes prisoner. Did he also help you capture the girls?' Ally took over in asking the questions.

'No, but he'd sure take the credit.'

Ruth kept that creepy, psychotic grin on her face. She was totally different to the others. She knew how to push certain buttons on the detectives, getting the reaction from them she wanted.

'The only help I got was from my fellow sister, Esther. And you're soon going to find out how much fun she really is,' Ruth continued, hysterically laughing, leaning back in her chair with her arms folded.

Ally whispered in Jacob's ear as Ruth smirked at them. Her solicitor was petrified and worried about what was going on in the room.

'That makes her sister Pestilence,' she whispered.

'Which means we might have a huge problem on our hands,' he said.

Ally and Jacob turned their attention back to Ruth.

'One more question, Ruth. Do you know what your sister, Esther, is planning?' Ally asked.

'It's a secret,' she answered, putting her finger to her lip before laughing again.

'Interview terminated at 5.34 pm,' Ally announced before stopping the tape. 'Thank you, Ruth. You can return Felicity now.'

Ally and Jacob left the room with Felicity's solicitor close behind them.

'I think she's going to need a new solicitor,' he said, before scurrying off.

'Well, that was...' Ally was speechless.

'I know,' Jacob replied after a slight spot of silence.

The pair of them were dazed and exhausted from the interview. Neither of them knew if it was an act or whether it was genuine. Barnes came running down the corridor to meet them as they wandered back to the CID.

'Are you two alright?' he asked.

'Yeah, just slightly freaked out,' said Ally.

'We need to work out who Esther is. Finding a fourth person, suffering from Dissociative Identity Disorder within our radius, could narrow down who our next suspect will be. Hopefully, we can get them in time before more bodies start piling up,' Jacob expressed his concerns and his next step.

'I'll talk to Ethan,' Ally announced before leaving him and Barnes in the hallway.

'How are you, Jacob?'

'I'm fine, be better when we've got all four of them behind bars,' he replied.

After the crazy day he had, Jacob had forgotten all about envelopes filled with photos he'd been receiving. He'd not even given it a second thought. Someone had been targeting him, watching him, and at this moment, he didn't care.

They entered the CID when Barnes called everybody into the briefing room. Once everyone was inside, Barnes filled them in on the investigation, no matter how weird the details were. Some laughed and sniggered, but Barnes gave them the stare, making it known he could still scare his officers. This was no laughing matter to him. It was as serious an investigation as any other, even if it was borderline strange.

Once the briefing was over, Jacob wandered outside for some fresh air, reflecting on the disturbing and slightly terrifying day he'd had. He thought the strange and weirdness was behind him when he discovered Lily was the head of the cult that had killed a group of local women, but he was wrong. It was like it was magnetised to him, like a plague. *Why do I have these visions? And why do I always get these supernatural cases?* It was like the powers that be wanted him to solve the strange crimes.

Ally exited the building and leant on the same rails in which Jacob was leaning on.

'Hey,' she greeted him.

'How'd you find me?'

'It's not hard,' she chuckled. 'You're either getting fresh air or...' She stopped, knowing the words she was about to say next, would hurt him. 'I'm sorry,' she apologised.

'What for?' he asked.

'I think we both know what I was about to say next.'

'About my drinking problem?' She stayed silent and ashamed. 'It's fine. I'm trying every day. One step at a time, but I'll get there,' he tried to make her feel better.

'Jacob, do you really think these people are telling the truth? That they are the four horsemen?'

'I'm not ruling it out. There are so many things I'd like to tell you...'

'I've got time,' she smiled.

'Maybe one day,' he returned the smile. 'Shall we get back to work?' He removed himself off the railings.

They both walked back inside the station to witness their colleagues running around in a frantic panic.

'What's going on?' Ally asked Barnes, who was halfway through putting his coat on.

'Another body has been discovered, covered in blood,' he announced to them.

The pair of them chased after Barnes as he sprinted for the car park. As he jumped inside his Jaguar, Ally and Jacob followed. Ally in the passenger seat and Jacob in the back. They had no idea whether this body would be connected to their case, but it had to be. They needed it to be.

Chapter 19

Scarlett arrived home later that night. It had been a busy day, let alone a busy week. She couldn't wait to climb into her own bed, but her home phone was bleeping with messages that hadn't been listened to. She didn't have the time nor the strength to sit there and listen to calls about where she was and others that would possibly ask if she was alright after they'd heard the news.

She flicked on her hallway light and fell flat on her sofa, too exhausted to move. Before she realised it, her eyes were closing slower and slower until she fell into a deep sleep. It wasn't long before she was awake again. Her dreams quickly turned to nightmares as all that was on her mind was her kidnapping and being held prisoner. Her strong will and bravery suddenly turned to mush thinking about the past few days and what she'd been through. Tears started to flood down from her eyes, her thoughts remained on her trauma and the other victims inside that room.

A noise startled Scarlett, making her jump out of fright. Her heart beat fast as she slowly removed herself from the sofa, one foot at a time. She crept towards the window to see a cat balancing itself on her garden furniture. Scarlett sighed with relief, knowing there was nobody outside waiting to pounce on her again.

Deciding she needed a drink, she headed towards the kitchen and opened the cupboard, removing half a bottle of vodka and pouring herself a glass. After a sip, she started to relax slightly. *That's better*, she thought, lifting the glass back to her lips and emptying it down her throat. Images of her kidnapping came flooding back, the moment she was taken and hurled into the back of a van. The colour of the van and the face of her kidnapper was still blurry.

Pouring herself another glass of vodka, she made her way back to her sofa, hoping it would send her straight off to sleep. She perched on the edge, knocked back the drink and spread herself along the sofa, laying flat, trying to close her eyes. She hoped for a fantastic night's sleep, but she knew that wouldn't happen.

As Scarlett lay awake, she listened to the sound of silence. Nothing but stillness filled the air. It was awfully quiet, not even the sound of traffic was hitting her ears. Her eyes just stared above at the ceiling. She needed to sleep but didn't want to, as the thought crossed her mind that somebody may be spying and waiting for her to drift off. Her tired eyes blinked slower and slower until she fell asleep. Nothing could wake her, not even the sound of someone breaking in.

Barnes drove his Jag up to the police cordon outside of the car park on Birmingham High Street. As they exited the car, they showed the uniformed officer their police badges before entering the crime scene where they were met by Sarah and Brian.

'What have we got?' Barnes inquired.

'A couple arrived back at their car when they noticed a pool of dried blood outside the back doors of the van,' Sarah informed them as they approached the van on the second floor.

The group arrived at the van which was surrounded by forensics. Chloe Fisher circled the van taking photos of all the evidence laying nearby. The back doors of the van were wide open and all the peering eyes could see the battered body of a woman lying in her own blood.

'Are there any cameras around here?' Barnes asked.

'Just your usual security style ones,' Sarah replied. 'Ethan's already checking them out.'

Barnes peeked in, getting a good look at the body, and noticed Julia Higgins in a white forensic suit, checking over the body, which was surrounded by tools and workman's equipment.

'Evening,' he greeted.

'Joe,' she announced his presence.

'Have you got an idea of how she died?'

'I can't give you a definite answer, but by the ligature marks on her neck
I think she was strangled, but I don't think it killed her. Her head seems to have been hit by a heavy object

on more than one occasion. My initial guess is the assailant strangled her, thought they'd killed her, but when she woke, they got scared and grabbed the closest object and hit her repeatedly with force, bludgeoning her to death. Found her driving license inside her bag. Her name's Natalie Dixon.'

'Have you got an estimated time of death?'

'From the dried blood to the decomposition of the body, I'd say the time of death would roughly be around two days.'

'Thank you, Julia. Can you get back to me when you've got confirmation?'

'Of course, Joe. Don't I always?' she smiled.

Barnes just smiled and nodded before he strolled back to his team to give them an update.

'Julia has just confirmed our victim's name is Natalie Dixon. She died of blunt force trauma to her head after attempted strangulation. Julia has a rough time of death of the 23rd which matches our time frame with Jack Roberts' blood-stained clothes and the night we arrested him,' he explained. 'Julia has also theorised what might have happened.'

'Let's hear it then, boss,' Ally spoke up.

'She seems to think our assailant tried to strangle Natalie, thought they succeeded until she woke up. Then they hit her hard in the head with an object to finish her off,' he informed them.

'Problem is, there's no murder weapon,' Sarah told him.

'Well done, Sarah,' he laughed. 'Guess whose just nominated themselves for a murder weapon search?'

Everyone laughed, except for Sarah, who gave Barnes a sarcastic smile as she placed on latex gloves and began to lead the search of the car park. Barnes strolled over towards the security office with Jacob and Ally, to see what Ethan had found.

'Have you got anything?' Barnes asked.

Ethan glanced up from the monitor to see Barnes, then returned his eyes to the screen.

'Yes, boss. Come have a look at this.'

The three of them crowded around Ethan and the footage. Once he pressed play, Ethan saw his boss smile with glee.

'We've got him!' he cheered as his eyes fixated on Jack Roberts, exiting the transit van. 'Ethan, burn me a copy please.'

Ethan said nothing, just nodded, and Barnes skipped happily back to the scene. Ally and Jacob followed close behind again.

'I just can't believe that is the same guy we met, crying on his doorstep,' Ally said.

'I know. It goes well with the D.I.D theory,' replied Jacob.

'And I'm starting to believe it even more after seeing that footage. I don't think he meant to kill his wife.'

'Sometimes killers can put on the best performances, worthy of an Oscar.'

They caught up with Barnes who was informing Brian on the footage when Sarah returned clutching an evidence bag in her hand. Inside the clear bag sat a bloodied hammer.

264

'Guess what I've found,' she smiled with a cheesy grin.

'The missing piece of the puzzle,' Barnes said. 'Brian, I need you to see if this van has been reported missing. Sarah, can you look into our victim and her past? We need to find out if she knew Jack Roberts and if this is connected or just some random killing. Jacob and Ally, I need you both to re-interview Jack and see if he can elaborate on who this woman is to him. I'll inform her parents of what's happened here.'

All of them dispersed and went their own ways with their current tasks, leaving Barnes staring into the van, taking one last look at Natalie Dixon, laying inside unrecognisable.

Belle arrived home to a dark, empty apartment. *Where is everyone?* she wondered as she made her way through to the kitchen. She worried about Kate after seeing her storm out of the cafe to meet the guy who claimed to be her real father. *What if he's taken her? I'm sure she's fine.* Horrible thoughts kept drifting through her mind.

Belle switched the kitchen light on and placed her dinner in the oven. After her shift, she'd gone for a few drinks with Ben, trying to take her mind off Kate and their argument, before arriving home. Her ears could hear keys jingling from the door. Kate made an appearance as she arrived home and Belle stormed over to her, angry and upset from worrying.

'I've been worried about you!' she shouted. 'Where have you been?'

'With my dad. My real dad,' she replied with a cocky tone.

'You can't trust this man, not yet anyway. There must be a reason why your mum never told you about him,' Belle tried to explain, but Kate just walked past her, not giving her the time of day. 'You can ignore me all you like, but I'm worried for you, Kate, and so are your brother's.'

Kate turned back to face Belle. 'I've told you, they're not my brother's. And you're not even family, so why do you care?'

She slammed her bedroom door shut, leaving Belle alone once again. She released a tear from her eye, thinking about what Kate had said. "*You're not even family*." Them words hit Belle hard. She thought she'd finally found a family, but she must have thought wrong. Feeling the need to move on, Belle searched through websites on her phone, looking for a place to rent. *It's going to be a long night*, she thought.

She sat down on the sofa, flicking through her phone, when she decided she needed some background noise. So she turned the TV on, and her eyes witnessed the horror of a news story. The reporter was telling the story of a body found inside a van. The news crew had snippets of the car park and the detectives coming out. Belle caught a glimpse of

Jacob and his team. She knew he wouldn't be home anytime soon and that she'd be all alone with her thoughts.

She decided to call Ben, asking him to meet as she didn't want to stay in the apartment a minute longer. He agreed to see her and go for dinner, so she turned the oven off, grabbed her coat and headed for the door. She paused momentarily, wondering if she should talk to Kate, but the anger rose up inside of her by her comment earlier. She shut the door behind her, not giving Kate a second thought.

Barnes arrived at Natalie Dixon's parents home, not wanting to break the news to them. As he stepped up towards the front door, Barnes noticed it was slightly ajar. Pushing the door open slightly he poked his head through, unsure of what he'd find. Making his way through the hallway, something caught his eyes below him. A few dark spots on the carpet, he wondered if it was what he thought it was. *Could it be blood?*

Barnes entered the living room, still too dark for him to get a clear image of his surroundings. His fingers found the light switch and once the light reached the room, all he could see was a man and a woman tied to chairs, decomposed.

'I think I've found Mr and Mrs Dixon,' he said, pulling the phone from his pocket. 'Jacob, I've found her parents and they're dead. They appear to have been tortured. I need you and Ally to press pause on that interview for the moment and get down here.'

'Yes, boss,' Jacob replied before Barnes hung up.

Barnes called it in and arranged for another forensic team to canvas the house. A thought crossed Barnes' mind. *Did he grab Natalie from her home? But why kill her parents? It's defiantly starting to look as if this was a targeted murder.*

Ally and Jacob arrived moments later, seeing Barnes sat outside of the house.

'What happened?' Ally asked.

'I came up to the house and saw the door was open. I entered and found them in there like that,' Barnes explained.

'Okay, boss. Forensics should be here shortly,' Jacob informed him.

'I don't get it. Why would Jack Roberts want them dead? Plus there are no signs of blood or lacerations on either of them. This doesn't fit Jack's M.O,' Barnes continued.

'Maybe it wasn't,' Jacob spoke up his theory.

'What do you mean?'

'Don't forget, we still have a fourth suspect out there.'

'Esther!' Ally yelled.

Forensics and other police officers suddenly arrived on the scene. The police cordoned off the house, while the forensic team got themselves ready.

Upon entry, the forensic officer swabbed the blood on the carpet before moving through to the living room while the rest of the team travelled into other rooms. Julia Higgins pulled up outside the police cordon and Barnes rose to his feet to greet her.

'What happened here?' she asked.

'More death and murder,' Barnes explained in one sentence.

'Is it our victim's parents?'

'I presume so. We've not had confirmation yet.'

'Right. I'll go and get myself ready,' Julia said before walking away.

An hour passed before Julia exited the house and informed Barnes of her first analysis of the bodies.

'They were injected with some kind of substance. I won't know what until the autopsy. There are no lacerations, no signs of torture. This doesn't fit the same profile as our last victim,' Julia explained.

'Whose blood do you think could be in the hallway?'

'Maybe their daughter? This might have been where she was taken.'

'Thanks, Julia. We'll come by your office tomorrow,' Barnes informed her before she went back to her car. 'I'm gonna head home,' he announced to the team. 'We'll pick up from where we left off tomorrow.'

Barnes strolled back to his car, sat inside and sighed loudly. He was exhausted and his eyes were sore. His thoughts drifted from the case to his ex-wife, wondering how she was as he removed his phone from his jacket, placing it to his ear.

'Hi, Vanessa. Sorry to call you so late. I've just been wondering how you are?'

'I'm getting there. I'm just so glad you were there,' she said. 'I don't know what might have happened if you weren't.'

'I'm just happy you're okay and getting better.'

'Joe, why don't you come over?'

'I don't think that's a good idea, V,' he replied, not wanting to say no, but he didn't want to have his heartbroken for a second time. 'I'll speak to you soon.'

Barnes ended the call and started his ignition to start his drive home. He needed a good night sleep, but the nightmares of his torture always stopped that from happening.

Jacob unlocked the door to his dark apartment, wondering if anyone was home. Dropping onto the sofa he flicked the television on and watched the news. The first feature was about the local canal and the graffiti artists, then they began to talk about the murder he was investigating. He'd had enough murder for one day, so he turned it off and picked himself up to go to bed.

As he entered his room, he thought he heard movement coming from outside the bedroom. His initial thought was an intruder, but then remembered he lived with two teenage girls. Opening his bedroom door, he caught a glimpse of a drunken Belle stumbling into the apartment.

'Belle?'

She paused still, squinting her eyes at Jacob to catch a glimpse of him. She began to speak but the words didn't make sense from drunken slur. She stumbled to the sofa and fell on top. Jacob helped her get comfortable and grabbed a blanket to place over her. Belle was asleep within minutes, leaving Jacob to return to bed.

Laying there, thoughts of the case whirled around his mind. Thoughts of the victims, the suspects and their alter-ego's, the horsemen were all he could think about. His eyes began to close as he drifted off into a deep sleep.

Something spooked Jacob, making him sit up and stare into the corner of the room. Movement in the darkness caught his eye, spooking him.

'Is someone there?' he asked.

Nobody answered, but Jacob's eyes caught an outline of someone's body. As he squinted to get a better image, he noticed two eyes staring into his from the shadows.

'Who are you?' Jacob shouted. 'What do you want?'

But the figure never answered, frightening him even more. They leant forward, entering into the light, revealing their true face. Jacob's vision became blurry as the figure's face became more clear, and suddenly Jacob woke from his dream.

The blinding light from the sun, peering between the blinds, warmed Jacob as he awoke from his nightmare. His body was covered and dripping in sweat, so he jumped out of bed and ran straight into the shower. The cold trickling water cooled his overheated body.

Once he cleaned himself, Jacob headed to the kitchen for breakfast, where he was met by Kate. She sat quietly eating her breakfast, not wanting to speak to Jacob. She raised another spoonful of cereal as he entered.

'Good morning, Kate,' he greeted her, but she stayed silent. 'Kate, please talk to me. We need to move past this. I'm sorry for keeping it from you, but you've got to understand why I did it.'

Kate said nothing, just removed herself from her seat, grabbed her coat and bag and headed out the door. Jacob tried to follow her as she exited the apartment but she slammed the door in his face. Belle lifted herself off the sofa in a jumping movement as the door slammed.

'Is everything okay?' she mumbled.

'Just Kate,' he briefly explained, walking back to the kitchen.

Belle followed him. 'Jacob, I've got to tell you something.'

'Okay,' he replied, shuffling about in the fridge.

'She's been speaking with her dad,' she announced to him.

'Belle, she's a grown kid. She can speak to him as much as she likes.'

'I know, but I don't think she should. There must have been a reason why her mother kept him from her.'

'As long as she's safe and happy, so am I. I just hope she can forgive me.'

Barnes entered the station at 8.02 am, and locked himself away in his office, shut the blinds, keeping the world out. He was extremely tired and didn't get much sleep. Julia Higgins called just after 8.30 am, bringing him out of his daydream and back to reality.

'Morning, Joe. I have the results on the post mortem of Natalie Dixon and her parents. My initial thoughts were correct with Natalie's death. She was strangled but that's not what killed her. It was the blunt force trauma. But her parents were killed by a poison injected into their bloodstream through a needle in their neck. They died twelve hours later as the symptoms began to take effect.'

'Wow, that's a lot of information to take in this early in the morning,' he joked.

'This is no time to joke, Joe,' she snapped.

'I'm sorry, Julia.'

'We might be looking at a major incident if you don't find their killer.'

'What do you mean?'

'I think whoever they are, they're planning something big. Those women who were locked away, I believe they were guinea pigs for an experiment. I think the suspect is going to advance the poison. I've contacted the specialists in the public health sector as well as...'

Barnes cut her off, 'What's going on, Julia?'

'I think we've got a terrorist incident on our hands,' she announced, shocking Barnes to his core.

'Thanks, Julia,' Barnes said before putting the phone down.

He sat in his chair momentarily, just for a few seconds before he got on the phone to his senior officer to inform them of the situation. Another half-hour passed when Jacob entered the office, with Ally tailing behind him. As they sat down at their desks, Barnes exited his darkened office and marched towards them with haste.

'Everyone in the briefing room in an hour,' he shouted for everyone to hear. 'Contact Sarah and Brian, I want them here for this too,' he asked Ally and Jacob before heading back into his office.

'I'll call them,' Ally said, picking the phone up off her desk.

'What do you think that's about?' Ethan asked from the other side of Jacob's desk.

'I have no idea,' Jacob replied. 'He might have discovered something.'

Ally put the phone down and zoned in on their conversation.

'Sarah said she'll call Brian. Any ideas on what Barnes is going to say?' she asked them both.

'Not really, but it sounded important,' Jacob answered.

It was 9.13 am when Sarah and Brian burst through the doors, rushing in as if they were late.

'What have we missed? What's the big news?' Sarah questioned them, gasping for breath.

'We don't know yet, the briefing's at ten,' Ally informed her.

'Good, I'm glad we're not late,' she sighed with relief as she turned and walked to her desk.

Barnes called the briefing at 10 am, and everyone flooded into the room and took a seat around the table. Barnes stood at the top of the table with the investigation boards behind him.

'I don't really know how to start this meeting,' he started. 'This morning I had a call from Julia Higgins who worked through the night doing the post mortem on our victims. Her theory for Natalie Dixon's death is correct, but her parents were murdered by someone else. They were poisoned by an unknown substance, which killed them within a twelve-hour time scale. Julia seems to think whoever is in control of this substance is modifying it to spread at a quicker rate. This is now labelled as a major terrorist threat. From the information we've collected, we think our suspect is going by the alias Esther. She might possibly be suffering from Dissociative Identity Disorder like our other suspects. I don't want anybody to tell family or friends or the public. We need to keep this under wraps for now. Please be careful out there and if anyone has any questions, please come and see me in my office.'

The crowd dispersed, leaving the team of five sitting in their seats. Barnes remained standing at the front of the room.

'A terrorist incident?' Ally said, unsure of what she had just heard.

'That's what I said, DI Miller.'

'I can't believe it, sir,' Jacob spoke up.

'Jacob, Ally, I need you both to get as much information out of Mr Roberts as you can. Sarah and Brian, you two need to ask Felicity James if she or her alter-ego know anything more,' he barked his orders.

'Yes, boss,' Sarah agreed, before dragging Brian out of the briefing room.

'We need to find this woman before this situation gets any worse,' Barnes said, scared and frightened.

Chapter 20

'Mr Roberts, we need to know who the fourth horseman is?' Ally asked.

'My name isn't Mr Roberts and I don't know anything other than her name is Esther.'

'Is Esther her real name or her alias?'

'What do you think?' he smirked.

'We've got no time for your games!' Jacob shouted and banged his fist on the table.

'DS Wright, you guys are barking up the wrong tree. I don't work with other people. If you're looking for her accomplice, you should be looking into my sister.'

'We've already got detectives interviewing her as we speak. We want to know if you have any relevant information that could help us locate her,' Ally interrupted.

'I don't, sorry,' he replied with a smirk across his face.

'We know you killed Natalie Dixon.' Jack continued to smile at Ally. 'We have CCTV evidence of you leaving the van in which we found Natalie's body. What we don't understand is, why are Natalie's parents dead? And on the same night? But killed differently?'

Jack placed his elbows on the table again and leant forward. 'And you think I killed them?'

'No. Your M.O is totally different. This killer was more cunning and planned. Your murders are messy and unskillful,' she replied, trying her best to aggravate him. 'We also think whoever killed the parents was working with Felicity... Sorry, I mean Ruth. Isn't that what you horsemen call her?'

Jack sat back in his chair, continuing to smile, angering both Ally and Jacob as time was of the essence. He kept his mouth shut, seeing Ally bursting with frustration because of it.

'Just tell us, why Natalie? What did she do to deserve to be killed?' Ally continued.

'Why should I make it easy for you by giving you all the answers? Why does there have to be a reason for why I killed her?' he continued to smirk.

'There's always a reason. You killed your wife because she was having an affair with your neighbour. Then your neighbour accuses you of murdering your wife in front of the whole street, so you killed him before he could get any closer to the truth, and this whole time you've sent us on a wild goose chase about a disfigured man, who you say, has been stalking you?'

'But you have no evidence linking me to those murders, do you? So, it's just hearsay.'

Ally was getting riled and Jack knew it.

'Hannah Jones is another piece of the puzzle that isn't fitting right. We know you killed her, but don't know why. She escaped from Felicity and you just happened to be there, taking a walk at the exact same place? I think you were working with Felicity and her accomplice, Esther. She called you, telling you that Hannah had escaped. You searched for her and when you found her, you killed her. Esther was also there when you kidnapped Natalie. Esther is the one who poisoned her parents. The connection is there, but what we don't know is why? Why did you and Esther kill Natalie and her parents?'

'That's a fantastic story, DI Miller,' Jack said while clapping his hands. 'But again, your job is to find out why.'

Suddenly there was a knock at the door, and Jacob announced a pause for the purpose of the tape before they stepped out of the interview room. Ethan was standing there, anxious about something.

'What is it, Ethan?' asked Ally.

'I found something. I don't know how I missed it, but...'

'Ethan, get to the point,' Jacob cut him off short.

'Natalie Dixon is the doctor who treated Felicity James and Nathan Lawrence a few years back,' he informed them.

'What about a connection with Jack Roberts?'

'There isn't one.'

Ally stood still, thinking for a moment before turning to Jacob.

'Then why did Jack kill Natalie? Did he do it for the others?'

'Most likely. There's no link between him and Natalie, but there are links between him and the others, which means he's either doing their dirty work or he wants to impress his new friends,' Jacob added his theory.

'Are you still believing the split personality lies now?' she asked him.

'I'm not sure. I'm starting to re-think my first thoughts about Jack Roberts and his D.I.D diagnosis.'

'Let's hope Sarah and Brian are having more luck with Felicity,' she added.

Sarah and Brian sat inside the interview room alone with Felicity. Her confident alter-ego was sat across the table from them.

'Felicity...'

'Ruth,' she interrupted.

'Ruth. Can you please tell us why you and Esther wanted to keep those women hostage in the farm shack?' Sarah commenced the interview.

'For fun,' she replied shortly and grinned creepily.

'What was Esther's plan with these women?'

Ruth let out a screech of a laugh. 'She wanted to kill them, slowly and watch them decompose.'

'What do you mean? Is that why you starved them, to watch them die slowly?' Sarah continued asking questions.

'No, that was my plan. That's how I like to kill.'

'Is that because you're Famine?' Brian asked, trying his best not to laugh, but he slipped out a smile.

'Yes.'

Sarah carried on. 'So, that means Esther must be Pestilence?'

Ruth nodded.

'What is she planning to do? Obviously, her plan is the big plan,' Sarah said, knowing it would annoy Ruth.

'All our plans are big plans, it's just she's not sat inside a prison cell,' she said, disappointingly.

'Then help us and her plan won't get as far as yours,' Sarah pleaded.

'I know what you're trying to do, detective, and it's not going to happen,' she sat smiling, infuriating Sarah.

Then there was a knock at the door and they paused the interview. When they exited the room, they caught eyes on Jacob, Ally and Ethan, standing there.

'This better be important?' Sarah asked them.

'Oh, it is,' Jacob told her.

'Felicity and Nathan Lawrence were both patients of Natalie Dixon,' Ally informed Sarah and Brian. 'Natalie was their doctor and we know Jack Roberts killed her but don't know why. There's no connection between Jack and Natalie, but we know Jack killed her and he killed her for a reason.'

'So, you want us to ask the question to Felicity?' Brian asked.

Jacob and Ally nodded before Sarah and Brian re-entered the room and commenced the interview.

'Ruth, if what you say about having another personality is true and that is your name, we know

Natalie Dixon was your doctor. She was murdered last night by Jack Roberts. What we are trying to figure out is why? There's no connection between Jack and Natalie, but there is between her and you. Did any of you ask Jack to kill Natalie?' Sarah stated her theory.

'Good story,' she laughed. 'I'm finished with this interview now.' Ruth faded away and Felicity's personality came back, panicked and frantic. 'What happened? Why am I back in here?' she asked the detectives.

Sarah and Brian looked at one another, before terminating the interview and left the room. The pair of them wandered back to the CID and Sarah gave the team the nod to follow them into the briefing room. Barnes was sat inside as they entered, staring closely at the investigation board, and turned around as they strutted through closing the door behind them.

'What's going on?' Barnes inquired.

'She's not telling us anything. We have no idea why Jack killed Natalie Dixon, no idea who Esther is and the more we poke, the less they talk,' said Sarah.

'I think I might have an idea who our mysterious Esther is?' Ethan piped up.

'Then please inform us, DC Robinson,' Barnes asked.

'I searched for any other people who booked into the hospital with certain qualities that matched the symptoms of D.I.D and also things that match our Esther and got a match. Her name is Jenny Reynolds. She was admitted a few months ago because of post-traumatic stress and self-harming and was under the watchful eye of...'

'Natalie Dixon?' Ally guessed.

'Correct, DI Miller,' he replied.

'Have you got an address?' Jacob asked.

'Yeah, I'll send it to you now.'

Jacob and Ally made their way out of the station as Ethan sent them the address of Jenny Reynolds. Sarah and Brian re-entered the interview room with gleaming smiles.

'Sorry to keep you waiting, Felicity. We really need to talk with Ruth again,' Sarah began.

'I have no control over when she takes hold.'

'The thing is, she holds information on our latest suspect and we need her to tell us where she is and what she plans to do,' explained Sarah.

'I don't hold the power to bring her forward, only she can do that. She comes and goes as she pleases,' she cried, nervous and scared of being imprisoned.

'Felicity, we need you to try to bring her out. I know you're scared but this could really help us.'

Felicity sat quietly, tears dripping down her cheeks, knowing that Ruth didn't want to show herself. No matter what was to happen at this moment, she knew she'd be locked up for the rest of her life.

Ally parked outside of Jenny's apartment building. Jacob's stomach rumbled as it hit 1.30 pm. The thought of food made his stomach groan louder, alerting Ally that he was hungry.

'We'll get some lunch after this,' she said.

'I was hoping you didn't hear that,' he laughed.

The pair of them jumped out of the car and walked towards the building entrance. There was an intercom with the names of the residents on it.

'Think we've come to the right place. Look,' Ally said, pointing to Jenny's name on the buzzer.

'We need to find another way in,' Jacob told her. 'The element of surprise.'

'I think you're right,' Ally replied, trying to think of another way inside.

Minutes passed before someone left the building, opening the door. Ally showed them her police badge before the woman let her inside the building.

'Do you remember what floor she lives on?'

'Yes, the second, apartment two,' Jacob answered.

They thought about taking the elevator but decided it might be quicker to take the stairs. As they reached the second floor, Ally peered around the corner to make sure the hallway was empty before they moved on to Jenny's apartment.

'Apartment two,' she announced quietly for Jacob.

Jacob knocked three times before announcing they were police. After waiting a few seconds, there was still no answer. Jacob tried pushing the door handle downwards, hoping for it to be unlocked, and when the door opened, his facial appearance showed how shocked he was.

'Usually, people lock their doors,' he whispered as they entered.

Jenny Reynolds' apartment was elegant and was as top of the range as they come. Ally started glancing around to find anything they could use in evidence, while Jacob's eyes caught a glimpse of a few photos hanging on the walls. A feeling of familiarity hit Jacob as he stared at what he believed to be their suspect. His eyes were diverted to a photo of Jenny with Ella Morgan.

'Ally, come check this out,' he grabbed her attention.

'What is it? What's wrong?'

Jacob continued staring as he couldn't believe what his brain was telling him.

'I've seen Jenny before,' he informed her. 'She was the friend of Ella Morgan.'

'One of the victims from our last case? The one with...'

Jacob stopped her and announced the one name he hated hearing. 'Lily.'

'Do you think there's a connection?' she asked.

'I don't know. I hope not. I put this Lily situation to bed. I don't want her ruining my life any further.'

Ally continued taking a look around the apartment, while Jacob took a photo of the pictures hanging on the wall and sent them to Barnes. Not five minutes passed before Barnes phoned him.

'Am I seeing this right?' he asked.

'You are, boss,' Jacob answered.

'Is there a connection between these two cases?'

'We don't know yet, sir.'

'Okay, call me if you find anything.'

Jacob ended the call and continued searching the apartment for anything that could help them locate Jenny. Time passed and more theories spun around in Jacob's mind. *Is the death of Ella what caused her to have post-traumatic stress and made her self harm?* Something wasn't adding upright.

'Something's not right,' he spoke up. 'Jenny was shaken up when she found out her friend had died. I don't believe it was an act. I also believe it's the reason for her having post-traumatic stress. But for her to go and be a part of all of this, no way.'

They moved on to the bedroom as they continued to discuss Jenny's personality and the facts when Jacob discovered a little black zipped wallet. They both watched in anticipation as he unzipped it, revealing needles inside.

'As a police officer, Jacob, we go by the facts and here we have needles and empty vials inside. If we send this off for testing and it's a match, we have our suspect. We have our Esther,' Ally told him.

Moments later, teams of uniformed officers showed up on the scene, digging through drawers and cupboards. Barnes turned up to help not long after the officers arrived. Ally's phone began to buzz, while she read through notebooks at Jenny's kitchen counter. It was an unknown number.

'DI Miller,' she answered, but there was a slight pause before the other person spoke.

'Good afternoon, Detective Inspector,' the female voice greeted. 'I hope you find what you are looking for.'

'Who is this?' Ally demanded to know, grabbing the attention of Barnes and Jacob.

'I think you know who this is.'

'Esther?'

'Bingo.'

'What do you want?'

'I think you know everything at this point. The body I've taken hold of, the people I've killed.'

'We know you've been helping Felicity...' Ally said before she was interrupted.

'Ruth, you mean? Please use their real names, DI Miller.'

'No. Their real names are Jack Roberts, Nathan Lawrence and Felicity James. And yours is Jenny Reynolds. I've had enough of this second personality bullshit. It ends now!' she shouted down the phone at her.

'Do you want to know what got Natalie Dixon killed?' Jenny asked.

'Please inform me.'

'Making deals with the devil.'

'I don't understand what you mean.'

'She was arrogant, thinking lightning couldn't strike in the same place more than once. I hear Jenny's screams every minute of every day. Felicity, Nathan and Jenny wanted her dead for what she did to them.'

'I don't believe you.'

'I don't care what you believe.'

'Why her parents? Why did you kill them?'

'For fun. They were a test to see how the modifications worked,' Esther chuckled. 'And there's more to come.'

'Why the girls in the farm shack?' she continued trying to get answers.

'They were going to be part of my experiment, but stupid Ruth got in the way.'

'So, starving these girls was not part of your plan?'

'No. Has Ruth not told you who she is?'

'If you mean in your fictitious world, then yes, she has.'

'Then you know that wasn't part of my plan, just her's.'

'Why did you call me?' Ally asked.

'To tell you that you'll have another body on your streets within the next twelve hours. See you soon, DI Miller,' she answered before the phone went quiet.

'What's wrong?' Jacob asked.

'Who was that?' Barnes questioned her.

'That was Jenny Reynolds, or should I say, Esther. There's going to be another body within the next twelve hours,' Ally announced.

Chapter 21

Kate met her father again that afternoon, unaware to Jacob and Belle's knowledge. They sat inside the restaurant, tucking into their dinner when Craig began to stare at her.

'Why are you staring at me?' Kate asked.

'I just can't believe how much you look like your mother,' he explained. 'I'm glad we can do this.'

'So am I,' she smiled, forgetting about everything for a moment.

'You shouldn't be too hard on your family. They don't know me and wanted to protect you and keep you safe.'

'But they lied to me and kept secrets from me. How can I trust them again?'

'Because look at what they've done for you since your mother died. Your brother took you in and kept you safe, gave you a roof over your head. He didn't know you weren't his little sister, but when he did, did he throw you out? No, he didn't. He took care of you like nothing happened.' Kate screwed up her face, not wanting to listen to him, even though she knew he was right. 'All I'm saying is, go easy on him. He still loves you like you're his sister,' he continued.

She nodded as a tear started to form in her eye. Knowing she was wrong about how she treated Jacob and Belle, it was time for her to make amends.

'Can you excuse me for a minute?' she asked her father and he nodded in response.

She removed herself from the table and exited the restaurant to make a quick phone call. Her hand trembled as she didn't know how to apologise to Jacob for how she'd treated him. Kate flicked through her recent contacts and called Jacob's mobile. It rang a couple of times before going to voicemail. She sighed and entered back inside, joining her father back at the table.

'No answer?' Craig asked.

'Straight to voicemail,' she replied.

She tucked back into her food and grabbed her glass, chugging the cocktail down her throat.

'Slow down,' her father laughed.

At that moment, Kate's heart sank as she noticed Belle and Ben walking in through the front door, hoping Belle wouldn't notice her. But it was too late for her as Belle locked eyes with her.

'Come on, Ben,' Kate heard her say. 'We'll find somewhere else.'

Kate rose off her seat and rushed towards her.

'Belle, wait.' She approached her. 'I'm sorry for the way I've treated you. I know I've been a bitch...'

Belle laughed at her. 'A bitch? Kate, you made me so depressed. You told me how we're not family...'

'I know and I'm so sorry. I really am,' she interrupted her. 'I know my words don't do much, but please accept my apology?'

'I'll think about it,' Belle replied before turning around and exiting the restaurant.

For the second time, Kate rejoined her father at the table just as dessert arrived. Craig noticed something was wrong by the change in mood upon her face.

'Is everything alright?'

'I don't know,' she answered keeping her head bowed. 'She's mad at me.'

'Who was that?'

'Her name's Belle. Jacob took her in when her friend was murdered last year. We've been quite close, up until the secrets anyway.'

'I feel like I've seen her before,' Craig muttered under his breath.

'Well, she does live with me.'

'Anyway...' he said, glancing downwards at his dessert. 'This looks delicious.'

Kate had a burning question to ask while watching him scoop his ice cream into his mouth.

'Why did my mum leave you?'

Craig choked on his dessert, wondering how he was going to answer her question.

'I'm going to be honest with you, Kate,' he started. 'I was an abusive husband. I'd come home drunk and off my face with drugs and alcohol, then I'd take it out on your mum and hit her. And I mean I hit her hard enough to send her to hospital on more than one occasion.'

'I guess that's why mum was always so skittish,' she recalled.

'And that's my fault,' he began to cry.

Kate placed her hand on his back and tried to console him. It was upsetting to her seeing him like this, even in the short space of time she knew him.

'I'm sure you're sorry for how you were in the past, and I'm sure mum would've forgiven you if she was still here.'

Sitting inside the car while Ally floored it back to the station, Jacob thought about the hidden uncle that he never knew existed. *Is this how Kate feels? Betrayed? My family holds too many secrets.* He was so angry that his father had a secret life that he never told his kids about as well as other secrets. He clenched his fist at his thoughts.

'Is everything alright?' Ally asked, noticing his fist.

'Yes,' he lied, turning his head to the window, not making any eye contact.

'You're lying,' she guessed.

'I don't want to bore you.'

'Jacob, whatever it is, you need to get it off your chest, otherwise, it will eat away at you.'

'I just don't know what to do.'

'What with? Is this about your secret uncle?'

'How'd you know?' he released a slight chuckle. 'He wants to talk to explain everything, but my father lied to us his entire life. My sister isn't my sister and my father isn't her dad. He kept that from us as well as his family and I don't know why. I want to get to know him, but I'm too angry with my dad right now.'

'How does Kate feel at the moment?' she asked.

'Betrayed and angry, and now...'

Ally interrupted. 'And now you know how she feels.'

'Yeah,' he lowered his head in shame.

His phone started to buzz in his hand. Seeing Kate's number, he couldn't bear to speak with her while Ally sat next to him, so he placed the phone back inside his pocket, silenced the buzzing and ignored it.

'Have you told your brother?' Ally continued.

'Not yet. I'll call him later, I just can't find the words right now.'

'When we get back to the station, I want it to be the first thing you do,' she demanded.

'Yes, boss,' he laughed.

Ally smiled along with him. Making him happy made her happy and she truly deep down, loved making him smile. She felt extremely carefree and relaxed around him and her love for him was growing by the day.

'Have you made your mind up yet?' he asked her, hoping she'd stay in Birmingham.

'On the job in Hawaii?' He nodded in response. 'Not yet. It sounds like a great opportunity. Sun, sea, sand...'

'...And murder,' he jumped in and finished with a giggle.

She laughed along with him. 'Everything inside is telling me to jump with both feet, but my heart is telling me to stay. I've just joined this incredible team who've made me feel so welcome, and then there's you.'

He turned his head in a quick motion, looking at her as she continued to keep her focus on driving, not wanting to look at him.

'Me?'

'Yes. Jacob, you must know by now how I feel about you?' He stayed quiet, not wanting to answer. 'If there is something between you and me, then I'll stay. I know we've only known each other for a short time, but I feel this strong connection between us and I don't want to leave knowing we could have been something.'

'I don't want you to give up a dream job because of me,' he lowered his head again.

'If you don't feel the same way as I do, then just tell me.'

The car stayed quiet as Ally pulled into the car park. The awkward silence made Ally feel upset and wanting to burst out in tears. She thought he didn't want to be with her.

As the car pulled into an empty space, Jacob jumped out of the car, quicker than he'd ever done before, and phoned his brother, trying to get out of answering Ally's question.

'Hi, Adam,' Jacob said to his brother, as Ally exited the car and entered the station. 'I've got something to tell you.'

'Jacob, I was just about to phone you.'

'Why? What's wrong?' Jacob asked concerned.

'I'm going through Dad's house as we agreed, and I've found something. Maria had hidden a few letters from Kate's father. I'm really worried about Kate if she's meeting this guy.'

'Why, Adam? What have you found?' Jacob kept asking, wanting his brother to get to the point.

'He abused Maria, but that's not why he went to prison. He killed someone, Jacob. He got angry and beat them to death,' Adam informed him.

'You don't think he'd do anything to Kate, do you?' he worried.

'I wouldn't rule it out. He's dangerous, Jacob.'

'I'll call her now,' Jacob said before hanging up on his brother.

Scrolling through his phone book, he stopped at Kate's number and called her, only to hear the beeping of an engaged tone. He tapped a text message to his brother explaining before he headed inside the station.

As he made his way through the grey hallways and walked into the CID, Jacob's eyes were met with a huge group of officers, buzzing around the office.

'What's going on here?' he asked as he approached Ally.

'The terror threat has become real. We've been given more officers, resources and equipment in helping us track Esther down,' Ally explained.

'Wouldn't this be a job for counter-terrorism?'

'Yes, we're working with them. Barnes demanded us to work with them as it ties in with our case. After all, this was our case first.'

Jacob marched over to Barnes, who sat alone inside his office, watching everyone running around, and slammed the door shut.

'Boss, what on earth is going on? Ally's just told me counter-terrorism is here and we're working with them?' He started to rub his hands over his head in panic.

'That's correct,' Barnes replied calmly. 'Just take a second to calm down.'

He placed himself in the chair opposite Barnes. 'So this is a real terror threat? I can't believe this case has gone from a simple domestic murder to people with a personality disorder, to then being a terror threat.'

'I know, it's a lot to take in.'

A knock at the door reminded Jacob of the busyness outside of Barnes' office. It was the lead officer from the counter-terrorism unit, Steven Hemmings.

'I'm calling a briefing in a few minutes, Joe. Just to update everyone and I need you there too,' Hemmings said.

'No problem,' he replied, still sitting in his chair. 'I'll be there in a minute.' Steven Hemmings nodded and shut the door behind him. 'Jacob, I know you've got a lot going on at home. You don't have to be here.'

'I'll be fine. I do have one thing to ask you though.'

'Fire away.'

'Did you know my father had a twin brother?' he asked and noticed a straight look upon his face.

'Look, Jacob. I'm not going to lie to you. I knew,' he revealed.

'You knew? You knew this whole time and never said anything?'

'There's a lot about your father you don't want to know.'

Barnes noticed Hemmings giving him a wave through the window and shot out of his seat. He opened the door and left Jacob still sitting in his chair.

'Are you coming?' he asked Jacob.

Jacob snapped back to reality from thinking about what Barnes had said. Once he jumped out of the seat, he caught up with Barnes.

'We'll discuss this later,' Jacob whispered upon entering the briefing room.

Barnes joined Hemmings at the front of the room, while Jacob sat between Ally and Sarah at the table. The room was full with both teams filling every centimetre. This was a huge case to the team and it frightened most, though Jacob noticed how calm Ally was, like it wasn't the first time she'd been involved in a case this big.

'How are you so calm?' he whispered in Ally's ear.

'This isn't my first rodeo, kid,' she whispered back, then started giggling.

'Good afternoon,' Hemmings started. 'If you don't already know me, my name's Steven Hemmings. The counter-terrorism team are now working with DCI Barnes' team in finding our assailant called Esther. We believe her real name is Jenny Reynolds and she is suffering from Dissociative Identity Disorder. She could be armed and dangerous so I need everyone to be on their guard.'

Barnes began to give some information, taking over from Hemmings. 'Jenny has got her hands on a man-made disease which she is intending to use. We believe it has been altered since she last used it. We also have no idea how many hostages she's got, if she even has any, who she plans on using this virus on. I know it's not much to go on, but she's linked to other murders and suspects. She's a dangerous woman and we need to find her as soon as possible.'

'Any questions or new information, please see myself or DCI Barnes,' Hemmings finished before dispersing the team.

Barnes left and walked back into his office, sat at his desk and sighed loudly. It had been a long couple of weeks and he was feeling incredibly drained. Not giving him a minutes peace, the phone on his desk rang. It was the prison in which Lily was being housed, informing Barnes that she wanted to speak to Jacob. He'd kept the calls a secret for days, not wanting to bring Lily back into his life, but he'd seen what his father's secrets had done to him as of late.

Barnes put the phone back down, denying Lily the right to speak to Jacob. He glanced out the window and saw Jacob and Ally giggling together, making Barnes realise that Jacob had moved on. He was stuck in a dilemma. He rose up and called Jacob into his office. Barnes' hands were sweaty. He was feeling nervous and worried about how Jacob would take it.

'Sit down, Jacob,' he insisted. 'I've just had a call... Well, I've had calls all week from the prison...'

'I don't want to see her,' Jacob jumped in.

298

'Are you sure? You need to get answers from her to get closure.'

'I've already put her behind me,' he replied. 'I'm not about to reopen old wounds, boss.' Jacob got off the chair once again. 'Is that all?'

Barnes nodded and Jacob left with thoughts of Lily and the questions he sought. Lily was all he could think about all afternoon. As he sat at his desk, Jacob blurred the sounds out around him, staring into space and clicking his pen.

'Jacob, are you okay?' Ally asked him.

He snapped back to reality. 'Yes, sorry, Ally. I'm fine.'

'No, you're not.'

He sighed. 'Barnes has just told me that the prison keeps calling. Lily is requesting to see me.'

'And are you going to go?' she enquired.

'Part of me wants to stay away from her and let her rot, but the other half of me wants all my questions answered. Plus I want to know why she sent me those photos.'

'Then go, Jacob. Otherwise, you'll never get the answers you seek.'

'You're right,' he replied.

Jacob had too much going on in his life right now and couldn't concentrate on the case at hand. *Barnes is right. I need to step away from the case*, he thought as he traipsed nearer to Barnes' office. He knocked on the door and entered slowly, not wanting to leave the team during this difficult time.

'What is it, DS Wright?'

'Boss, I've been thinking about what you said. I know it's not a good time with what's going on right now but...'

'Jacob, you can have some leave. With everything that's happened in your life, your dad's death, my disappearance, you stuck by the team. Now you need to sort your life out, go and sort it. We'll be fine,' he comforted him.

Jacob replied with a smile as he rose to his feet and left. Walking to his desk, he grabbed his coat and left without saying a word. Ally and Ethan lifted their heads from their work and watched Jacob stroll out of the station.

'Where's he going?' Ethan asked Ally.

'To get some answers,' she replied.

Chapter 22

Jacob arrived outside his apartment. Worrying if Kate was inside, he slowly opened the door. Hearing talking and laughter, he thought Kate and Belle had made up but got a shock as he entered to see a strange man sat opposite Kate.

'Oh, Jacob. I didn't think you'd be home yet,' Kate said surprised as she turned her head to see who was entering.

'Who's this?' he asked, worrying about the answer.

'This is my father, Craig Ross.'

'Nice to meet you,' Craig said, holding out his hand for Jacob to shake it.

Jacob ignored him and looked at Kate. 'What's he doing here?'

Craig sat back down quietly and upset.

'He's my Dad, Jacob. You can't just ignore him and hope he'll go away,' she yelled.

'I know who he is and I don't want him in my home,' he shouted back.

'Look, I'm not here to tear you away from one another. I just want to get to know my little girl. I've already lost out on so much of her life because of my wrongdoing. ' He turned his eyes to Kate. 'I'm going to go. I'll see you soon.'

'Okay,' she replied.

Craig walked to the door before turning back to Jacob. 'It was nice to meet you, Jacob. Thanks for looking after my girl.'

Kate shut the door behind him, then gave her brother an angry glare. 'How dare you!' she continued yelling.

'How dare I? This is my place, Kate, and if I don't want him here then you should respect my wishes,' he continued the shouting match.

She huffed before going inside her bedroom and slamming the door behind her. Jacob headed to the kitchen, grabbed the bottle of whiskey and poured himself a glass. He calmed down once he'd taken a sip. Belle walked in as he released a sigh.

'Is everything alright?' she asked.

'No. I don't think it'll ever be alright,' Jacob started to break down.

'What happened?'

'She brought him here.'

'Her dad?'

'Yes.'

'What happened?' she asked.

'Not much. He left without a fuss.' Belle grabbed the whiskey bottle from his hands and grabbed herself a glass. 'What do you think you're doing?'

'Drowning my sorrows,' Belle explained.

'What sorrows?'

'All of this. I'm fed up with it all.'

'Me too, and now I'm told that Lily wants to see me,' he explained.

'And are you going to?'

'I have so many questions about everything, but I don't want to see her. She hurt me, Belle. I can never forgive her for what she's done, so if it's forgiveness she wants, she won't find any from me.'

No words were spoken, they just stood in the kitchen with nothing but their thoughts and whiskey glasses.

'How's it going with Ben?' Jacob broke the silence.

'Great. He makes me so happy.'

'I'm glad. Seems like your life is on the up,' Jacob smiled.

'I know and it's all because of your kindness,' she replied the smile.

She kissed Jacob on the cheek before making her way to her bedroom. Jacob remained in the kitchen, sad and alone, before deciding it was also time for him to go to bed. He had a big day ahead of him, full of questions and hopefully some answers. He lay his head on the pillow and drifted off quickly.

The station was flooded with officers, making Barnes feel overwhelmed and needing some fresh air. He swung his coat over his back and placed his arms through before leaving his office.

'Where are you going, sir,' Ally questioned as she watched him leave with his coat on.

'Just stepping out to get some fresh air,' Barnes answered as he left the CID.

Once he made it out to the car park, Barnes felt the cold nights breeze against his skin. His warm breath released, creating a cloud of smoke. A chill made him shiver as he glanced up to the sky.

Ally stood alongside him. 'What's on your mind?'

'Everything,' Barnes smiled.

Ally chuckled. They both stood silent for a moment, not knowing what the future was going to hold.

'It's been a strange couple of cases. Witches, Horsemen of the apocalypse, are we ever going to have any normal cases?' Ally said.

'I do hope so,' he replied. 'I'm getting a bit fed up of this supernatural crap.'

Ally laughed. 'So you do believe they could be telling the truth?'

'Maybe. I don't know. It all sounds a bit crazy.' There was another slight pause of silence before Barnes turned to walk back inside. 'Think we should get back to work.'

Ally followed him back inside the bustling station. No new information had been found, neither did they have any new phone calls from Esther. Officers were trying their hardest, backtracking the horsemen's last movements. Barnes entered his office, shut his blinds and removed the bottle of vodka from his drawer. After taking a swig, Barnes took a deep breath and took another mouthful. His life had gotten crazy and become a living nightmare the more he thought about their cases. *Witches and Possession? I must be going mad.*

Jacob woke the next morning, had breakfast, showered and hit the road to visit Lily in the slammer. His heart pounded as he drove closer to the prison, not wanting to see the woman who lied to him before killing his father. His life would never be the same again because of that woman.

Jacob pulled into the car park and reminisced about their good times together before the memories of the night he found his father dead, came flooding back. His hand clenched tight around the steering wheel. He exited his car with angry thoughts on his mind as he entered the building.

As he approached the entrance, the prison officers did the usual checks before letting him near the inmate. Once that was out of the way, they sat him in an open room while he waited for Lily to enter. His hands were full of sweat as he began to panic.

Minutes passed before she finally entered the room. Her appearance wasn't quite the same as the last time Jacob locked eyes on her. Her hair was messy and her skin pale. She shuffled along with her hands cuffed together for his safety.

'Jacob, it's good to see you,' she greeted him while the officer sat her down.

'I wish I could say the same,' he replied angrily. 'So, what was so important that you wanted to speak to me?'

'I wanted to explain.'

'Explain? You killed my father!' he shouted.

'Because he killed my sister!' she yelled back at him. 'Look, I didn't call you here for a shouting match. I just want you to hear the reasons for my actions.'

'Go ahead then, I'm listening,' he folded his arms and leant back in his chair.

'As you know, my mother went missing. My sister took care of me when we were younger until that night your father... Well, let's just say that was the night I was put into care. I spent many years trying to find out what happened to my mum, but she found me.'

Jacob leaned in, interested in her story. 'What do you mean she found you?'

'You wouldn't believe me. You'd think I've gone crazy,' she leaned back, turning away from any eye contact with him.

'Try me,' he replied, knowing how crazy his past experiences had been.

'She spoke to me in my dreams, gave me instructions to bring her back.'

Jacob interrupted. 'Back from where?'

'She's trapped somewhere, Jacob. Somewhere she can't get out of.'

'Is that why you had all those women killed?'

Lily released a tear from her eye. 'Yes. I thought it would bring her back, but then she came to me again in my dreams while I was on the run, telling me that wasn't going to bring me back, but the diamonds would.'

'Diamonds?'

'Yes. Barnes knows all about them, which is the reason why I kidnapped him and tortured him, hoping he'd tell me where they were.'

'And did he?'

'Yes.'

'So where are they?'

'Somewhere safe.'

'In evidence?'

'You'd think so, but no. I think you need to ask your boss that question,' she answered.

'Why kill my father? Did he know something more about your mother?'

'He killed my sister. It was nothing more than revenge.'

'But why? He treated you like a daughter. Did that mean nothing to you?'

'I couldn't just let him get away with what he had done just because of my feelings for you.'

'Did you enter our relationship, knowing what you were planning to do to my father?' he asked.

'Yes, but I fell deeply in love with you and still am,' she answered, trying to grab his hand, but he pulled away.

'Then why? You could have just let him live and got over what happened to your sister.'

'You can say that because it's not your family member. If it was the other way around...'

'I wouldn't have killed someone!' he shouted at her again.

'Are you sure about that?'

He stayed silent, thinking about what she'd said. He was so angry and wanted to kill her for what she'd done to him and his family, that he knew she was right. He would've killed someone.

'Why the photographs?' he continued to question her.

'What photographs?' She was confused.

'The one's you've been sending to the station and the apartment,' he answered.

'Jacob, I don't know what you're talking about.'

'Don't give me that rubbish.'

'I think you've got another admirer because I didn't send them,' she replied.

Jacob sat quiet, reviewing her answer. *If she didn't send them, then who did? Who's been watching me?*

'Something wrong?' she asked.

'I'm done here,' Jacob replied, lifting himself off his seat and walking towards the door.

'I'll be seeing you soon, Jacob,' she said calmly as he carried on walking.

Jacob was searched again upon leaving. He exited the building shortly after, entered his car and sighed, not wanting to believe Lily. *She must be the one that sent the photos.* Jacob started hitting the rim of the steering wheel as hard as he could out of anger. He was so angry, he screamed out loud before he started to cry.

He'd had enough of all the problems he faced. His sister, his ex, and his hidden uncle. Not to mention the crazy case he'd been trying to solve with his team. He was a broken man. Minutes later, Jacob wiped his tears, took a deep breath and started the ignition, driving home with nothing but the thought that someone had been watching his every move.

Upon arriving home, Jacob felt the sudden urge for another drink, not realising Kate was still home. Pouring the whiskey into a glass, he noticed her sat on the sofa, scrolling through her phone. He grabbed his glass and sat in the armchair beside the sofa, then took a swig from the glass.

'Kate. I'm really sorry about yesterday.' She glanced up from her phone. 'I know you want to get to know your father and I just want you to know I have no problem with that. I'm sorry for my behaviour last night. I was totally out of order. I've just got a lot going on at the moment,' he said before tears started to roll down his face.

Kate just stared, then moved over to him and gave him a hug. 'I'm sorry too. I've acted so childishly and spoilt. All you tried to do was look after me and I threw it back in your face. Can we move past this?' she asked, trying to comfort him.

Jacob nodded. 'Yes. Just promise me one thing?' She nodded in response. 'Just be careful.'

She nodded again. The pair of them hugged one another again, letting go of their anger and issues, throwing them away and forgiving each other as Belle entered witnessing them embraced in their hug.

'I see you two have made up?'

The pair turned their attention to Belle and smiled at her. Kate approached Belle and threw her arms around her.

'What's this for?' Belle asked.

'Because I've been a bitch. I'm really sorry for how I've treated you,' Kate apologised, then let go of Belle.

'Apology accepted,' Belle smiled with joy. 'We good now then?'

'Yes, we're good,' Kate answered. She turned back to Jacob. 'Why the change of heart anyway?'

'A similar situation. Just found out Dad didn't just keep a secret about your father, but also kept his past hidden from us. Just found out we've got an uncle and that Dad was a twin.'

'How did you find out?' she asked.

'He found me. I thought I was seeing things but I approached him and he told me who he was. He wants to explain everything, but I don't know if I want to know.'

'Wow, and I thought my family was screwed up,' Belle smirked and they all laughed along.

'Are you going to meet him?' asked Kate.

'I want to but I don't know if I should. I know nothing about the man and it seems like I know nothing about Dad now either.'

'But if you don't take the chance, you'll be sat forever wondering what if,' Kate said. 'I took that chance with my Dad and I knew nothing about him. He says he's sorry for his past and he wants to be a part of my future. Take the chance, Jacob, otherwise you might regret it.'

'I think Kate's right. You should get to know him and see what he has to say,' Belle agreed with her.

'Okay,' he replied, standing to his feet. 'I'll give him a call.'

Jacob strolled towards the kitchen, pulled his phone out and dialled the number his uncle had given him.

'Hello,' a voice answered.

'Hi, it's Jacob.'

'You ready to talk?' his uncle asked.

'Yes. Meet me at the cafe on Martineau Way in an hour,' he gave him a time and place, before ending the call.

Jacob arrived just after 3 pm and saw his uncle sat inside, holding a cup of coffee. Standing outside the cafe looking in, Jacob stared at his uncle while thinking about his father. *Why did my Dad keep him a secret? Did my Dad even know anything about his family?* Jacob couldn't delay a minute longer. Too many questions ran through his thoughts as he entered the cafe.

'Hi,' Jacob greeted him as he sat down at the table.

'I'm glad you came,' Dan replied.

'I need answers and right now you're the only one who can give them to me,' Jacob got straight to the point.

'I'll tell you anything you need to know,' he smiled.

'Did my father know he had a brother?'

'Yes. He also knew your grandmother before she passed away. You also have another uncle, but he doesn't know about me, you or anybody else. Your great grandfather kept him when he was a baby and your great grandmother helped my mother escape after she had me and your father. We're triplets and it's only me and your father who look alike.'

'My other uncle, why does he not know about the family?'

'He was poisoned by your great grandfather, inheriting the family company, his wealth and beliefs. Now he's as corrupt as him,' he explained.

'Why did my father keep you all a secret?' Jacob continued asking questions.

Dan started to laugh. 'What is this? An interrogation?' He stopped laughing after seeing Jacob's serious face. 'He wanted to keep you safe. Your uncle is a dangerous man, Jacob and so was your great grandfather.'

'Why? Who is he?'

'His name is Malcolm Harrington. He runs Harrington Labs. Stay away from him, Jacob. He's not the type of person you want to approach.'

'Why did your mum run away?'

'Because my grandfather wasn't her father, he was my Dad's. My father has been missing since before I was born. My mum always said he was trapped in another world, but me and John always thought she was crazy until we got older and did some digging. Which is one of the reasons your father joined the police force. We found information on Harrington Labs. People were going missing and still are.'

'Missing?'

'Yes. Went to work and never came home. We're still investigating it.'

'We?'

'I work for an organisation called S.T.O.R.M.'

'I've never heard of them,' Jacob told him.

'That's because they're off the radar,' he explained.

'What's the meaning behind S.T.O.R.M?'

'Don't laugh,' he smiled. 'It stands for Supernatural Tactical Operational Response Military.'

'Supernatural?' he smiled, though he didn't want to explain what he'd been through the past year, seeing ghosts that helped solve his case.

'I told you not to laugh,' he replied with a smile.

'I don't think it sounds crazy,' Jacob said, making Dan give him a strange look.

'What makes you say that?'

'Last year I started seeing the ghosts of my victims. I know that sounds nuts, but it's true. And then there's Lily.'

'Elizabeth Blackwood? We know all about her,' he admitted.

'You do?'

'Yes. Her family have been on our watch list for a while,' Dan continued.

'What do you mean?'

'Her mother went missing when she was younger, am I correct?'

'Yes,' Jacob answered, unsure of where this conversation was going.

'Her sister started a cult and began ritual killings when your father was an active police officer. Your father was given the order to kill her.'

'So, he did kill her,' Jacob said, beginning to get angry, banging a clenched fist on the table.

'No. He disobeyed his orders.'

'Why?'

'He couldn't go through with it. He kept saying something about trying to bring her in for questioning, but it was too dangerous. She was too dangerous.'

'Was my father working for S.T.O.R.M?' Jacob kept the questions coming.

'Yes, on the side.'

'What about my boss?'

'Joe Barnes? He doesn't work with S.T.O.R.M but knows of us because of John. Your father told him all about me and about our operation. I think it was him that stopped your father from completing his orders on Daisy Blackwood,' Dan explained.

'What about Lily? If her sister was so dangerous, then why is Lily still alive? She completed her sister's plan, so why is she still in prison and not on the slab?'

'Because we might need her. The night you caught her accomplices, did you notice any lights flicker?' Jacob thought for a moment. 'What about the slight earthquake? You ignored the signs of her plan completing.'

'When I went to see Lily earlier today, she mentioned something about diamonds. She mentioned Barnes had put them somewhere safe, but not in evidence. Do you have these diamonds?' Jacob asked as he began to piece things together.

'That's confidential,' Dan answered.

'I take that as a yes then,' Jacob smiled, knowing he'd got the answer he wanted.

'Jacob, there's another reason I asked to meet you. I want you to be a part of our operation at S.T.O.R.M.'

'What? Do what my father was doing? No, thank you,' he replied.

'Just have a think about it. We're on the same team, and after all, we are family.' Dan got up off his seat after finishing the last of his coffee. 'Just sleep on it, okay?' He tapped Jacob on the shoulder before leaving the cafe.

Jacob didn't know what to do. His uncle had another motive, but he'd come away with more questions than answers. Something positive had come out of this meeting. At least he knew he wasn't going insane and what he saw could be real. *But if the supernatural exists, that means our suspects could be telling the truth, and Barnes would know that*, he thought.

He wanted to phone Barnes and shout at him. He knew more than he said about everything. *Why'd he stay silent?* Jacob decided to speak to him face to face. He left the cafe, entered his vehicle and drove back to the CID.

Chapter 23

Barnes' office was surrounded by phones ringing, people talking and busybodies running all over the place. His head was pounding with an ungodly pain. He opened his desk drawer and grabbed the paracetamol that lay beside his bottle of vodka. He popped two tablets out of the plastic wrap, chucked them inside his mouth, then washed them down with the half bottle of vodka. His head rested on the back of the chair as he closed his eyes, trying his best to block out the constant ringing in the background.

There was nothing but silence as he sat resting with his eyes closed, nearly drifting off to sleep. Then a sudden knock on the door brought him out of his slumber and back to the annoying ringing of phones. *Goddamn it*, he thought silently.

'Come in,' he shouted above the noise. Jacob entered and sat opposite him, red-faced, staring at him angrily. 'I thought I told you to take some time off?'

'Oh, I am. Guess who I've had the pleasure of meeting today?'

'I knew this was coming,' Barnes sighed, knowing his headache was about to become much worse.

'Why'd you keep it all from me? You knew about Elizabeth Blackwood this whole time. Why didn't you say something?'

'I didn't know she was Lily, plus I didn't know about Elizabeth Blackwood until we discovered that information. I don't work for S.T.O.R.M, only your father did,' he explained.

'But you knew about my uncle. Why did you never say anything about him to me?'

'That was your father's place to tell you. Remember, I'm your DCI, a family friend. I'm not a part of your family, so it was up to them to tell you, not me.'

Jacob thought about his words for a moment. *He's right. I expect too much from him.*

'What about the diamonds?' he continued his line of questioning.

'What are you talking about?'

'The diamonds from the crime scene. They're not in evidence, are they? Lily kidnapped and interrogated you because she wanted to know what you'd done with them.'

'You already know where they are, don't you? That's why you've come in here asking me all these questions.'

'Well, I wasn't going to get the answers from you. You're just as bad as my father.' Jacob rose from the chair. 'Just tell me one thing.' Barnes nodded. 'You know about S.T.O.R.M and that they deal with the supernatural. Do you believe our suspects are who they say they are?' Jacob asked.

'A part of me does, but so many people get out of jail time by pleading insanity. I've seen it loads of times, whether or not they're telling the truth,' Barnes answered.

Jacob gave a slight disconcerting smile, before leaving his office. He had a choice to make. Join S.T.O.R.M and have joint intel on his case, or carry on as normal, always knowing that his cases might not always be normal. It was a hard decision for him to make.

Barnes remained seated, trying to rid himself of his headache. The CID was flooded with detectives and counter-terrorism officers, bouncing from desk to desk, collaborating their information with each other.

Another knock on the door. *For goodness sake*, he thought as he sat up in his chair.

'What!' he yelled as Steven Hemmings entered.

'Just want to know if you've got any new information to share? My teams come up blank,' Hemmings asked.

'No, nothing.'

'What did he want?' Hemmings referred to Jacob.

'Oh, nothing. Unrelated to the case,' Barnes answered truthfully.

'I'm going to move the operation over to counter-terrorism and I want your team in with us,' Hemmings offered. 'I've already spoken to your Superintendent and she's agreed.'

'No problem,' he replied, leaning back in his chair while Hemmings left.

Giving it a minute, Barnes got on his feet and opened the door to the hustle and bustle. He got his team's attention, clicked his fingers and pointed to the briefing room, signalling a private meeting.

Once they had all entered, Barnes shut out the noise before he brought the news to their attention.

'Hemmings is moving the investigation to his counter-terrorism unit and we've all been cleared by the Super to join him.'

'But sir, we've got our case to close,' Sarah voiced her concern.

'I know, but this is classed as our case and who better to be included than the people who know the suspects and all aspects of the case,' Barnes replied.

'I'm not sure about this, boss,' Ally raised her thoughts.

'Well, we're a part of this now, so there's no more room for discussion.'

'I found something just before you called this meeting, sir,' Ethan directed at Barnes.

'Carry on, DC Robinson,' Barnes said.

'Well, I was trying to find a connection, as you asked. One thing did pop up. All patients under Natalie Dixon were given an experimental drug to help with their conditions. This drug has more than one chemical that can trigger dissociative identity disorder,' he explained.

'Do you think Natalie Dixon is the main reason why our suspects have multiple personalities?' Barnes questioned.

'I believe so,' Ethan replied with certainty.

'Looks like Natalie's become more the villain than the victim,' Sarah said with a cocky tone.

'What company created the drug?' Ally asked Ethan.

'Harrington Labs,' he answered.

Jacob was parked outside his apartment building, debating going to the pub for a drink to suppress his craving or go inside to his family. Minutes passed with still no decision. He knew he shouldn't, but the drink was the one thing that numbed all the pain he'd thought about and been through. His life had become increasingly difficult since his first big case. *Becoming a detective was harder than I thought.*

The engine purred as he pondered. A decision was made as he pulled away, looking for the nearest boozer. The craving had grown stronger as he drove around until his eyes caught hold of a bright sign for a local pub. Jacob found somewhere to park and bolted out of the car as fast as he could.

Upon entering the pub, he strolled to the bar and ordered a pint of lager, hoping it would stop the craving and calm him down. He started to shake as he lifted the glass, then the lager touched his lips, calming him. Seconds later, the glass was empty and he ordered another. Memories of his old life came flooding back while he gulped the second pint down. His childhood, his mother, his father and their happy life as a family. *But that's all in the past*, he thought. Another empty glass sat on the bar as he shouted for a third.

'Slow down, mate,' the barman said.

'Mind your own business,' Jacob replied nastily, while the barman pulled another pint for him.

Jacob paused. He noticed his behaviour and apologised before suddenly heading for the exit. The fresh air hit his burning hot face and he placed his bum on the edge of the curb. *What's happening to me?* He cried. He'd hit rock bottom at a rapid pace. The night they'd arrived at Alex Baker's home to find him dead and Belle sobbing in the bedroom appeared in his thoughts. It was as if someone somewhere was trying to give him a reason to carry on and get past the difficult times. He helped Belle after that night, giving her a reason to live.

'I can do this,' he said as he pulled himself up onto his stumbling legs. Jacob's phone suddenly began to buzz. 'Hello,' he answered.

'Jacob, it's Ally. I've got some news. Can we talk?'

'Can you pick me up? I'm on Steelhouse Lane.'

'Sure. I'll be there soon,' she agreed and hung up the phone.

Twenty minutes later, Ally arrived and Jacob got inside the car.

'Have you been drinking again?' she asked, smelling the booze on his breath.

'Yes,' he hung his head in shame.

'You need help, Jacob. If not for yourself or me, then for Kate and Belle. They need you.'

He nodded and Ally sped off. The car was silent for a minute. Jacob rubbed his forehead upset, knowing how silly he'd been.

'What did you want to talk about?' Jacob cut through the awkward silence.

'The team's been moved to counter-terrorism to help with the case,' she started.

'Why?'

'Hemmings thinks we'd be better off using their resources.'

'But this is our case.'

'I know, but he'd already gone behind Barnes' back and spoke to the DSI,' she explained.

'What an arsehole,' Jacob lost his tongue.

'That's not even the best bit,' she carried on. 'Ethan discovered that Natalie Dixon treated all our suspects with an experimental drug that has ingredients which can bring on dissociative identity disorder.'

'Do you think this could affect our case when it goes to court?' he asked.

'Maybe. They might even plead insanity anyway.'

'Is anybody looking into the company Natalie had gotten these drugs from?'

'Ethan's trying to get in contact.'

'Has there been any other cases of these drugs triggering dissociative identity disorder?'

'Possibly. Sarah and Brian are on that case,' she informed him.

'Do we know the name of the company?' he asked.

'Harrington Labs,' she answered.

The car returned to silence as Jacob's facial expression changed. Ally turned her attention off the road for a split second to see why he'd gone quiet.

'Is everything alright?' she asked, concerned after seeing a shocked look on his face.

'You said Harrington Labs?' he repeated.

'Yes.'

'Pull the car over.'

Ally followed his order and he jumped out of the car at lightning speed. His mind was racing all over the place. *Harrington Labs. My uncle's business is involved in my case. I need to tell Dan.* Jacob removed his phone from his pocket.

'Dan, I've got some information,' he said as his uncle answered. 'It's about Harrington Labs.'

'Who are you talking to?' Ally asked as she exited her car.

Jacob placed his finger against his lips, telling her to be quiet. 'Meet me at the station and I'll tell you what I know,' he said before hanging up.

'Who were you talking to?' Ally demanded an answer.

'My uncle. I'll tell you and the others everything when we get back to the station.'

The team grouped into the briefing room with Jacob's uncle, Dan, sat with them. Everyone wondered what was going on as they took their seats around the table. Jacob stood up front, ready to explain what he knew about Harrington Labs and his family's history.

'Why are we all here, Jacob? We've got work to do,' Sarah piped up in her cocky tone of voice.

'It's about this experimental drug and Harrington Labs.'

'Please enlighten us,' Barnes said.

'Harrington Labs was created by my great grandfather and is now in the hands of my uncle,' he started to explain before everyone turned their heads to look at Dan. 'No, not that uncle.'

'My other brother,' Dan took over. 'My mother had triplets, myself, John and Malcolm. I never knew my father. He went missing before we were born. My mother gave birth to us at my grandfather's house. He took Malcolm away as he was first born, then she had me and John and my grandmother hid us from him. My mother managed to escape, with help from my grandmother and our mother kept us hidden from them. Once my grandfather died, Malcolm became the sole heir to his fortune, including Harrington Labs and to this day, he has no idea that I exist.'

'So, your brother is the head of Harrington Labs? I still don't know what this has to do with the case,' Sarah said.

'Does anybody remember where Ava Lewis' parents worked?' Jacob asked.

Ally answered, 'Harrington Labs?'

'Yes. And her parents worked with someone else's mother...,' he continued.

'Lily's,' Barnes replied with surprise. 'Two cases which are kind of connected. How weird.'

'Now this part is going to sound strange, but if you look into the history of Harrington Labs, you'll find missing people cases dating back years. I think Lily was telling the truth about her mother. I think my uncle and Harrington Labs had something to do with her disappearance.'

'Should we bring Hemmings up to speed?' Ally turned to Barnes.

'Not just yet. Let's see what else we find first,' he said.

'What hospital did Natalie Dixon work at?' Jacob asked out of curiosity.

'Birmingham City,' Ally answered. 'Why?'

'Mia Clarke was a nurse...' Jacob walked out of the room and marched to his desk, logged onto the computer, staying in his thoughts. Everyone followed him over and crowded around him. 'Mia Clarke was a nurse at the same hospital Natalie Dixon treated her patients. Mia also murdered Will Shepard inside that hospital.'

Every member of the team seemed surprised at the revelation.

'Jacob, if you don't mind suspending your holiday for the time being and diving straight back in? We could really do with your help on this,' Barnes asked.

'No problem, sir,' he smiled, happy to be back in the saddle.

'Can you and Ally head to the hospital and ask around about Natalie Dixon and Mia Clarke? We need to know if they were friendly and see if there is a connection between both cases, or if it's a coincidence,' Barnes continued.

They both nodded and left with their coats on as Dan followed them out. He pulled Jacob to one side.

'Have you made your decision yet?'

'Not yet, but I'll keep you in the loop. Common courtesy,' Jacob smiled and patted his uncle on the top of his arm.

Chapter 24

Ally parked her car outside Birmingham City Hospital. Jacob sprung out of the passenger seat and proceeded to the entrance. He was in his own world with thoughts spinning around inside his head, forgetting he'd left Ally behind.

'Wait up!' she shouted.

'Sorry, Ally,' he snapped back to reality. 'I was somewhere else.'

'Figured,' she smiled, trying to grasp some breath back.

Once inside the reception area, the pair approached the desk, flashed their badges and asked to see Natalie Dixon's office. They were chauffeured by Daksha, a nurse who knew both Natalie and Mia.

'Here it is,' Daksha said as she opened Natalie's office door.

'Thank you, Daksha,' Ally said as they walked in.

'Would you mind staying around for a minute?' Jacob asked her. 'We've got a few questions to ask you.'

'No problem.'

'Did you know Natalie and Mia well?' Jacob began questioning her.

'We weren't friends. I spoke to them both a few times but that was about it. I can't believe Mia was involved in murdering all those women. She seemed so nice.'

'Did Mia and Natalie ever speak? Were they friends?' Ally asked as she searched Natalie's desk.

'They spoke a lot, sometimes about patients. I don't know if they were friends but they definitely spent a lot of time together,' answered Daksha.

'Do you know if they ever met outside of work?' Jacob continued questioning her.

'Probably. I can't recall.'

'Was there anyone else they spoke to a lot?' Ally switched back to asking the questions.

'What is this about? Was Natalie involved in Mia's murders?' Daksha asked.

'We believe it may have something to do with Natalie's murder and our current investigation,' Jacob informed her.

'Oh my God,' she said, shocked about what they'd told her.

Ally continued digging around Natalie's office with her latex gloves covering her hands. Jacob placed his notepad and pen back inside his pocket, whacked on his gloves and helped Ally in the search.

After a few minutes, they gave up. They couldn't find a single shred of anything that could help them. Ally ripped the gloves off her hands with frustration.

'Thank you, Daksha,' Jacob said as he pulled his gloves off and followed Ally out of the office. 'You seem a little angry.'

'Frustrated more than anything, mate,' she replied. 'I thought maybe we'd find something, but we've found absolutely nothing.' Ally turned back to Daksha, wanting to ask another question that sprung to mind. 'Sorry, I've got another question to ask.'

'Fire away.'

'Does the hospital have a contract with Harrington Labs to trial patients on experimental drugs?'

'No. All that sort of thing needs to go through the appropriate chain,' she explained.

'Thank you. If we need anything more we'll contact you,' Ally shook her hand before catching up with Jacob. 'Looks like doctor Natalie Dixon was giving out experimental drugs off the books.'

'So, she had a secret contract with Harrington Labs? If she got caught she'd have lost her job,' Jacob said.

'Would've been better than losing her life,' Ally replied, lifting her eyebrows at him.

'If I were a doctor with a secret stash of drugs, I wouldn't hide them here,' Jacob spoke his thoughts.

It turned 8.43 pm when Jacob and Ally arrived at Natalie's home. Crime tape still stuck to her door as Ally ripped through it, opening the door and entering the property. They both wore their latex gloves and searched through the entire house. Drawers were being emptied and contents rifled across the room. They didn't know what exactly they were looking for but hoped they'd find something in relation to Harrington Labs and the secret meds.

'Find anything?' Jacob shouted to Ally from the dining room.

'Not yet,' she yelled back from Natalie's office.

Ally pulled out the filing cabinet drawer and flicked through the files of paperwork, each with a labelled tab. She stopped when she noticed the file named Harrington and removed the contents inside. It was a contract with Natalie's name at the top, explaining their agreement in which she'd give the trial of the drug to certain categories of patients. She was paid a sum of £10,000 for each subject and their results. The bottom was signed by Malcolm Harrington.

'I've got something,' Ally bellowed.

Jacob came rushing in. 'What is it?'

'It's a contact between Malcolm Harrington and Natalie. It explains how he'd pay her £10,000 for each person she'd given the drug to and their result of how they were affected,' she explained. 'If this isn't enough evidence to pay your uncle a visit, then I don't know what is.'

'Dan did say he was not to be trusted. How could he risk putting these people's lives in danger?'

'Greed? Control? There are many reasons companies do these sorts of things, Jacob. It doesn't mean it's right though.'

'I'll call Barnes and let him know,' Jacob insisted. He left the room and called DCI Barnes. 'Hi, boss. We've found a contract between Natalie and Malcolm Harrington explaining their agreement and her payment. Can Ethan dig through Natalie Dixon's financial records to see how many payments were made from Harrington Labs?'

'I'll get him on it right away,' Barnes replied. 'Are you guys going to pay Malcolm Harrington a visit?'

'When we've wrapped things up here,' Jacob explained.

'Okay. Keep me updated.'

Jacob placed the phone back inside his coat pocket while Ally stood beside him clutching an evidence bag with the contract inside.

'Think we'd better get this to the station and visit Harrington Labs in the morning,' she said.

'Good idea,' he replied. 'Though, I do think we should pay Mr Harrington a visit tonight.'

Once they sat inside Ally's Ford Mondeo, Jacob called his uncle to inform him of their findings as he'd promised.

'Dan, we found something at Natalie's house.'

'What did you find?' he asked Jacob.

'A contract binding Natalie to give Harrington Labs information on her patients she'd trialled the drugs on. The offer was £10,000 for each patient report. We visited the hospital and they have no contract with Harrington Labs which means Doctor Dixon was doing illegal activities off the books,' Jacob explained.

'The problem is, why is Harrington Labs interested in certain patients with different conditions that can cause dissociative identity disorder?'

'That's something I hope Malcolm can answer.'

Malcolm Harrington drove through the gates of his home and onto his drive, parking right outside his house. Opening his front door, he was greeted by his wife. The walls were incredibly tall, giving the hallway a high ceiling with a grand staircase in the middle.

'Good evening, honey,' she greeted him as he stepped one foot through the door, holding a glass of bourbon whiskey.

He grabbed the glass from her, smiled and necked it back. 'It's good to be home. Dinner smells good,' he said, sniffing the air.

'It'll be ready soon,' she replied before walking back into the kitchen.

Malcolm strolled across the large, grand hallway, and over towards his study. He slowly and quietly closed the doors behind him, trying not to make too much noise. He sat at his expensive oak desk and relaxed in his comfortable leather chair. He placed the empty whiskey glass on the desk, closed his eyes and released a sigh. It had been an exhausting day at work and the investors of Harrington Labs were making his life incredibly difficult.

'Dinner's ready,' his wife, Janet, shouted from the kitchen.

When Malcolm entered the dining room, his wife and son, Aaron, were already sitting at the long, elegant dining table. Food placed neatly in the middle in different dishes and bowls, letting them serve themselves. Malcolm sat at the head of the table like always.

'So, Aaron, what did you do at school today?' Janet asked him.

'Nothing much,' he mumbled in teenage fashion.

Malcolm tucked into his food, trying his best not to delve into the conversation as he didn't want to discuss his difficult day. The three of them sat in silence, eating away at the food on their plates. Once Aaron had finished, he took himself off to his room, leaving Malcolm and Janet alone to finish their meals.

'I don't know what's gotten into him,' she started to strike a conversation with her husband.

'He's a teenager. It's what they do.'

'I know, but he used to be a happy boy. Now he just mopes around the house.'

'He's got plenty of friends at that school of his. That Kyle kid, for example, they've been friends for years.'

'I know but I can't help feeling like something is wrong,' she continued.

Malcolm lifted his body off his chair, grabbed his plate and began to walk into the kitchen. Janet always looked too much into things, finding problems that weren't there. Malcolm strolled back into the dining room and kissed his wife on the cheek.

'I've got some work to finish,' he informed her.

Janet sighed. 'You've just got home. Can it not wait until tomorrow?'

'Nope, I've got the investors on my case again. I've got to get it finished tonight, ready for tomorrow,' he explained.

Malcolm entered his office again, closing the door behind him. Sitting in his chair, he pulled open the drawer in his desk and removed a Glock. He placed the gun on the desk and started to take deep breaths. He pulled the gun up beneath his chin, his hands shaking and tears rolling down his eyes.

The doorbell rang, stopping Malcolm from pulling the trigger. He quickly placed the gun back inside the drawer, then slammed it shut as he got off his seat and hurried towards the front door. He stood still for a second before opening it, worried about who was on the other side. *I was just about to kill myself, why am I worried?* he thought.

On the other side of the door, stood a man and a lady no older than thirty-five.

'Mr Malcolm Harrington?' the lady asked.

'Yes, that's me,' Malcolm answered.

The lady rummaged through her pockets before placing a police badge in his face. 'Detective Inspector Ally Miller,' she informed him. 'This is DS Wright.'

'What is this about?' he questioned them.

'Can we come in? We need to ask you a few questions.'

He moved out of the way so they could enter. 'We'll talk in my study.'

Ally and Jacob entered the house, both glancing around at the elegant and spacious hallway.

Janet shouted from the kitchen, echoing through the hallway. 'Who is it, dear?'

'Just the police. They've got a few questions to ask me,' he shouted back before closing the doors to his study. 'So, what is this about?' he asked them.

'What's your involvement with Doctor Natalie Dixon?' Jacob asked, taking a good look at the tall, dark-haired man, whose appearance didn't resemble his father or Dan one bit.

'She works at Birmingham City Hospital. I've had a few dealings with her, trying to get some of the top dogs at the hospital to use a trial of a drug my company is producing,' he answered.

'That's not the truth though, is it?' Jacob continued.

'What's that supposed to mean?' Malcolm shouted at him.

'What my colleague means is we've found a contract between you and Doctor Dixon, stating that your company will give her £10,000 for each report of her patient's reaction to the drug you supplied her with,' Ally interrupted.

'That's absurd!' he continued to shout.

'But it isn't, sir. What about the missing employee cases your company has had throughout the years?'
'I'm not saying another word without my solicitor present.'

'Okay, Mr Harrington. We'll be seeing you again soon,' Ally finished before she and Jacob left the Harrington house.

How dare they! his inner thoughts shouted. He panicked slightly, knowing it wasn't only the investors he was worried about. The thought of suicide crossed his mind again, but he knew he was too much of a coward to try it again and succeed. He was a man in trouble and not just by the hands of the law.

Chapter 25

'Malcolm Harrington denies having known about the contract we found inside Natalie Dixon's home office. He's lawyered up, making it incredibly difficult to speak to him now on the evidence we have,' Jacob informed the team.

Every member of the team sat around the conference table in the briefing room, listening to the information Jacob was feeding them.

'Another thing we discovered was that Natalie was good friends with Mia Clarke. We can't be sure of any meetings but that is something we need to look into more,' Ally said.

'We've found something too,' Sarah started. 'Each of our suspects has been tested and there have been traces of the drug in them, including Jack Roberts. We've also looked into your missing people cases from Harrington Labs and I think you're right, Jacob. Missing people cases dating back over twenty years.'

'Shit,' Jacob said, shocked about what he'd just heard.

Ethan started with his information. 'I traipsed through Natalie's financial records like you asked and there were a few payments made by Harrington Labs. Malcolm Harrington is either lying or he knows nothing about the contract and someone else within the company is doing illegal activities.'

'So, we're dealing with a company that is illegally supplying a doctor with experimental drugs which caused the patients to manifest dissociative identity disorder and has a history of missing employees,' Barnes summed everything up. 'We'll all go home and get some rest and meet back here tomorrow morning. After the last couple of weeks, we could all do with the rest.'

Everybody got up from their seats and left the room. Barnes walked off into his office as everyone else grabbed their coats from their desks.

'Any plans for tonight?' Ally questioned Jacob, placing her arms through her coat sleeves.

'No. Kate's out with her dad and Belle's out with Ben. Might just be a meal for one,' he laughed.

'How about I cook?' she smiled. 'If you don't mind, that is?'

Jacob began to stutter, not wanting to say no. 'That'll be great.'

They both walked out of the office together and got inside the Mondeo. Jacob became nervous, even though he had strong feelings for her. He wanted to express to her how he felt but didn't want to rush because of how his last relationship with Lily turned out.

Opening his apartment door, Jacob got butterflies in his stomach. Ally put the shopping bag on the kitchen counter which was filled with ingredients they'd picked up at the local supermarket beforehand. She started to unload the bag and then started to slice the onions and peppers.

'Where are your pots and pans?' she asked Jacob as he ripped off his tie.

'Bottom cupboard to the left of the sink,' he answered. 'I'm just going to get out of these clothes.'

Ally raised an intrigued eyebrow. 'Oh, yeah.'

'I'm putting other clothes on,' he laughed.

As he entered his bedroom, he thought about how comfortable he felt when she was around. Ally made him feel loved and cared for, even though he knew there were others out there that loved him, but not the way that she cared for him.

After changing his clothes, he re-entered the kitchen to see Ally in full swing. *It smells incredible*, Jacob thought. *She seems to be enjoying herself*. Ally decided to put some music on. Her phone blared summer anthems while she danced and stirred the pot of sauce. Jacob chuckled at her as he sat watching from the breakfast bar, but Ally dragged him to his feet and danced with him.

'Time to let your hair down, DS Wright,' she laughed as she pulled him onto his feet.

Jacob was reluctant to dance at first but Ally was very persuasive and within minutes, Jacob was dancing along. It was the best fun he'd had since he and Belle played crazy golf. The music stopped and between gasping for breaths, they both laughed at the enjoyment they'd both had.

They gazed at one another. The laughing had stopped and they continued gasping for breath but their eyes continued to lock on to each other. Jacob stepped closer. Time seemed to slow down as the two of them edged closer together. Ally trembled as Jacob stood directly in front of her, gazing into her eyes. His lips leaned in closer to her's before touching in a passionate kiss. Ally had dreamt about this moment for so long, fantasising about him and scenarios like this. He pulled away momentarily, giving her time to breathe.

'I'm sorry,' he apologised.

Ally opened her eyes and said softly, 'What for?'

'For being so intrusive,' he explained.

Ally said nothing, just looked him in the eyes again before launching her lips on his full throttle. She didn't stop. Ally was in the moment and she took Jacob with her. They'd both longed to be loved and nothing else mattered at that moment. Ally ripped Jacob's t-shirt off after releasing lips for a split second but were back together in a few short seconds.

'I've only just got changed,' he joked, making Ally chuckle slightly.

They continued their passionate kiss while manoeuvring themselves to the bedroom, taking off a piece of clothing with every step. As they reached the bed, they'd stripped down to nothing more than their underwear.

They both took a moment's breath as Ally pushed Jacob on the bed, towering over him. She sat on top of him, kissing his neck while he undone her bra strap, and slowly slid it off from around her shoulders. Everything happened slowly as if the pair of them wanted to savour every moment.

Jacob pressed his lips against her chest, kissing every inch of her. They felt incredible, forgetting everything in their heated moment of passion.

Barnes knocked on the door. His stomach was fluttering with nerves before Vanessa opened it. She smiled as she noticed him standing in front of her.

'Joe, it's good to see you. Do you want to come in?'

'If that's okay? I know it's late but it's been one hell of a month,' he laughed and she did too. 'I just wanted to see the girls.'

She opened the door wide enough for him to enter. Her affection for him grew stronger since his kidnapping and her being held hostage. She loved him and always did, even through the divorce, but she couldn't keep being second place to his job. She wanted to be a part of his life again but knew he wouldn't give up the job for her.

Barnes crept upstairs with excitement. The twin girls were fast asleep, but that didn't bother him, he just wanted to see their little faces. Standing over the top of them, fast asleep, made him feel warm inside, forgetting his troubles.

'Beautiful, aren't they?' Vanessa said, also gazing at their babies.

'I've missed them so much.'

'I'm so happy you survived that...'

'I needed to. I didn't want anything to happen to you and the girls. I needed to stay alive for our family,' he interrupted her.

'And I'm so glad you did, otherwise, they'd have no mum or dad,' she released a few tears.

Barnes held her in his arms, still staring at the girls, not wanting to move from this moment. He hoped one day they'd be a family again, living under the same roof, happy and content.

Vanessa glanced up at Barnes as his grip loosened. Her feet lifted on their tip-toes and she placed her lips on his, shocking Barnes, but that didn't stop him from carrying on. He finally felt like he belonged again. Vanessa started to become more intense and passionate, placing her hands on his cheeks, then around his neck while not losing the connection from his lips. Barnes pulled away, unsure if this was what she truly wanted.

'What's wrong? Vanessa asked.

'I just don't want you thinking I'm taking advantage,' he said.

'This is what I want, Joe. That's if you want it too?'

It didn't take more than a minute for Barnes to make up his mind and launched back fiercely into another intense kiss, tearing off Vanessa's clothes.

'Ouch,' she cried out, still trying to kiss him.

'What is it?' he queried.

'Still sore from the gunshot wound,' she told him.
'I'm sorry.'

'Just shut up and kiss me,' she demanded, locking lips with him again.

They both stumbled to the bedroom and tumbled onto the bed. Vanessa lay on her back as Barnes removed her trousers. His eyes caught sight of her pink, laced underwear as she lay waiting for him. He lay on top of her, pulling her down her pink underwear and thrust himself inside her. She felt a rush of emotions and pleasure. They both felt a sudden release of all their pain and troubles as they kissed the night away. Barnes was finally back where he belonged, in the arms of his wife.

Sarah sat on the rooftop terrace bar on Frederick Street with her date opposite her. Drinks between them, laughs and jokes flowing, it was safe to say Sarah Taylor had let her hair down. She was having a great time for a change. Her date was a dark-haired girl called Claire, who she'd found through a dating app a few months ago and they clicked straight away.

'I can't believe the number of times we've been out and I still don't know what you do for work?' said Claire.

'If I told you, I'd have to kill you,' joked Sarah.

Claire laughed along. 'No, but seriously, what do you do? You know all about me and I hardly know anything about you.'

'If you really wanna know, I'm a Detective Sergeant within the police force,' she informed her.

'You're pulling my leg.'

'I can assure you, I'm not.'

'What sort of things do you investigate?' Claire asked intrigued.

'Murders,' Sarah announced. 'Do you remember the murders of young women last year?'

'Yes. Did you investigate that case?'

'With my team, yes.'

'I heard something about it being ritual cult killings?' Claire fished for more information.

'I can't say much more about it,' Sarah shut her down.

'Wow, such an interesting career. I don't think I'd have had the balls to join the police.'

'It's a hard job but even in the darkest of times, I enjoy it,' she smiled.

'Well you only get one life, you might as well live it,' Claire returned the smile.

'I've really enjoyed tonight. I'd love to do this again next week if you're up for it?'

Claire nodded. 'I've had a good time too. Call me when you're free from your busy schedule,' Claire laughed. 'Do you wanna get out of here?'

Sarah was cautious, not wanting to miss her chance at happiness, but her past relationships crumbled too fast. Her heart was telling her to jump but her head kept her back. Not knowing which to pick she sat quietly.

'If you don't want to, then that's fine. I don't want to push you into anything,' Claire continued after noticing Sarah's silence.

'It's not that I don't want to, I do, but I want to take it slow.'

Claire smiled while placing her hand on Sarah's. 'That's fine with me. Whatever you want, babe.'

Ethan returned home, hung his coat on the hook in the hallway before swinging the living room door open. His girlfriend sat firmly on the sofa, grasping a mug of tea in her hands.

'You're home early for a change.'

'Busy day tomorrow. The boss wanted us to get some rest,' he said, flopping on the sofa beside her.

'Wanna talk about it?' Ruby asked.

'Not really,' he answered, tucking himself between her arms for a hug.

Ruby was a pretty girl with dark hair and a dyed red tint. Ethan fell for Ruby as soon as he saw her at a friend's party and connected straight away. Ethan had asked her to help him dig into his family's history to try and find his biological parents. He was adopted as a baby and suddenly decided it was the right time to find his birth parents. When he was younger it hadn't bothered him, but as he got older, he felt he should know his heritage.

'I've got something to tell you,' she spoke up.

Ethan sat up, looked at her and asked, 'What is it?'

'I think I've found your birth parents,' she announced.

Ethan was shocked, even though it was what he wanted and asked her to help. His stomach flooded with a sick feeling from nerves and anxiety. He stayed quiet for a couple of seconds.

'Are you okay?' Ruby asked with concern.

'Yeah, I just didn't think you'd find them that fast, that's all,' he answered, still shocked at the news. 'What are their names?'

'Anna and Dean Turner,' she informed him.

'So, my name would be Ethan Turner,' he pondered.

Ruby laughed. 'I prefer Detective Constable Ethan Robinson.'

Ethan gleamed a huge grin before hugging his girlfriend tightly. She was the one good thing he had going in his life. When things became difficult at work, he knew he always had Ruby to come home to. They continued their night watching whatever rubbish was on the TV before heading to bed. *How did I ever become so lucky, finding the girl of my dreams?* he thought as he followed her to bed.

Chapter 26

Jacob stirred and opened his eyes. The bright light from the alarm clock shone 6.20 am in his face. He lay still, watching Ally as she slept perfectly, not wanting the moment to end. It was close to 6.30 am by the time Jacob decided to move. He gently got up, trying not to wake her as she lay fast asleep. He jumped straight into the bathroom, showered, washed and brushed his teeth before sneaking into the kitchen to make her breakfast. He threw some bacon on the frying pan and watched it sizzle while he poured her a fresh cup of coffee.

By 7.20 am, he opened the bedroom door holding a tray with a full English breakfast, orange juice and a mug of coffee.

'What did I do to deserve this?' she asked, smiling at him.

'Just being you,' he smiled.

The pair of them heard Kate and Belle's bedroom door open and they freaked out slightly, knowing the girls probably knew Ally had stayed the night.

'Oh my God. They're going to know,' she panicked.

'It's okay. I'll try and get them out before we have to leave.'

Jacob left the bedroom, closing the door behind him, to see Belle and Kate standing in front of him. He jumped slightly from fright, not realising how close they were.

'Why's it smell like bacon out here?' Belle enquired.

'I made myself breakfast,' he lied.

'Jacob, in the whole time I've lived here, you've never once made breakfast,' she laughed.

'She's got a point,' Kate butted in.

'Well aren't you two the little detectives this morning?' he laughed nervously before strutting into the kitchen.

They both followed him, giving each other a strange glare like something was wrong.

'What's going on, Jacob?' Kate asked.

'What do you mean? There's nothing going on,' he continued to lie.

'She's here, isn't she?' Belle raised an eyebrow and smiled cheekily.

'Who do you mean?' he avoided eye contact.

'Ally? She stayed the night, didn't she? You dirty dog,' Belle continued to joke, making both her and Kate giggle.

'Maybe,' he admitted.

'It's fine by us. We quite like her,' Kate said with confidence.

Jacob smiled before ushering them off. 'Don't you two have to get ready for work?'

The pair huffed at him, knowing he wanted them gone so she could sneak out. Jacob walked back into the bedroom to see Ally buttoning up her blouse. She'd picked at the breakfast, but her nerves stopped her from eating.

'I'm going to be doing the walk of shame if I turn up at the station like this,' she said.

'I had a really good time last night,' Jacob announced.

'Well of course you did,' she joked and winked at him. 'Jokes aside, I did too.' She kissed him on the lips.

'Shall we drop by yours first, so you can change?' Jacob asked.

'If you don't mind? I don't really want people to gossip.'

They both sneaked out of the apartment and raced to Ally's place, before their eventful day at work.

'Have you thought any more about that job yet?' he asked nervously.

'I don't think I'm gonna take it. I've got everything I need right here,' she grinned.

Brian was first in the dark, unlit office. He flicked through some of the paperwork on his desk while he waited for the others to arrive. Next in was DCI Barnes, who had a slight skip in his step, smiling profusely.

'Morning, sir,' Brian greeted him.

'Good morning, Brian,' Barnes replied before whistling into his office.

What's going on with him? he wondered. *Barnes is acting unusually peculiar this morning.* Sarah arrived next in the same sort of manner and plonked herself at her desk, not realising she was being watched.

'You're rather chirpy this morning,' Brian said, glaring at her with a confused appearance.

'Am I not allowed to be happy?' she frowned, making Brian slump back into his work.

Another half an hour passed before Jacob and Ally entered, giggling like school children. Brian's thoughts wandered from his work as did Sarah's. Everyone noticed the strange behaviour from DI Miller and DS Wright. Brian finally clicked about why everyone was so happy.

'I know what's going on?' he shouted. 'Barnes whistling, Sarah smiling and you two giggling. You all got some last night,' he roared with laughter.

Ally and Jacob stopped giggling, worried they'd been found out.

'Sit down, you moron,' Sarah shouted, knowing he was probably right.

Barnes was leaning on the door frame of his office, watching everyone. 'If that's the only case you've solved in the last six months, DC Edwards, then God help us all,' he joked, making everyone in the office roar with laughter.

Brian sat down with embarrassment, lowering his head back into his work.

'Has anyone seen Ethan this morning?' Jacob asked, noticing he wasn't perched at his desk like usual.

'No. Usually, he's the first one here,' Sarah answered.

Seconds later, Ethan strolled in, not noticing people were staring at him. He removed his arms from his coat, placed it over the back of his chair and sat down.

'DC Robinson, is everything alright?' Barnes asked him.

Ethan glanced up. 'Yeah, why? What's wrong?'

'Well, usually you're the first one here,' Jacob answered.

'Sorry to be off schedule,' he laughed slightly. 'Got stuff going on.'

'If there's anything we can help with, let us know. We're all family here,' said Barnes.

'Thank you, sir,' he replied before returning to his screen.

'DS Wright, DI Miller, can I see you in my office?' Barnes asked politely. They both wandered inside and Barnes shut the door behind them. 'Are you both heading to Harrington Labs this morning?'

'Yes, sir,' they answered at the same time.

'I want to know what you find right away. Hemmings is busting my balls on what new information we're withholding. Call me the minute you find anything.'

They nodded as they left his office and walked back to their desks. Minutes later, Sarah approached Ally clutching some files from Natalie Dixon's home computer.

'I think you should take a look at these.'

'What are they?' Ally enquired.

'These are the files found on Natalie Dixon's home computer. They are the patient files on who she gave this experimental drug to,' Sarah explained. 'Names, addresses, the lot.'

'Thank you, Sarah.'

Ally flicked through each case file, coming across names of people they already had in custody, but also others who'd had the drug.

'Jacob, come and have a look at this,' she said. Jacob approached and leant over her shoulder to take a look at the file in her hand. 'Recognise this lady?' she asked.

'Is that Charlotte Roberts?'

'Yes. These are the people Natalie signed up for trials of the drug.'

'But why is Charlotte on that list? And why is Jack Roberts showing sign of taking the drug if it was his wife taking them?' Jacob started raising questions.

'Maybe she wasn't taking them. Maybe she was dosing Jack with them for some reason.'

'Did she sign up for the experimental drug, not for her but her husband?'

'She was having an affair, maybe she wanted to poison him?'

'I'm looking at the missing people reports of Harrington Labs employees. They date back longer than we initially thought,' he informed her.

'How long?'

'So far, about forty years.'

'Shit,' she replied shocked.

Jacob returned to his desk. Scrolling through the missing people reports on the computer, he came across a familiar surname. Blackwood. *Lily was right. Her mum did work for Harrington Labs and she is missing. Cassandra Blackwood had been missing since the year 2000. The last place she'd been seen was at work.* There was a photo on the case file, showing Jacob her mother's appearance. *She looks just like her mother*, he thought. Jacob stood up, walked over to Ally and informed her of his findings.

'Lily was right,' he said.

'What?' she replied, confused about what he was saying.

'Her mother's disappearance. She was right. Cassandra Blackwood's been missing since the early 2000's and the last place she was seen was Harrington Labs,' he shared his information.

'Christ!' she yelled slightly.

The pair of them waltzed into Barnes' office, catching him off guard and making him jump with fright.

'What do you two want?'

'You said to come to you if we had any new information,' Jacob said.

'What have you found?' he enquired.

'Sarah gave me some files they'd found on Natalie Dixon's computer, regarding her patients who she trialled the experimental drug on. One of these patients was Charlotte Roberts,' Ally informed him.

'Jack Roberts' wife?'

'Yes.'

'But his test came back positive for the drug, didn't it?'

'Yes, sir,' she answered again. 'Our initial thought is, she was drugging her husband.'

'But why?'

'We don't know yet, sir.'

'I found something too,' Jacob piped up. 'Searching through the missing people cases in relation to Harrington Labs employees, I discovered Lily was telling the truth about her mother.'

'Explain?' Barnes asked.

'She worked there and it was the last place she was seen back in February 2000,' Jacob explained to Barnes.

'Okay, so you think your crazy, manipulative, psycho ex-fiancee was telling the truth?' he sarcastically replied. 'Did you somehow forget what that woman did to me, DS Wright?'

Barnes was raging with anger and Jacob knew this, not just by his remark, but because he called him by his police title. Ally bowed her head in silence, not wanting to say a word.

'No, sir, I haven't,' Jacob answered calmly. He turned his head to Ally and whispered, 'Can you give us a minute?' Ally left the two of them in the office alone. 'I think you seem to be forgetting something as well, sir.'

Barnes' face was red with fury. 'What do you think I'm forgetting?'

'I know everything. About S.T.O.R.M, the diamonds, the lot,' he announced.

'DS Wright, whatever your uncle has told you...'

Jacob interrupted, 'He hasn't told me anything, Sir. Don't forget, we're all detectives. The pieces have started to fit into the puzzle. I know you gave Dan the diamonds that night.'

'Accusations like that would have Anti-corruption on my arse and I could be dismissed as well as prosecuted,' Barnes started to worry.

'Which is why I haven't said anything. I know they are in a safe place and not in evidence.' Barnes started to relax, but still tense. 'I'm going to ask you again. How long have you been working for S.T.O.R.M?'

'I'm not. When we started to believe Elizabeth Blackwood was committing ritual killings, me and your father contacted Dan and told him everything we knew. The night of the raid, when we caught Ava, I saw the diamonds on the floor. I couldn't take the risk of anyone else picking them up, so I took them and gave them to Dan to keep them locked away,' Barnes confessed. 'If anyone finds out, I'll be sacked. No one will believe the real story.'

'But won't they need it for the investigation?'

'There are only two people that know about the diamonds and they're the two people in this room.'

'They called out to me, you know.' Jacob said, making Barnes stare at him confused. 'The diamonds. I heard whispers coming from them.'

'What did they say?'

'I couldn't hear them. Do you think our four suspects are telling the truth about their alter-egos?'

'I think they're crackpots who want a lighter sentence by pleading insanity. There's too much evidence to prove their condition was brought on by the drug they were trialling.'

'But do you think the supernatural exists? Do you not think something might be controlling them? After all, look what happened a couple of months ago,' Jacob said, hoping Barnes would tell the truth.

'To be honest, I don't know,' he answered honestly. Jacob got up off his seat and went to exit the office. 'Jacob, this conversation was just between us, wasn't it?' Barnes asked, hoping Jacob would stay quiet about the missing evidence.

'Yes, sir. Our little secret,' he smiled before leaving Barnes' office.

Jacob returned to his desk where he was greeted by another envelope that sat firmly upon his desk. His hands began to shake nervously and he frantically glanced around to see where it had come from. *More photos*, he thought. He placed his hand on the envelope, worried and scared to find out what was inside. He ripped the seal open and slid out the piece of paper from inside.

"*I'll be seeing you soon, DS Wright.*"

The note was like the ransom style note they'd found at the crime scenes of their last case. *Who is this person?* he asked himself. Ally caught sight of Jacob's terrified face and wandered over to him with worry that he was keeping something secret from her.

'Is everything okay?'

Jacob stayed silent, shaking vigorously from fear and panic. He had no idea who this person was or what they wanted from him. He knew it wasn't Lily as she was locked away in a prison cell, which made him freak out even more. He was afraid of the unknown. The unknown of who they were.

'I've had another package,' he told Ally, handing her the envelope. 'We were only in Barnes' office for a couple of minutes and somebody has managed to dump this on my desk, undetected.'

She scanned the note with her eyes. 'This looks the same as the ones we found at the crime scenes last year.'

Jacob nodded. 'Is this ever going to end?' He plonked himself down in his chair and placed his head in his hands, leaning his elbows on his desk.

Ally placed her hand on his back. 'We'll find out who's sending these to you,' she comforted him.

An hour had passed since Jacob opened the envelope. Everyone's eyes glued to their computers while Ally returned to Jacob's desk. She towered over him.

'I think I've worked it out,' she said. 'Harrington Labs just sent us a list of their employees and one name stuck out. Scarlett Jones.'

'Isn't that one of the women you saved from Felicity James' farm house?' he asked.

'Yes. Let's start at the beginning. We have four suspects. Nathan Lawrence, Jack Roberts, Felicity James and Jenny Reynolds. Each of these is known to have had the experimental drug in their system at some point because of the trial conducted by Doctor Natalie Dixon. We started with Jack Roberts, who killed his wife in which we believed was because she was having an affair, but if you remember he confronted Mr Hussain and told him he already knew. So, why kill her now?' Jacob shrugged. 'We know Charlotte Roberts was on Natalie's list of patients but Jack had the drug in his system.'

'Maybe he found out Charlotte was trying to poison him?' Jacob said.

'Yes and that's why he killed her. Not because of the affair, but because she was trying to kill him. Then we move on to Felicity James, who captured women and starved them to death, one being Scarlett Thatcher before she escaped because of us.'

'Someone else related to the drug.'

'Then we've got Natalie Dixon murdered, along with her parents, who were given a dose of a mutated version of the drug. It all relates to this company and their production of the drug,' she finished explaining her theory.

'Do you think the Lab is a target?' Jacob asked.

'It may be a possible threat,' Ally agreed.

'We better inform DCI Barnes,' Jacob replied, rushing to his office, bursting through the door. 'Boss, we think Harrington Labs is going to be targeted.'

'Are you sure?' Barnes asked worriedly.

'This whole case might be about getting revenge on the people behind this drug,' Ally informed him.

'Why would they want to take such drastic action?'

'I've been looking into the D.I.D condition and if the other personalities feel the main host is threatened, they could take action. There's been a few reported cases of it happening. Not to mention that certain aspects of this drug can cause death over time, which Harrington Labs have ignored and why there was so much secrecy around it,' Ally continued explaining.

'I think you two need to head over there and ask a few more questions before we take any action,' Barnes said before returning to his paperwork.

'But, sir...' Ally tried to

'DI Miller, I can't phone Hemmings on a hunch. I need something more concrete,' Barnes interrupted. 'Now I suggest you two go and find out the reason why Jenny Reynolds is a threat to the company more than just because she popped a few pills,' Barnes finished rudely.

Ally stormed out, slamming the door wide open and marched angrily to her desk, grabbing her coat and exiting the CID. Jacob remained shocked inside Barnes' office.

'DS Wright, don't tell me you need to be told twice?' Barnes raised an eyebrow.

'No, sir,' he answered, leaving and closing the door gently behind him.

Jacob followed Ally out of the station and got inside her car, where he witnessed her red, vexed face.

'Arghh,' she yelled, releasing her anger from within. 'Why's he ignoring us?'

'He's right. We don't have any evidence about why she wants to attack Harrington Labs. Let's just get there and ask Mr Harrington if he knows Jenny and any reason why she'd want to hurt them,' Jacob calmly replied to her.

Ally calmed down. 'You're right. But my gut is telling me something is going to happen there.'

Barnes remained seated, hidden away in his office, filling out the remaining paperwork which had sat on his desk for weeks. His head pounded as the craving returned. His eyes removed off the paperwork momentarily and focused on the desk drawer below. *No, Joe*, he talked himself out of it. His sight returned to the files. This was always the boring part of his job and he always hated it. The phone on his desk rang out, giving him the distraction he needed.

'DCI Barnes,' he answered.

PC Bell from the station's reception was on the other end. 'Sir, we've got a situation down here. You've been requested.'

'I'm on my way,' he replied, placing the phone down and marching his way down to reception.

He rushed out of the office and locked eyes with Sarah. He snapped his fingers at her, Brian and Ethan, instructing them to follow him as he burst through the doors out of the CID. Walking through the corridor, they heard a commotion. *What's going on?* Barnes wondered. They were greeted by dozens of police officers, surrounding Scarlett Thatcher, who had marks and rashes across her skin. Her face was unrecognisable because of the number of cysts and rashes that covered her.

'Scarlett? What's going on?'

Scarlett was so upset, crying hysterically, she couldn't find the words to talk. Barnes approached her slowly and carefully, knowing she was in trouble.

'What's happened?' he continued.

'She wants me to send you a message,' she stuttered, frozen with fear.

'Who? Who wants to send me a message?'

'She said her name's Esther, but her real name is Jenny Reynolds. She used to work with me at Harrington Labs,' she answered his question.

Barnes froze for a moment, knowing this was either a distraction or a trap. 'What's the message, Scarlett?'

'I am. She's injected me with the drugs.'

'What drugs?'

'The one I sold to Natalie Dixon,' she burst out in more tears. 'She's enhanced it. She told me it wasn't ready, but we were in a rush to hit our targets, so I didn't listen to her.'

'What's she planning?'

'Death and destruction,' she cried. 'She's going to release it.'

'Where's she going to release it?'

'Harrington Labs.'

Barnes' face turned white and Sarah noticed.

'Sir, are you okay?' she said.

'Ally and Jacob, they're in danger,' he told her. 'I sent them to Harrington Labs.'

Chapter 27

Ally quickly flew her Mondeo into a space and the pair of them entered Harrington Labs. Once inside, they were greeted by Malcolm's receptionist who made them wait in the lobby for ten minutes before Malcolm burst through the doors and invited them into his office.

'I've told you already, that wouldn't be my signature on that document and you can speak to my solicitor.'

'Calm down, Mr Harrington,' Ally started. 'We think someone in your lab forged your signature to get that untested drug into human guinea pigs.'

'You think I'm telling the truth?' he said with a shocked tone.

'Maybe. We need to know who your chief of staff is here?' she continued asking questions.

'I'll get you a list,' he replied, shuffling through drawers and cabinets in his office. He placed the files on his desk for them to investigate. 'There you go.'

Ally and Jacob flicked through each file, taking a lot of care and attention to details. Then Ally noticed a name and recognised the photo. She tapped Jacob to get his attention.

'Look who's Chief of staff,' she said.

'Scarlett Thatcher?' Jacob read the name out loud.

'Yes. I think maybe she's the one who forged the signature.'

'But why?' Malcolm asked.

'That's something we'd hope you'd tell us?' she replied.

'Why would I know?'

'Are you telling us you have no idea what happens inside your company?' Jacob asked with a cocky tone.

'I had no idea Scarlett was making dodgy deals in secret.'

Ally changed the subject. 'Do you know anybody by the name of Jenny Reynolds?'

'Yes. Jenny worked here for years, up until the end of last year when she went off the rails,' he began to tell them.

'What do you mean?' Jacob asked.

'She started shouting at Scarlett about stealing something from her. She lost control and hit her. I had no other choice than to dismiss her.' Malcolm continued.

'That's why she wasn't on the list of employees,' Ally whispered to Jacob.

'Why? Has Jenny done something?' Malcolm questioned them.

'We believe Jenny is a threat to you and all your other employees,' Jacob informed him. 'Do you know what Scarlett supposedly stole from Jenny?'

'Oh my God,' Malcolm exclaimed. 'No, I've got no idea.'

'Is Scarlett working today?' Ally asked.

'No. She didn't turn up. I presumed it was because of her traumatic experience.' Malcolm began to fit the pieces into place. 'She's got Scarlett, hasn't she?'

'I don't know,' Ally replied.

'She kept taking a couple of personal days because of her ordeal and I thought today was the same,' Malcolm continued.

'Don't worry. We'll send some officers to her place and make sure she's safe,' Ally informed him while glaring at Jacob to send officers to Scarlett's home. 'Mr Harrington, we need to start evacuating the building just in case.'

Malcolm nodded, staring out of the window of his office. Each lab was surrounded by glass windows and doors making them all visible from his office.

'Mr Harrington, are you listening?' she repeated.

'Yes, yes, sorry,' he panicked.

Barnes phoned Ally and she answered. 'Ally, get out of...' he shouted before the call cut off.

As Malcolm was about to raise the fire alarm, another alarm sounded, alerting the three of them. Ally checked her phone for signal but she had no bars, making her begin to lose her cool.

'What's that?' Jacob asked Malcolm.

'That's a contamination alarm,' he explained.

'What does that mean?' Jacob continued to ask.

'If there's a leak in one of the labs, the alarm system detects it and seals off the zone where the leak is.'

'Where's the nearest safe zone from here?' Ally asked her question.

'Right here,' Malcolm said.

'How long have people got before the rooms become sealed?'

'About a minute from when the alarm sounds,' Malcolm continued.

All the rooms locked and sealed themselves from the breach. The three of them watched in horror as a gas like fog, filled inside one of the labs, sending five people to what Ally and Jacob could only hope was a peaceful sleep.

'We need to get out of here,' Ally said, worrying about their fate. 'I don't want to end up like them.' She checked her phone. 'Still no bars. Have either of you two got signal?'

'No,' Jacob answered. 'She must be using some sort of communication jammer.'

The phone on Malcolm's desk began to ring. Three of them stared at one another in a confused gaze. None of them had any signal which meant the call was coming from inside the lab.

Ally picked up the phone. 'Hello?'

'I've cut all communications to the outside world. Everyone in this building will die unless you give me Malcolm Harrington. You have three hours,' the voice on the other end of the phone said in a harrowing tone before hanging up.

Ally realised the seriousness of the situation. She was terrified, not knowing if any of them would live through this. For all she knew, they only had hours to live.

Jacob Wright
will return
in

Hours to Live

Acknowledgements

Thank you to everyone who has fallen in love with the characters and enjoyed the first book in the Jacob Wright Series. The response and reviews I received from 'Secrets and Lies' was fantastic and has boosted my own confidence in writing. The journey has only just begun and you're all in for a crazy ride.
So to all the fans, I want to say a huge thank you. Without you this wouldn't be possible.

Someone else I would like to thank is Lauren for helping me fix any mistakes, and as you can imagine, there were a lot. Another huge thank you to Annette Bates for keeping me on track and giving me great feedback.

Last but not least, I'd like to say thank you to my amazing fiancee, Chantelle, for keeping me sane while trying to burst through my negativity. You are amazing and I truly couldn't do this without you by my side.

We have all had a difficult time during this pandemic. Some have lost people, including myself, but the one thing we must do is stay positive and talk to people when we're feeling low.

Printed in Great Britain
by Amazon

61502973R00210